This first edition of "The Best Revenge"
was autographed by the author
November, 1992

NOVELS

The Husband
The Magician
Living Room
The Childkeeper
Other People
The Resort
The Touch of Treason
A Deniable Man

PLAYS

Napoleon (The Illegitimist)
(New York and California, 1953)

A Shadow of My Enemy
(National Theater, Washington D.C.
and Broadway, 1957)

NONFICTION

A Feast for Lawyers

THE BEST REVENGE

THE BEST REVENGE

A Novel of Broadway

SOL STEIN

Random House · New York

Library of Congress Cataloging-in-Publication Data

Stein, Sol.
The best revenge: a novel of Broadway/by Sol Stein.
p.   cm.
ISBN 0-679-40231-4
I. Title.
PS3569.T375B4   1991
813'.54—dc20   90-53490

Manufactured in the United States of America
2 4 6 8 9 7 5 3
First Edition
Designed by Jo Anne Metsch

For Ruth Jandreau
and in memory of
Lady Zam and Louie

ACKNOWLEDGMENTS

During the decade in which this novel was fashioned, I had the welcome advice of three talented editors in my immediate family: Elizabeth, Patricia, and Toby Stein. The early comments by Renni Browne, David King, and most particularly Saul Bellow steered me toward the rapids and beyond. On certain matters I tapped the expertise of Daniel Chabris and Estelle Schecter. Nick Mayo's long career in the theater proved a gift. I am grateful to all of them.

Hamlet. My father, methinks I see my father.
Horatio. Where, my lord?
Hamlet. In my mind's eye, Horatio.

1979

BOOK I

Ben Riller

Entering my reception room is like lunging into a corner of bedlam reserved for people insane enough to be actors. There are always two, three, four of them without appointments waiting, some for hours, energized by aspiration, faces puffed with hope, determined to snare me while I streak, albeit fully dressed, the twenty-two feet to the privacy of my office. Or, as a legend of Broadway would have it, I stop because I am tempted to invite one of them, preferably a woman, preferably striking, in for a chat about her ambitions, a subject she is pleased to talk about as I search her face for the glint of talent that given the right words to speak will cause the central nervous system of an entire audience to tremble. Meryl Streep was not the first or last to sit in that straight-backed chair facing my desk exuding talent not yet recognized by the world.

Today, having combed my freeform hair with my fingers before opening the outer door, I stride in to see Charlotte behind the safety of her desk fending off the insistence of a shabbily dressed man who from the back seems old enough to have retired two decades ago. Charlotte is trying to signal me with her eyes.

Use a semaphore, I don't understand you!

I turn my attention to the worn leather chairs reserved for actor-supplicants, of whom there are three this morning.

Frank Tocia has worked television as a heavy for twenty years and still yearns for the stage. He nods, which from him means, "Hello, do you have anything coming up that might be right for me or should I go to my next sitting place?" To him I say, "Good to see you, Frank," which will inspire him to gossip well of me until his next visit.

Of course I see her! The young woman sitting next to Frank, exuding innocence, is a living trap for a middle-aged man fond of beauty. She must leave her picture with Charlotte. She must remove her radiance from this room before I invent a play that's perfect for her. "Good morning, Mr. Riller," she says, "I don't have an appointment." I want to hug her, tell her, "Child, actors don't have appointments, they have perpetual waits. Why don't you find an occupation you can depend on?" There are a dozen men in this city who would buy a theater in order to put her on its stage, which is not the recognition her pride lusts for. Charlotte will have to deal with her. I am far too vulnerable.

The geriatric who'd been wrangling with Charlotte spots me at last. Some of the best actors in the world are close to eighty. Their age-lined faces exude character. In the movies you can do repeated takes, but in theater the scourges of the body haunt eight performances a week. Old people chip at my heart. I see my father, Louie, in every one of their faces. Though he was only fifty-two when he was swept away, in my demented mind he ages a year every year that I get older because I find intolerable the idea that I am now one year older than my father was when he died. It aches to turn an old man down. I smile as he approaches me. I think he wants to shake my hand.

What he wants to do, it turns out, is to provide me with personal service of a subpoena.

I try to hand it back to him, but he's out the door with a gait a younger man would envy.

The face of the spine-straight woman in the third chair clicks a synapse in my memory bank, but what is her name?

"Hello," I say, saluting with two fingers, my trademark immortalized by Hirschfeld in a swirl of Ninas on the front page of the theater section of *The New York Times*. "I hope you haven't been waiting long," I say, as Charlotte, her hand over the mouthpiece of her phone, announces clear across the room, "It's Mr. Glenn calling from Chicago for the fourth time. He doesn't believe you're not in."

"I'm not in yet," I say. "I'm still in the reception room."

"He just said, 'Girlie, tell your boss to pick up the phone.'"

"What did you say?"

"I said my name isn't Girlie."

Charlotte Neville should have been a playwright and not have taken on the most demanding task of the American theater as my personal assistant. As a blackmailer Charlotte could be instantly rich. She knows secrets of mine even I have forgotten.

Now what I'd almost forgotten was the woman with the familiar face. She uncrosses her legs. I see them, I see them. In a single upward movement, she stands. I reach to take both her hands in mine, and she, instead, puts out her cheek for a kiss. I kiss my saluting fingers and touch her cheek. "Safer," I say, and she dutifully executes a hearty laugh, and says, "The whisper on the street is that Ruth Welch has had it with the play. The moment she leaves I want you to call me, Ben." She slips me a piece of twice-folded paper. "It's my private number."

Is this a seduction or a petition? Who is she?

"In fact," she adds, "if I can borrow a script now, I'd be ready to read for the part if she takes off without notice."

"Ruth Welch will never leave this production alive," I say. "Besides, you're much too beautiful for the part."

I know, I know, she would forgo her beauty for a leading role. Mephistopheles, you need to work the theater district more. Everyone is ready to deal.

In another instant I am inside my office, safe from the innocent ingenue whose precursors warmed and cursed my past. On all four walls posters of plays sing my history.

Thank God for my private john. I lock the door behind me, unzip, and instruct its aim.

Washing up I cannot avoid the mirror. My hand-combed hair is a nest of ripples, spirals, twists, and coils. I succumb to convention and use a comb, thinking, Why has no barber ever found a way of taming this mane? Or at least suggesting that I let him try a little something that will make the gray strands match their neighbors? I ball up the paper towel and arc it toward the basket. Two points! I encourage the mirror to notice the dimple in my right cheek.

At my desk, I reach for the phone to call Ezra. On the back of my left hand I see the wandering shape of a vein, a blue worm under the skin. My right hand seems perfectly normal for a man of fifty-three. The left, sensing my disapproval, lets the phone back down into its cradle. If I transport that hand to Dr. Heller, he'll say, "There's nothing wrong with you, Ben. Take a vacation." How does he know God's plans for me? I'm in the business of surprises. Doctors are surprised by surprise. They have no business practicing medicine.

I buzz for Charlotte. I want to know if she can see the difference between my two hands.

Advancing on my desk, she says, "Ben, don't give me anything else to do until I finish the loyalty letters."

I'd better forget my hands.

"Charlotte, what's the name of that woman?"

"The ingenue?"

"The older one who knows me."

"Harriet Barnes, she understudied Duse and Bernhardt."

"You must learn to be kinder, Charlotte. Didn't she star in *Breakway?*"

Heading for the door, Charlotte says, "I'll get rid of both of them. I've got fourteen of those letters to go."

They were all, of course, to previous investors who'd profited mightily from Ben Riller productions and, afraid of a lion of a play, had passed on *The Best Revenge.*

We've shared opportunities in the theater, the letter said, *that have enriched our cultural heritage and produced a handsome return on investment at the same time. While there's never a guarantee that a particular production will work, my instinct and experience both tell me that* The Best Revenge *is worth my while. Shouldn't it also be worth your while to be a limited partner of mine once again and share the benefits of this production? There are a few units still left, and I'll save one of these for you until I get your phone call. As ever.*

As bullshit. Most of the units were left, not a few. And the hard-assed recipients of my loyalty letter probably won't bother to call. No is no. Not this one. Too chancy. Too many problems. See you next time if you're around.

Pick up the phone. Call him.

Get off my back, Pop.

Aldo Manucci always helped me.

I am not you. I can't waste time.

I told you the best way to move is like a duck, calm on the surface, paddling like hell underneath.

Pop, I don't need lectures.

Ben, you're an upside-down duck, paddling against the air and wondering

6

why you're not getting anywhere. Let Manucci help you the way he helped me.

To an early grave, Pop.

Louie would have spoken to me even if Charlotte were still in the room. The first time she ever caught me communing with him, she didn't point a finger to her temple as any other secretary would have. "It's okay," she said, "Joan of Arc heard voices, why shouldn't you?"

I buzzed her.

"Now what?" she asked.

"There's nothing in my in box except *Variety*."

"You want me to send you one of the letters I'm trying to type?"

"Where's my mail?"

"Censored. You don't want to read any of it. I'll put them in your autobiography file. What did the process server have?"

"I threw it in the wastebasket."

"I'll fish it out and send it over to Ezra. When you leave. Which is how soon?"

"Are they gone?"

"I'm all alone. Except for you."

Her first year here Charlotte had said to me, "I like your hair," a sentence that hung in the air between us for a week before I learned she was as wedlocked as I am.

I opened my office door a crack. How nice, just Charlotte typing away. I announced, "I'm heading for the theater to catch the rehearsal."

"Call Ezra," said Charlotte without taking her eyes off her work.

"I've got nothing more to say to him."

"He's trying to help, Ben."

"The only way he can help is to get rich quick and lend me the money." With the tip of my forefinger I slit my throat. "I am up to here with advice."

"I guess that includes my reminders as to who you're supposed to call."

"Charlotte, Charlotte, Charlotte, I don't need reminders. I need money."

Charlotte the Kind stopped typing and put the palms of her hands together. "If I had the money, Ben, you know I'd give it to you."

"You'd be crazy."

"Then why should anyone else invest? Who believes in you more than I do? Besides Jane."

Obeisance to the wife.

"I am not a religion. I don't want to be believed in. This play is a business proposition like all the others."

"It isn't, Ben."

"You read it?"

"You didn't hire me as a critic."

"You always criticize me, I don't see why you stop at a mere play."

"I had to see why everyone is saying no."

"Well?"

"I kind of liked it."

"You did?"

"In fact I thought it was pretty great."

I went around to Charlotte's preserve, her side of the desk. Her hands quickly went to her typewriter keys for safety.

"What are you doing?" she said.

"Don't scream." I kissed the side of her face.

"What do I know," she said. "Alex the Pencil hates it."

"I don't want accountants reading plays."

"He didn't read it. He just did the numbers."

"I'm going down to the theater."

"Call Ezra first."

"I'll take the kiss back if you say that once more."

Her right hand left the typewriter just long enough to wave her fingers good-bye.

"Farewell," I said.

Charlotte stopped typing. "Some of these are sure to come through, Ben."

In the unlikely event they all came through for a unit each, it would still leave us sixty yards from a touchdown and not a prospect in sight. Sending out the letters gave Charlotte hope. Hope is the immune system's first line of defense. Why should I interfere?

I walked past out-of-towners pointing at the marquees, snapping future memories, exciting each other about actually being on the Great White Way in person at last. Be warned, I thought, this place will snow you blind.

Broadway isn't Broadway anymore. I was down to letters nobody would answer.

Last night Jane said, "We need to be candid now."

Oh, come on now, Jane, I said, you were candid from the word go. Eighteen years ago you said, "Ben, I'm going to rescue you from all those clustering females because you're an energy machine, a human rocket, you get things done, and between your fits of temper you can be a vastly entertaining man."

That was then. What she said last night was, "Ben, stop clowning and pay attention. We need to be candid about money."

Money? Oh yes, the ultimate goad, spur, stimulus, incitement, the fundamental fuel in the drive to power. I remember it well.

Good women avoid weak men. Weakening men.

I almost tripped over Mustard, the legless wonder on his skateboard platform, cap held out. The *Times* said he took in more than a thousand dollars a day in good weather. Maybe he could give me a course in successful begging.

"How are you today, Mr. Riller."

I put my dollar in his cap. "Morning to you," I said and turned the corner.

I slowed my walk to the pace of my brain.

The last time I addressed cast and crew was when I jumped up on stage to announce a record number of theater parties for *Love or Marriage,* which meant they'd all be working for a long time. If I tried jumping up there today I'd break a leg, right, God?

Sorry to interrupt, everybody, I've got an announcement. We're broke. And you're out of a job, effective last payday.

Equity would want my scalp.

The public phones around Times Square double as urinals, but there was one free and I closeted the noise out and the smell in.

When Ezra got on, I told him what I was about to do.

"That's suicide," he said. "We need to talk this over."

"I'm entitled to close one play."

"It's not that simple, Ben. You've spent escrow money."

"You never complained about that before."

"Before, I saw more money coming in. I'm not a criminal lawyer, Ben. Spending escrow could mean—don't hang up."

"You're a mind reader, Ezra."

"You can't just walk into the rehearsal and close the show down. You've got to post notices. I've been trying to get to you for two days. That fellow from Chicago called me. What's his name?"

"Sam Glenn."

"That's the one. Why's he calling me?"

9

"Your name is on the papers, Ezra."

"He wants a certified check returning his investment. He says you wouldn't take his phone calls. Now he wants you to fly out to Chicago for a talk."

"How the hell can I do that in the middle of this?"

"That Glenn is not a nice man."

"I've known that since high school."

"He could be real trouble."

"Compared to what?"

"He's threatened . . . I need to talk to you, Ben, before—"

"I do anything stupid."

"I'll grab a cab and meet you at the theater. Don't talk to anyone before I get there."

"I don't want you at the theater."

"I'll meet you wherever you say, only swear you won't talk to the cast first. Promise?"

"What the fuck can I promise, I can't keep the hundred promises I already made," I said and hung the receiver on the black wishbone.

Why should I call Ezra? Won't everything he'll say be predictable? What I needed for a lawyer now was a gorilla, not a friend.

Two more blocks to the theater.

If in doubt, blow up the ship.

Does the captain get away in a lifeboat? Isn't he supposed to go down with the ship?

In the theater, the sea of seats rippled downward, empty except for two in the fifth row occupied by the director and his boy. I sat down in back. The seat creaked.

Mitch craned his head around. He got up abruptly—not his usual inconspicuous way—and headed for the stage. He whispered something to the stage manager, who quickly came down the side steps to the auditorium and slid into Mitch's seat, a way of telling the cast he was watching the run-through in Mitch's place.

Mitch stole back to where I was. "Let's go outside, Ben, so we won't disturb the cast."

"Later."

"Not later, Ben. Now."

Once we were clear of the auditorium, I said, "Looks good, the five seconds I saw of it."

"Ben," Mitch said, "the word is bad. They say the investors aren't in, that the partnership can't close. Don't shit me, Ben. If it's gotten to the cast, it must be all over town."

I was trying to think of a lie when I heard Louie's voice.

Enough is enough. Tell him the truth.

Mitch said, "Stop daydreaming, Ben. If the show folds out of town, it'll butcher the cast. And murder me." Mitch's eyes wouldn't let go of mine. "Or do we close before we move out of town?"

I used to be able to tell wonderful lies.

Mitch was saying, "Everybody in the business knows I turn down five for every play I do. I've got my thing hanging out there. Tell me, Ben. Level."

I can usually put my arm around a gay man without feeling uncomfortable. This time I felt queasy because it was part of my deceit.

"I should have talked to you earlier, Mitch. You didn't expect financing this production would be a walk, did you?"

"Of course not. But we move out of town in ten days. It's panic time."

I took my arm off Mitch's shoulder.

"I guess I'd better tell you," I said.

"Tell me what?"

Tell him Manucci.

"You got time, Mitch?"

"Is it a solution?"

"Of course."

Mitch's smile could have cracked glass. "Don't tell me what it is, Ben, just do it."

He headed toward the doors of the theater, then turned to say, "Your word is good, Ben. I'll tell the others."

The moment before he went back into the auditorium, as if he'd forgotten something, he turned at the door just enough to blow me a kiss.

My lie galvanized me into a rapid stride back toward my office. Before opening the door I ran my fingers through my hair. Thank heaven, no more beseechers. Charlotte said, "Ezra told me."

"Told you what?"

"That he couldn't stop you from going down to the theater to close the play."

"He had no business telling you."

"He says you could end up in jail. Did you?"

"Did I what?"

"Close the play."

"I didn't have the guts. Why are you smiling?"

"I know you."

"Nobody knows me. Not anymore."

"That reporter from the *New York Post* called."

She handed me the slip. Larry Robertson. Page Six slime, read by the *Post*'s lawyers and then everyone else in town. I dropped the slip into the wastebasket just as I heard the phone ring in the outer office.

Charlotte buzzed. "It's him again."

"Ezra?"

"No, Robertson."

"All right." I wasn't ducking any more calls.

"Ben Riller," I said into the phone.

"Hi, Mr. Riller. I've been trying to reach you about a little item we're running in tomorrow's paper about the show. I'd just like to get your comment on the story around town that *The Best Revenge* may never open."

"Mr. Robertson?"

"Yes?"

"If I tell you you're wrong, your story will say 'Producer denies show folding,' right?"

"Unless you'd care to confirm that it is folding or make some other comment."

"I do," I said.

"Slowly, please," he said, "so I can take it down."

"Mr. Robertson," I said, "does your wife have syphilis?"

Robertson's voice shrilled, "What the hell kind of question is that?"

"I'll tell you," I said. "I've got an AP wire service reporter here finishing up an interview and he'd like to run a story saying '*Post* reporter denies wife has syphilis.' Well, has she or hasn't she?"

I could hear Robertson breathing. Then he said, "You win, Mr. Riller," and hung up.

Fuck him. The worst thing you can do is lie down in the snow.

Louie's voice in my ear was saying, *Italians are wonderful people, Ben, warm. Look how many times Manucci reached a hand out to help me. A phone call won't hurt.*

Just shut up, I shouted at him. I don't need anybody's advice.

A grown-up doesn't talk to his father that way.

If I didn't answer, he'd go away.

You can't get rid of me, Ben.

I don't need voices.

I told you to be a writer, not a talker like me.

I did what I could.

Not true. You did what people wanted you to do.

I had to make a living, Pop.

Did I use up my life so you could become a salesman like everyone else in America? In the newspapers they call you an impresario, what's that? A fancy salesman? A broker for other people's talents? A handler? *You were supposed to use the brains I gave you to write, every teacher said so.*

I needed money.

You had money.

I needed enough so I wouldn't end up a slave to someone like Manucci the way you did.

Careful, Ben, soften your voice. Manucci was my friend.

You always went to him for money.

The Rockefellers don't lend money to people like me. Who should I have gone to?

Manucci's a shylock.

Without Manucci my business would have gone down the toilet. We had to eat. Manucci helped me the way you helped Ezra when he was in a money jam.

I didn't charge Ezra interest. I'm not a moneylender.

Ben, I love you. I hoped you would never go broke like me.

Go ahead, curse me.

The biggest play producer in America is not going to like it in jail. God have mercy on you.

Don't do that, Pop. When I was a kid, you always talked and I listened. It's my life now, not yours.

That's true.

Now I'm going to shout into your grave, Pop, and you're going to listen.

Ben

I kept three things of my father's: a rotted-canvas-covered case that contained his World War I razor with which I took the first fuzz off my cheeks and called it a shave; a metal box filled with unredeemed pawn tickets that I never showed anyone, not even Jane; and a small maroon leather address book that contained, according to my mother, the names of all of Louie's alleged mistresses, in addition to friends, acquaintances, business contacts, our long-dead family doctor, and the unlisted number of Aldo Manucci, Louie's moneylender.

I'm famous for not being able to find anything I'm looking for. The address book, which I hadn't looked through in years, was, to my great relief, where it was supposed to be, in my locked desk drawer.

"No calls," I said to Charlotte, who'd followed me in.

"Not even prospects?"

"Take numbers. I've got a very important call to make."

"Jane wants to talk to you."

"Later."

"Ezra called her."

"I said later. Please shut the door gently."

I put a yellow pad in front of me on the desk. I placed a pen on the yellow pad. This is ridiculous, I'm not going to write anything, just call.

I expected whoever answered the phone to speak in the Italian intonations I remembered from long ago. The voice of the woman who said hello in English had no hint of an accent.

"I'm calling Mr. Aldo Manucci, please," I said.

The woman hesitated. Was Manucci still alive?

"Who may I say is calling?"

What a relief.

"My name is Ben Riller."

"Miller?"

"Riller with an *R*. Tell him it's Louie Riller's son."

"Oh," the woman said with an audible rush of air. "Can I help you in any way? Can I give him a message for you? It's hard for him to come to the phone."

"Is he sick?"

"Well, not sick sick," the woman said, "resting. He's eighty-eight, you know. Can I give him a message?"

Can I ask whoever you are to carry the message that I need over four hundred thousand dollars?

"My father—Louie Riller—was a good friend of Mr. Manucci's—"

"Oh, I know," the woman said. "I still have the cross he made for me when I was three. My uncle has arthritis. His sight is very poor, and his hearing, well, he can hear what he wants to hear, but it's difficult for him on the telephone, Mr. Riller. Can I give him a message?"

"Could I come to see him at a time when he's rested?"

"A social visit?"

That would be a lie. "I'm afraid I've been neglectful of my father's old friends," I said. "It's a business matter."

"Oh, Mr. Manucci is not in business anymore. He hasn't been for many years."

"He might make an exception. My father said that—" I hesitated. "If I ever got into trouble, I should go talk to Aldo Manucci."

"If you'll hang on," the woman said, "I'll ask." She was gone a long time.

"Sorry to have kept you. My uncle says to tell Bennie that the past is never past. He'll be happy to advise you. If the matter is urgent, you could come today, after he's rested and shaved. Would seven this evening be all right?"

She could have said midnight.

"Are you still in the same house on North Oak Drive?"

I remembered the Little Italy of my childhood in the northeast Bronx in images of its people, the imperious shouts of old women dressed in black, the teenagers playing stickball gesturing with three fingers and yelling obscenities at cars that disrupted their game.

Though I saw no stickball games in progress, my BMW seemed too conspicuous on these streets narrowed by parked cars on both sides. I should have taken Jane's Toyota for this visit. I drove slowly, noticing the walkers carrying portable radios—that was new—and the stoop sitters, as of old, looking at my unfamiliar vehicle as if it were a foreign invader.

I had almost forgotten about the hierarchy of houses, the tenements from which families hoped to move into the attached row houses with their tiny vegetable plots in back, and then the stand-alone houses covered with imitation brick siding except for the largest house— which I recognized as if suddenly coming upon an old enemy— covered with imitation stone siding, set back from the street, surrounded by a wrought-iron fence with a gate that used to be locked.

I was able to park at the curb directly in front. I reached across to lock the glove compartment and saw three teenagers looking at me through the windshield with expressions learned from gangster movies on TV. They expected what from me? A declaration of war? I smiled and waved at them, destroying their poses.

I checked to make sure the door lock held. Then, looking over the roof of the car as if it were a battlement offering temporary protection, I took in the house. I remembered the legend that once in the 1920s someone had been heaved out of a third-story window and had been pierced by one of the spikes of the wrought-iron fence. Though he was still alive and screaming for an hour or more, nobody came to get the man off, not even the police.

The gate was not locked. I went through, closing it behind me, watched by the kids near the car. After twenty feet of flagstone path —I remembered Louie saying how expensive flagstone was—I went up the three steps to the front door. There was no name on the doorbell.

The woman who answered my ring was in her mid-forties, a dark-haired, olive-beautiful, Mediterranean presence.

"Is this the Manucci residence?" I asked.

"Come in, Mr. Riller," she said, smiling. "Your face is the same as in the newspapers."

"You were very kind to arrange this meeting."

She stepped aside so that I might pass her. "You won't remember me," she said. "When you were here long ago, I was just a baby."

Was she the niece Manucci chose to be his fortress-keeper when his wife died? Had he not allowed her to marry?

She showed me to the sitting room. "I'll get him," she said.

I looked around. No one decorated homes like this anymore, pieces of furniture put in place over time, each without aesthetic connection to the others. The painting of the Madonna on one wall was an untalented piece of street art. If Manucci rescued me, perhaps I should buy him a worthy painting of the Madonna. He wouldn't recognize it as worthy but as an insult to his own.

At last she wheeled him in, a shrunken human stuffed by a careless taxidermist. He was trying to hold his head up to see me, an eye clouded by cataract. He took an unblinking look, then let a rich smile lift the ends of his mouth as his voice, still bass though tremulous, said, "Ben-neh!" which made my name sound like the word "good" in Italian.

"Mr. Manucci," I said, and took his hand in both of mine, which were cold. His hand was warm, for he had long ago abjured nervousness about anything that life might bring him.

"You a much big man now," Manucci said. "In papers all time Ben-neh Riller present, Ben-neh Riller announce, Ben-neh Riller big stars, big shows. You bring Gina Lollobrigida here I kiss her hand. I kiss her anything," he laughed. "Magnani, you know Magnani, she more my type. I tell people here I know you when you just a little Jew kid this high." He held his hand up flat to show my height when he saw me last. "Your father, Louie, he just a shrimp, how you get so big? Oh, this my niece, Clara. I call her Clarissima, she best woman ever in my life."

Clara nodded, blushing.

"Clara go two colleges," he said. "Last one where all snob girls go, whatsits name?"

"I'll leave you two," she said.

"I tell you something," he said. "Don't stand like idiot, sit, sit, I sit all time."

I pulled a chair close to him.

"That's good." He sighed. "How's your father?"

I wasn't sure I'd heard him right. "He's, well he's been dead a long time."

"I know, I know. He talks to me once in while. He must talk to you, too, no?"

We understood each other.

He went on. "Clara tell me you coming, I near cried. I miss your father. I don't mean business. I had all business I need. I mean Louie stories, jokes, make all women here laugh, cry, he could been Don Juan the whole Little Italy if your mother not such a beauty dish herself. People I do business with old days make my pocket so rich I can't spend if I live two hundred years more, but Louie he make my heart rich every time he come here. He was like family, I tell you."

Unembarrassed by the rush of his emotions, he brushed his eyes with the back of his sleeve and said, "Anything I can do for son of Louie I do. What kind of trouble you got?"

I told him a short version.

"Your investors stink," he said. "No loyalty. Clarissima!" he shouted. "Bring Strega!"

From the other room Clara said, *"Momento."*

"You in trouble, Ben-neh?"

I nodded.

"Money trouble?"

I nodded again.

"Who with?"

How do I explain?

"Everybody?" He laughed. "Always that way. Never mind. You try banks?"

I nodded. "No dice."

His laugh was raucous, spittle glistening in the cracked corners of his mouth.

"Very good, no dice. Must remember. Banks take no chances. God bless stupid banks make Manucci family rich."

Clara put two cut-crystal glasses with Strega between us, disappeared.

"How much you need?"

"Four hundred twenty-nine thousand dollars," I said.

He emitted a whistle. "Ho boy," he said, then leaned forward. I was afraid he might fall out of the wheelchair. I pulled my chair closer to his.

"Know something," he said, "don't give half that much to one party even when I was king around here. Never mind. Nineteen seventy-nine dollar nothing. When you was boy, Ben-neh, five cents buy big ice cream, five dollars get someone off street for good. Last week my friend Paolo paid one buck for a shoeshine, you believe that?" The old man sighed for the past. "Never mind. You need all one time?"

"Yes."

"When you need? Yesterday! Everybody always need money yesterday. Right?"

I nodded.

His face turned hard. "I got bad news for you. I no do this no more fifteen years maybe. When you lend, you got to collect. You got to be stronger than the *stupidos* who collect for you. When my legs go, eye goes, pecker goes, I say, Aldo, retire."

He read the utter disappointment in my face.

"Wait minute. Rule of life: After bad news, good news. My son Nick, he do this kind business. Clara!" She must have been close. He turned his head to her.

"Get me Nick, he home now, quick."

As she dialed a number, the old man said to me, "You know Nick?"

"I just met him once when we were kids. In this room." Clara handed him the phone. The old lion addressed Nick in Italian, orders to a subordinate. I recognized a few essentials, Louie, my name, the amount of money. There were raised voices on both sides, then Manucci said something sharp in Italian, and calmly handed me the phone. "He remembers you. Here, you and him talk."

I took the phone.

"Hey," Nick said, "Long time. I saw your picture in the papers. You haven't changed. How're you doing?"

"Hello, Nick," I said, aware of his father watching me. "How's it with you?"

"My wife says I get a year older every year. You got to tell me your secret. We should get together. You heard my old man? He said when Louie Riller is dead a son of Louie Riller's is like a son of his, real old country. That makes you my brother, right? That's a big number you need. Want to come see me tomorrow?"

"Sure," I said. "Of course. Thanks. When?" He set the time, asked for the name and phone number of my accountant so he could get some facts, told me his company was called The Venture Capital Corporation, and gave me the address.

The Seagram Building?

Before I left, the old man said two things. "If Nick no help you real good, you call me." He looked at Clara, motioning her to move his wheelchair closer to me. "I have nice farm in Sicily I go every year till doctor—*stupido* first class—he say no more airplanes. You, Ben-neh, you stay on my farm no charge. No one look for bigshot Jew-producer in Sicily. One year, two years, everything calm down, you come back. Take wife. Take *bambini*. Leave mess for everybody else clean up." He laughed.

"My *bambini*," I said, "are in high school. They don't know any language except English. My wife wouldn't know what to do on a farm."

"What's matter? She not smart? She learn, no?"

"She might leave me."

"That's no wife."

"Louie wouldn't want me to run away."

He sighed. "I forget what Turks you Jews are. Do one thing for me. One."

He leaned his head very close to mine, as if to keep what he said from Clara, who was standing at a discreet distance.

"Ben-neh?"

"Yes, Mr. Manucci."

"You come to my funeral, okay?"

I nodded, extended my hand to confirm the agreement. He closed both his hands around mine with hurting strength, his eyes blazing. "If you no there," he said, "I jump from coffin, find you, cut your throat." And just as suddenly he let go of my hands, roared with laughter. "You believe that?"

I nodded.

"You better believe, Clara call you. Go!" he said.

I nodded good-bye to Clara, but it was difficult to take my eyes off the old man's face, which I was certain I would not see again until I joined the line in front of the bronze casket to pay my respects.

Outside, the air seemed fresh like after a lightning storm. I was breathing hope again.

I noticed the three boys sitting on the hood of my car, pretending they didn't see me coming. I guess they thought I was someone from Manhattan who would beg them politely so they could hold their hands out for commerce to get their asses off my BMW. I unlocked the driver's side, got in, turned on the ignition with a roar, and started forward, giving them a bare second to scoot off the car. I knew the ways of the street once. As I zoomed away, I caught a glimpse of their squashed bravado in the rearview mirror.

B e n

The Seagram, for all its copper-clad simplicity, was once for me the Taj Mahal of New York, a slab thrusting thirty-eight floors up from Park Avenue as much to capture the attention of the heavens as of the passersby below. In years past I'd thought of it as an enclave for companies that know how to use interior space for the benefit of business. I daydreamed then of having my offices in the Seagram Building, but I was expected by actors and investors to stick to the West Forties, close to Sardi's and, of course, the theaters themselves. Over the years, whenever I lunched at the Four Seasons or took a late night supper at the Brasserie, I'd sneak an upward glance at the huge building that held them both. If no bombs fell, the Seagram would survive any person in it. Not bad, Louie would have said, for that *pisher.* Meaning Nick Manucci.

I scanned the lobby for Ezra. I had warned him to be here on time. It was three fifty-five and he was late.

As I searched for The Venture Capital Corporation on the lobby directory, a gray-uniformed elevator starter asked, "Can I help you, sir?" If I'd been wearing my usual clothes—slacks and an open-throated shirt—he wouldn't have called me *sir.*

"No, thanks," I told the man in uniform. I'd just found the room number. What difference did it make if this fellow found out I was here to see Manucci? A voice behind me made me turn.

"Traffic," Ezra said, glancing at his watch. "Let's go."

"No briefing?" I asked.

"If I interrupt, let me," Ezra said. "Stick this memo in your case. If he wants facts, hand it to him. It's sanitized."

Ezra followed me into an already crowded elevator. As I watched the lighted numbers track our fast climb, I remembered how when I was a kid I would stir my anticipation of adventure by thinking of each floor of a building as a *story*.

Today, my story was on the thirty-second floor. The gilt lettering on the impressive, grained-wood double doors of suite 3218 had the name we were looking for. Those doors were nine feet high, not to admit giants but to give those entering a sense of the limitations of their size. I expected the entrance to be locked, but the knob turned readily. The reception room surprised me, a Max Ernst on one wall and a Zao-Wou-Ki on another. Coming from behind a desk, a young lady sheathed in silky polyester a mite too slinky for an office, with a touch of British accent said, "How good of you to be so prompt, Mr. Riller. Is this gentleman with you?"

"Mr. Hochman is my lawyer."

"I see. I'll tell Mr. Manucci's secretary you're both here."

As she spoke on the intercom, I felt Ezra's elbow in my ribs. He nodded toward the lithographs, and whispered, "I wonder who had the good taste to steal those for him."

"You've seen too many gangster movies, Ezra."

From across the room, the receptionist said, "Mr. Manucci is just finishing an overseas call. He won't be a moment. Please have a seat."

The coffee table displayed virgin copies of *Forbes* and *Business Week*.

"Can I get either of you a cup of coffee while you're waiting?"

Ezra declined with a headshake.

"Just had some half an hour ago," I said. "Thank you."

She smiled. "I recognized you from your photographs, Mr. Riller. I still read the theater pages before the news."

Her smile strained for my attention. My eyes wandered to her sheathed body, the indented waist, the arching hips.

Our family album contained sepia and gray photos of Louie with three or four women. Sometimes only one woman, gazing at him. Even after he married, the attention continued. Is it because of Louie's example that I have never been able to do without the attention of women, which is, of course, a hazard through life?

"I'm an actress," the receptionist said. "That is, I used to be."

I knew what was coming.

"I had to earn a living."

"May I know your name?" I asked.

"Gertrude Atherton."

"I'll remember that," I said, as I always did, the shortest way to conclude that kind of conversation on a note of hope.

A sharp buzz caused her to pick up the phone. "Mr. Manucci's secretary will be out in a second."

And she was, standing just beyond a framed doorless doorway leading to the inner offices. As I walked through, an alarm went off, just as they do in airports.

As I stepped back, Miss Atherton laughed uncomfortably, holding out a plastic tray. "You must have quite a few keys or a lot of change. Could you drop them in here while you pass through?"

I put my key case, car keys, and a lot of change on the tray. "That's what did it," Miss Atherton said, her voice trying to make light of the procedure.

I passed through the portal. No alarm. Miss Atherton handed the tray to me so that I could repocket my things.

I passed the plastic tray to Ezra. "Very up to date," I said.

Ezra put a metal pillbox next to his keys on the tray. "You should carry those pills for me, Ben. I only take them when I'm going to be around you."

The secretary led us past two closed doors to the corner office and gestured to the open door. Beyond it we could see sofas and chairs, a Dufy on the wall, and, as we stepped forward, in the distant corner a man coming toward us with an energetic stride. Not quite as tall as I was, a natural blond beginning to gray, in his face a strong elegance his father did not have. He looked as if he ought to be a Ford Foundation executive—until he spoke.

Pumping my hand, he said, "I'm pleased to see you." His voice barely betrayed the gritty consonants of his childhood.

"We met," I said, "at your father's house."

"I remember." He shook Ezra's hand as Ezra introduced himself.

"Let's get away from the desk," Manucci said and guided Ezra and me to a sofa facing an armchair. "Please understand, I don't know anything about your business. I'm not prepared to put a contract in front of you today"—this at me in particular—"and you didn't have to pay a lawyer to come. I'm seeing you because my father called."

"I understand."

"I need a briefing."

I nodded. "Mr. Hochman prepared a short memo with the facts," I said, opening my attaché and handing it to him. "I should explain that Mr. Hochman isn't just my attorney. He's a close friend."

"Good," Manucci said. "Maybe I should have brought a close friend." He chuckled. "How about some coffee, with a little anisette, maybe?"

I remembered the Sunday morning long ago when Louie announced that for a change he wasn't going to pay his respects to Aldo Manucci alone. Our family had been invited to Sunday dinner with their family, an honor, an event. My mother refused. Louie begged her not to be difficult, this was very important. Zipporah insisted that he was going out of fear of not going. "He makes a beggar out of you," she said. Louie's fury frightened me. "Manucci never makes me beg. You make me beg you to come with me. Do you think he invites customers for Sunday dinner? We are friends now, Italians, Jews, it doesn't matter, our blood might yet cross."

I remember, later that day, my mother wanting to tuck the cloth napkin under my chin to keep the spaghetti sauce off my grown-up shirt and my only tie. I took the napkin from her. I could do it myself. And I remember the food, veal, and eggplant, and zucchini—I remember asking its name—and at the end, a cheesecake totally unlike the ones Louie brought home from the Jewish bakery, and with it, coffee and anisette. A drop or two was poured into my cup, though I was only twelve, with my mother protesting and Aldo Manucci saying, "It's all right, next year he's a man according to you, right?"

My nod now gave Aldo Manucci's son license to pour steaming black brew from the sterling silver coffee pot into the small, hand-painted porcelain cups. From the sideboard came the bottle of anisette.

"Just a drop," I said.

"For flavor," Manucci said.

What might he have become if his father hadn't been a money-lender? Even when I was twelve I couldn't imagine myself sitting at a workbench the way Louie did day after day, fashioning metal into jewelry. To escape Louie's fate, I accepted proffered roles—stage manager and finally producer—instead of pursuing my own. Had Nick Manucci followed his father out of respect? Or did he have no choice?

"This is a little different than your father's business," I said.

"A little. Your father was a jewelry maker, right? Little rings, things like that."

I nodded.

"Your father used to say what a creative kid I got. I'd have guessed you'd end up a writer, something like that."

"Oh," I said, "play producing can be fairly creative."

The word *fairly* hung in the air.

Ezra said, "Mr. Riller once called producing secondhand fucking, remember, Ben?"

What the hell's gotten into Ezra?

He had Manucci laughing.

"Mr. Manucci," Ezra went on, "a producer is a rat just to the people he works with. If Ben had become a writer, he'd have to rat on everybody."

Manucci guffawed. "Hey, this lawyer friend of yours is okay."

As soon as Manucci lowered his eyes to look at the memorandum in front of him, Ezra gave me his Cheshire Cat smile.

Manucci, looking up, said, "Understand, you didn't give me too much time. My father caught me at home yesterday evening. Lucky I was able to get my accountant at his house. He got in pretty early this morning to make some calls. According to this," he tapped the memo, "your record is exemplary." He let the word lie there for a moment. "Fourteen hits out of seventeen times at bat. Anybody else come close besides DiMaggio?"

Ezra and I laughed, as the circumstances required. I noticed how the creases in Manucci's trousers were more sharp-edged than good taste would have permitted. *Ben,* I could hear Louie saying, *you are a snob like your mother. The important creases are in the brain, not in the pants.*

I must make Nick comfortable with me, the way Louie would have made his father comfortable. I must bring him into my world because that is where he would be putting his money. Lightly, lightly, I said, "DiMaggio wouldn't have made it in the theater. In our business, if you bat three hundred, you're dead."

Manucci nodded. Did that mean he was buying in? My heart was a bird flapping its wings, too big for its cage.

"Merrick," I said, "is the Babe Ruth of Broadway. Actually, I was involved in eighteen productions. In my first, I was one of three co-producers."

I watched Manucci's laugh subdue into a genial smile. Louie had always said, *If a man's face improves when he smiles, it might be possible to trust him.*

"Was it a flop?" Manucci asked. "The first one."

That first production had me bounding out of bed in the morning, my happiness manic as I helped put director, cast, costumes, and set in place. And all the time Louie's voice was like a megaphone in my head. *Don't get so excited about a business deal. A business deal is not a woman.* I wanted Louie to shut up. Theater wasn't business.

Manucci was studying me over the top of his porcelain cup. "You were going to tell me if your first one was a flop."

Pay attention, Louie was shouting, *as if your life depended on it.*

Shut up, Pop, life doesn't depend on any one deal.

If this doesn't work out, what will you do, sell suits? Stop daydreaming, the man is waiting for your answer.

"That first play ran five months, Mr. Manucci. It sold out only on Saturdays. We didn't advertise much. Word-of-mouth kept it going. The ticket brokers didn't send us people. People who saw it sent us people. We made a small profit."

"How small?"

"Maybe fifteen percent on the investment. I'm guessing. It was a long time ago."

"If you made a profit on your first one, you've got a right to be proud."

He's not asking me the name of the play.

You're not looking for a cultural companion, pisher. *Talk to him in the language he understands. Money.*

"If a play's a smash, you can make four, five hundred percent," I said.

Manucci wasn't smiling. How many hundred percent did he make on his loans?

"What was the name of that play?" Manucci asked.

For a moment I couldn't remember. I glanced over at coach Ezra.

"It was called *A Long Way to Tipperary,*" Ezra said.

"World War One?" Manucci asked.

"No," I said. "The hero is first-generation Irish. His father came from Tipperary."

"I hope you don't mind my questions, Mr. Riller."

It's his ball game, Louie was saying, *let him pitch.*

I thought, You're wrong, Louie. We take turns pitching or it's no ball game.

27

"Mr. Manucci," I said, "I hope you don't mind a question from me."

"Be my guest."

"From your first business deal, did you learn anything?"

Manucci thought a moment. Smiling at the memory, he said, "The first time I lent anybody big change I learned never pay attention to a guy's suit. This guy wore a terrific suit. He hadn't paid for it. He took a long, long time to pay me."

I was aware of Ezra laughing along with Manucci now, an audience of two waiting for my response.

"From the *Tipperary* run," I said, "I learned that if you build a better mousetrap, without lots of publicity nobody knows about it. Even the mice stay away."

Ezra nodded. I was keeping the mood light.

"I also learned that it's too late to start promoting after you open. If you want a smash, you've got to set it up that way from the start, at least one name actor for the theater parties, roll the publicity long before you're in production, feed the gossip columns, and when you open in New York, advertise as if you were Ford launching a new car."

"Like the Edsel?"

I let him relish his crack for a moment.

"Like the Mustang," I said. "You have to get behind whatever you're launching."

"Even if it's a lemon."

"I don't produce lemons, Mr. Manucci."

"Maybe not so far, Mr. Riller. Maybe this one'll be your first. Suppose the critics don't like what's-its-name?"

"*The Best Revenge* is its name," I said. "If you've presold enough theater parties, it doesn't matter much."

"How much?"

"If the production gets good word-of-mouth from the theater parties, it'll run."

"What happens if you don't get theater parties, like on this one? Mr. Riller, I made one phone call before you came, somebody in your business who owes me, and from what he said it sounds as if your investors think your new play is controversial. Do you agree with that?"

Manucci sure was thorough. I said, "I've had my share of inoffen-

2 8

sive hits. I decided it's time to have an offensive one. A lot of people thought John Osborne and Harold Pinter offensive at first."

"Did they pay off?"

"Some did. Some didn't."

"Mr. Riller, you sound as if producing plays isn't exactly a business."

Ezra interjected. "Depends what you mean by business," he said.

"A business," Manucci said, "is when you get to take out enough more than you put in to be worth the trouble. It seems to take a lot of trouble to put a play on."

"Compared to what?" I said.

"Compared to what I do."

"Mr. Manucci," Ezra said, "all of Mr. Riller's plays are part of a mix. Some are pure commercial for visiting firemen. Some are for serious theatergoers. If either lands big, they get everybody. A few of Mr. Riller's productions will continue to generate income long after we're gone."

"Can you borrow against that future income?"

"Not really," Ezra said.

"Mr. Hochman," Manucci said, sipping coffee again as if it might lubricate his harsh consonants, "an asset is something you can borrow against now. Posterity is not an asset."

Ezra started to speak. Manucci cut him off.

"If Mary my wife becomes Mary my widow and needs what's in my safe deposit box, she don't want to find future income. She wants to find cash money. No posterity, no prestige. Fellows in the fantasy business sometimes lose track of what's real." He sighed and turned to me. "I hear the *Times* man has more clout than the rest put together. Ever try buying him?"

What do you do with the type of mind that imagines that what you can do on the docks you can do with the *Times?*

"I don't think that would work."

"It works in every business I know. A hundred buys a traffic ticket from a cop. If Lockheed wants an okay from the Jap government, it costs a lot of millions. Everything else is in between. You think a critic who makes sixty thousand a year won't take thirty for one review?"

"It's not done."

Manucci stood up. "How the fuck do you know it's not done? Maybe you don't do it. Maybe it's done with presents, not cash.

Maybe it's done by giving a paid annuity to somebody's mother. Maybe it's done by not doing something."

I didn't understand.

"Not breaking legs. Mr. Riller, if I put money with you I got to know you're a realist."

The intercom buzzed. Manucci went over to his desk, held the phone to his ear. What am I doing here? I looked at Ezra.

He gestured, palms down. Take it easy.

Louie in heaven, I thought, it wasn't like this when you went to see Aldo, was it?

Manucci was saying into the intercom, "No. No is no." He disconnected whoever was on the line, then said, "Did you tape that, honey? Terrific. Now hold the calls for a while." He was still seated at the desk across the room when he said in a voice that seemed to boom, "How come a guy with your track record is having such trouble raising money for your new play?"

Ezra interjected, "When Mr. Riller organized this partnership—"

Manucci, on his way back to the sofa, cut Ezra off. "Mr. Hochman," he said, "if I advise your client to do anything illegal, you speak up. Otherwise you keep quiet because this is a meeting between him and me and you are an observer, understand?" He turned to me. "Please," he said, "continue."

I tried to speak casually. Nothing was to be gained by telling Manucci how desperate I was. Why else would I come to his father or to him?

"Most of the people who invest in the theater," I said, "figure the downside gamble is a tax write-off against ordinary income, costing them thirty to fifty cents on the dollar net. That's if you lose everything, which is rare. This year most of my steadies have taken a bath in the market, short term and long term. They can't use losses."

I couldn't tell whether he believed me. He sighed. "What's in it for you?"

"In a loss situation? The production usually contributes some part of the budget to my office overhead."

Manucci laughed. "You spend a year of your time for some office overhead? I hear guys who produce movies can make three hundred big ones as their fee on a flop."

"If a play's a success, as general partner I get fifty percent of the profits once the investors have their money back." Why did my voice sound as if a mechanical monkey were talking?

"I'm like the movie producers," Manucci said. "I like to see mine, win or lose."

"I understand."

"What I understand," Manucci said carefully, lowering his voice so that I had to lean forward to hear him, "is that sometimes an investor is entitled to a piece of your piece, is that right?"

"That's a matter of contention," Ezra said. "I've never permitted Mr. Riller to do that."

"Please, Mr. Hochman, don't use words like *contention*. There's always a first time for everything."

Ezra coughed.

"If you offered better terms than usual to some of your old-time investors," Manucci said, "maybe they'd have come up with the money."

"I couldn't have Mr. Riller do that. Word would get around to the others."

Manucci tapped his forehead. "Mr. Hochman, you think you're doing your client a favor by butting in? I tell you, any lawyer did me favors like that I'd put in a tube and mail back to law school." Manucci leaned forward in his chair, addressing me now. "Weren't some of your investors leery of your new one because it isn't a musical or a Neil Simon–type play that rakes it in?"

"My new one," I said, "is like the plays that have survived over the years, O'Neill, Tennessee Williams at his best."

"They weren't in poetry, were they?"

"Whoever described it to you as poetry in a derogatory fashion was misleading you, Mr. Manucci. Tennessee Williams used elevated language."

"He didn't do too well in the end, did he?"

"I produced one of his best plays. Would you deride Shakespeare for using elevated language?"

"There ain't no elevated anymore," Manucci said, "just the subway." He looked to see if we would laugh at his joke. When we didn't, he did.

"I wish you'd take a look at my new play. Will you read it?"

Manucci, leaning back into the sofa, said, "That's very flattering, Mr. Riller, but I don't know that I'm a judge. I know automobiles. I know horses. I know money. I know women. Now some of the women I see, they like to go to Broadway plays, it's very exciting to them, live theater, and I like them to be excited you understand, so it's mutually beneficial. I get to see shows that are good and some that are not so good, but what would I know personally? I told my accountant to ask around. He knows a couple of the people who've been in with you pretty steady. They talked as if they were friends of yours, not just investors. They admire the hell out of you as a producer, but they told my accountant they don't think this one has a hope in hell in today's market, that's why they're staying out. You lied to me about the reason."

In my circles, people don't call each other liars except behind the other person's back.

Ben, I never lied to his father. Pay attention. Don't lie. Use your brain.

"What my accountant tells me," Manucci went on, "is that in your business you're the general partner and the investors are limited partners, and when all the money's in, the partnership is allowed to start spending it and not before. He tells me this play of yours been in rehearsal for six weeks, you're headed out of town for bookings, and the partnership is a long way from closing. Is that true?"

I nodded.

"Who's been shelling out for the actors?"

"I have."

"Personally?"

"That's the only kind of money I've got."

"What about the set, isn't that expensive?"

"In this case, yes," I said.

"And it's built?"

"It had to be."

"Who paid for it?"

"I haven't yet."

"You're going to get the set builder mad if you don't pay."

I nodded, trying to smile.

"In fact," Manucci said, "I had a little talk with your set builder before you came. He says he's going to close you down out of town unless he gets paid."

"He'll get paid."

"Out of what? You've raised only twenty percent of the money you need and no more's coming in."

"Twenty-two percent," I said, hopeless. He'd researched everything.

I stood up so his eyes would have to follow me as I paced.

I said, "Mr. Manucci, you know I'm here to discuss an investment from you that would enable the show to go forward on schedule, but I have to be sure . . . the money is clean. I don't mean to pry—"

"You're prying," he cut me off. His face was chiseled stone. Then the muscles in his cheeks relaxed. I'd have hired him as a character actor in a flash.

"I don't know what you know about me, Mr. Riller. I'm going to tell you. When you sit down."

I retreated to my place on the sofa opposite him.

"When you pick a play, Mr. Riller, it's got to meet your standards, right?"

I nodded.

"Would you have produced *Let My People Come,* one of those things?"

"No."

"It's got to be something you want to be associated with, right? Right," he said. "I don't do narcotics because I don't want to be associated with something that hurts a lot of people I don't want to hurt. You understand?"

I nodded.

"There's nothing I do that would foul up kids," he said. "Besides, the hard stuff is dangerous for guys who run it because the cops've got a rod up their ass about narcotics. You know why?"

I didn't.

"Because they're jealous. You'd be too if you were a cop. You make thirty something a year after a long haul, and some low-level dealer's making that much a week? A cop does his twenty years, what kind of a civilian job does he get? Directing traffic to a teller's window in some bank? A drug dealer, if he doesn't get caught, he's got a lifetime career. The cops hate dealers for the same reason a lot of people hate Jews, pure jealousy. I don't want to get in the middle of that kind of psychology. Have a cigar?"

From the desk he brought over a box of Macanudo coronas.

"Only after dinner," I said, waving the box away. Ezra, offered the box as an afterthought, took one.

"Take another one for later," Manucci said, clipping off the end of Ezra's cigar.

"Can we get back to the business at hand?" I said.

Manucci's face froze. He'd offered the cigars. He liked telling me about his business. I'd made a crack about the source of his money, and that opened him up, and now I'd shut him up.

"Mr. Riller," he said, "the business at hand was your needing four hundred plus. I was explaining to you that every bill that crosses my desk is as clean as your wife's face. I don't think you want to listen, you just want to talk. You think you're up on a stage or something? You think you're in charge of this conversation? I'll tell you something, Riller, you aren't in charge of anything anymore."

My pride forced me to my feet.

"You going somewhere?"

How repair this? I looked at Ezra.

Manucci said, "If you're going, take your babysitter with you."

"Gentlemen, gentlemen," Ezra said.

I walked the rest of the way to the door as if I were underwater in a diver's heavy helmet.

Ezra came after me. "Ben," he said, "wait a minute." And in a whisper, "What'll you tell Sam Glenn?"

I needed to loosen my tie, undo the top button of my shirt so I could breathe.

Manucci's voice caught me. "Hey Riller," he said, "this is a business discussion, isn't it?"

• • • • • 4

Nick Manucci

Sure everybody said my old man was terrific, did they ever ask my mother or me for a reference?

With Mama he never went off the wall because she was going to be the mother of his bambinos, right? His fun was other women. With her he was like she was some religious figure who lived in the house. He gave orders to her just like he did to the priest.

Nice man. You think that body spiked on the iron fence flew there? You crossed Aldo Manucci and you crossed the River Styx at the same time.

In high school, come my senior year I had to talk college to him. You needed college for anything, right?

That terrific man didn't ask for a discussion with me about my life, he had it all figured out. "I want you go first class, Harvard, Yale, something like that. You become bigshot for big company, General Electric, General Motors, something like that."

Finished?

"Papa, with respect," I said. "I don't want to be part of General nobody. I want to be on my own like you."

"Maybe you don't have brains to be on your own. Maybe you not smart enough to go Harvard Yale."

"If you wanted me to be like you," I said, "why didn't you marry a woman as smart as you?"

"I married your mother!" he shouted.

"My brain is half yours. Maybe it's her half that isn't good enough!"

The old lion smacked my face so hard the mark stayed for three days.

I hung in my room like it was a cave, the shade down, the ceiling light off. I pissed in my baseball trophy so I wouldn't have to go down the hall to the toilet except when they were asleep.

I kept the door locked. I wouldn't let him come into the room even when he said through the door that if I apologized he'd make peace.

On the third day I let my mother in.

She stood there, holding her arms out to me. Not a word.

She held me tight against her breasts, patted my head, humming some Italian song from long ago.

It was like dope.

Then she said, "Nicko, he tell me what you say. I forgave you, Nicko. Now you forgive him."

That old moneylender sure knew how to put a proposition to your head. Pick any college. Major in anything. He'd *lend* me the money. But if I went to a college he approved of and majored in business, the money wouldn't be a loan, it'd be a gift.

I didn't want to come out of school owing him anything.

The only business school in the area I could get into was NYU, where I learned all the rules my old man violated. They taught us never confuse employees with people. My father confused them all the time. Also, some borrower give him a story, he'd give the borrower two, three more days. Soft! If one of his collectors goofed, he'd give him a warning before firing him, a waste of time. NYU taught us time was your asset, the more successful you were the bigger that asset. My old man wasted time listening to people's stories that didn't have anything to do with how much they could pay back. He was like a country grocery store, that's why he never made it out of Little Italy.

My father's way was horse-and-buggyville, getting hooked by customers' stories, meeting their families, that shit. My business was to sell money. The guys who borrow big from banks use the phone. The guys who borrow from me, they're not thinking about buying a car if they find the right model. They have a hard-on for money that won't let them think of anything else and it won't go away unless they get it. The little guy's got a MasterCard, he's borrowing every time he uses his plastic, he doesn't have to ask. The man who comes into my office couldn't make it if he had a hundred Visas in his pocket. He knows how much he needs. He can't walk to another showroom. It's a dangerous business. If a starving man walks into a supermarket, he'll steal. In this supermarket the goods aren't lying around on shelves. People starving for money can get crazy. Guys who put out oil rig fires, they get paid a lot, don't they? Guys like me put out a businessman's fire. When one of them welshes and you go to get your money and he puts his hands around your throat, he forgets it's business, he thinks he has a right to kill you. Which is why I frame deals so the guy knows I've got his short hairs, so he won't be tempted to welsh, or to get rough. My customers don't have a list of approved suppliers. It's either me or the mob, and who wouldn't rather deal with me?

When that Ivy League *putz* Riller and his nothing lawyer headed for the door, they were doing what a lot of them do, pretending to be heading somewhere when they had nowhere to go except back to me. I could see his lawyer stirring the sawdust in his brain.

Riller turned around as if I had him on a string. "Mr. Manucci," he said to me, "you're right, this is a business discussion. The real negotiator in the family is my wife."

"Oh? What does she do?"

I looked at Mr. No-Guts. I figured his wife for one of those Greta Garbo types that tries to make you feel you're part of the wallpaper. I'd have guessed she's an actress who gets her jobs through Mr. Big, then puts her ass out for him to kiss.

"She's a literary agent," Riller said. "She negotiates hard bargains every day."

I'd give her something hard to bargain for.

He said, "I'd like you to meet my wife sometime."

"It would be my pleasure," I said.

Riller reminds me of Boxhead Armitage, dean of admissions, the supersnob who needed to replace eight grand he'd slipped out of the college treasury, one bill at a time, for a necessity. Necessity my ass,

Boxhead spent all the dough on his new wife, a people-in-the-street-stopper. He brought her around to prove it to me. She looked like Princess Grace, and I treated her, putting a chair under her ass when she sat down, lighting her cigarette, all that. Boxhead was fucking stupid about the way he fixed the books. An audit team was on the way in. His collateral wasn't worth filing a UCC form for. I tried sending him away, but he pulled me aside and said as part of the deal would I like to spend a weekend with his Princess Grace? You'd never catch an Italian doing what these boxheads do. If these guys need dough bad enough, they let a stranger play with their best toy. If my father'd owed five million to Mussolini he wouldn't have let him play with home goods for one second even if one feel wiped out the debt. The only guy I ever personally took care of was the one who picked Mary for a pigeon and made the mistake of boasting about it.

When Armitage repeated the offer, I looked over at Miss Clean pretending she's paying attention to *New York* magazine. A weekend's too long for any broad, I told Boxhead, one evening's okay, and since he needed the cash immediately, how about today as watching her goods got my motor running.

Afterward, while I was driving her home, I knew why she'd agreed. It takes savvy to get one of those iceboxes warmed up. On her back that lady was no Princess Grace, she was a hollerer. I let her take the envelope with the cash to him. I made sure she knew it wasn't pay. It was a loan at ten percent a week. Maybe her Dean boy could get a loan from his rich mother he'd avoided seeing since he married Princess Grace. Mama Armitage, the way he described her, was supposed to be class. Maybe she saw through Princess Grace. As this princess was getting out of my car I thought of something. "Honey," I said, "any week you bring the interest, you don't have to make a payment on principal. If your husband makes the drop, I want ten percent of the principal, suit yourself."

You see how easy it is to keep a beautiful relationship going? I saw them together only once more, when Boxhead came to tell me that though he'd put the money back they'd traced what they called the defalcation and asked him to resign. He had to get a job in some other city, and there was still fifteen hundred on my books. At the outset I had told him one condition was no skipping town, not even the appearance of skipping town, or the whole loan comes due and payable immediately, and I had a surefire method of finding anybody anywhere.

Boxhead didn't know what to do, right?

So I told him it's simple. He and his Princess Grace go off in his Honda and leave her Porsche with me. When the fifteen hundred was ready, with the interest of course, she could fly east and pick up her Porsche from me person-to-person so to speak.

What could he say, no? She'd hound him till he'd come up with the scratch to get the Porsche back.

Anyway, Riller, who even looks like this Armitage, he's trying to be nice, so I told him, "Please have a seat. No reason for anyone to get excited. I was just trying to explain my principles since we're talking about being partners." To Hochman I said, "Did you know Mr. Riller's father and my father knew each other real well a long time ago?"

Hochman said, "I was aware of it." Why can't these guys say something straight out in English. *I was aware of it.* Shit.

It was Riller who piped up, "My father was very fond of your father."

Fond? My old man fell for that Yid's personality like it was some medicine he needed. He let Louie Riller become a suckerfish on him. "Louie nice man," he used to say. "Brains working allatime." My mother'd say, "If he's so smart, how come he always needs money?" She was pecking at my old man, you got to be careful who you lend money to, friends don't like to pay interest. The truth is she had a thing for Louie, finding an excuse to be around whenever he showed. Even a kid could see it. The guy was no George Raft, but when he came she fluttered her black dresses like a pigeon.

"I suppose you know," I said, "that my father made his first big money from renting women?"

Riller didn't say a thing. His cupid-lips lawyer didn't say a thing. I loved it.

My father never wanted straight people like Louie Riller knowing where he got all that money to lend out, but I was going to make sure these guys knew that Aldo Manucci's halo was made of a lot of nose-rings.

"That's okay," I told them, making my face serious. "The only bad part was that it made my mother ashamed. She wanted me to be Mr. American. She was worry-sick I'd wind up doing the same thing as my old man. Well, my mother died a happy woman because the sex revolution gave away free what my old man'd been selling. He always said the best money was in specialty service, high-priced fancies. When people started advertising their kinks in *The Village Voice,* my father decided that's enough. My money," I said to Riller, "is as clean as a virgin."

Riller coughed.

I like to negotiate with someone who is nervous.

He coughed again. Beautiful.

Finally he said, "I was merely"—get that, *merely*—"concerned that any investment in my play not be connected to Atlantic City casino money, anything like that."

I told him, "You're out of date, Mr. Riller. I was out of gaming before Atlantic City was back in. If a gambler can't make it, he blows his brains out in the men's room. If I wanted to spend my life doing business with sick people, I'd open a hospital. In fact I got two legit nursing homes in New Jersey. I make my money available to people who deserve it and can't get it someplace else. That's my principle. How many guys in show business live on principle?"

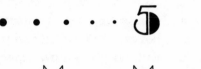

Mary Manucci

When I was a teenager I used to have a kind of private joke. I'd tell myself that my parents, Salvatore and Mary Carducci, didn't settle in one of the Little Italys on the East Coast but went on to Minnesota because everyone there was so blond. The truth is they came from a small town in the north of Italy, and everybody from there either went to Argentina or the United States, and those who came to America passed right through New York and went on to Duluth because all the others from their village had gone there.

My father, a refined-looking man, always wore his fedora at a slight tilt. Mr. Proud used to laugh when he referred to people who came from Naples as "four-legs" and from Sicily as "sheep lovers." He called me his *Principessa,* and implanted the idea that what I needed was an Italian boy who didn't look Italian.

My father, who, according to my mother, always had the smarts for business, didn't want to do what the other Italians were doing, fruit and vegetables or a barber shop. He had what he called "a real American idea," a store that carried imported children's clothes for people who didn't want to dress their kids in Sears Roebuck. Baby clothes with a European label caught the wind of snob appeal among the better-off locals. Pretty soon if you attended any baby shower in the so-called good neighborhoods, you'd see the piled-up boxes wrapped in candy-striped foil paper that proclaimed where the contents had been bought. My father's employees spent eight minutes wrapping a gift, with a ribbon in the form of a flower. People used to joke about buying empty boxes from the Carducci store because they made beautiful presents. Kids, as you know, grow out of clothes fast. If your precious started out in a Carducci outfit, you kept the image up by going back to Carducci's every time Precious grew a couple of inches. Distances in Minnesota mean nothing. People came from other counties before an important birthday. In the six weeks before Christmas we could have sold tickets to get into the shop. I grew up smelling success, but once I heard a dressed-up farmer and his wife leaving with an armful of pretty boxes say, "These wops sure know how to stock a store." At my junior prom, Olaf Swenson's son Pete, the handsomest boy in our class, asked me to dance twice in a row, and when we went out back with our Cokes, his blue eyes burning, he said, "Mary, you are absolutely number one. My mother says you're Catholic, is that true?"

That shook me. We got another jolt when my father refused a certain Mr. Sondergaard further credit because of his long-unpaid bills. Mr. Sondergaard left the store spluttering loud enough for others to hear, "Never shopping in this dago store again."

When it was decided that I go to college in the East, my father's excuse was that I should get away from home for a while, but I knew the real reason. I was eligible. And I had better be in places where I'd be more likely to meet good young men of Italian extraction so that my ears, which my father said could have been sculpted by Michelangelo, would never hear *dago*.

My father, who put a dollar in the collection plate when everyone else put a quarter, asked the priest about colleges where good Catholics go, and where there weren't too many Italians from places "down below," meaning south of Rome, which was for him a more important dividing line than the Iron Curtain. The priest said Manhattanville, Mary will meet wonderful girls there.

I was accepted by Manhattanville. In my sophomore year, on a trip to Bloomingdale's with a girlfriend, I met Nick Manucci, who looked like he might have come from Minnesota, tall, handsome, hair the color of white sand, and a name that rhymed with mine.

He danced like a professional. When he kissed me, it wasn't lips on lips like other boys, but lips on my neck, and just above my breasts, and behind my ear, and suddenly my mouth, never the same route twice, and always a way that made me aware of my body preparing itself for love. I wouldn't let him. We had to get to know each other first.

I took him to Searleham's, a men's clothing store that catered to well-to-do Protestants. I could see he instantly felt uncomfortable because he was wearing a fluorescent sports shirt. Over at the display case, I pointed to a button-down with a muted stripe. He nodded. At the tie rack, I fingered a paisley. He said okay. I could tell he wanted to get the hell out of the store fast so he could take off his shiny shirt and throw it in a Salvation Army dumpster.

He had a dark coat he wore when we went out. So after a couple of days I took him back to Searlham's and had him try gray gloves with his dark coat.

"Classy," was all I said.

"Thirty dollars for a pair of gloves?"

Of course he bought them. Once I said I wanted to give him a manicure. He resisted, as if it was something sissy. But I made a ritual of it, and he said it turned into one of the most erotic experiences of his life, and wanted a manicure soon again. His hands began to look well groomed, like my father's.

His voice had a slight coarseness to it, like Bogart's. I tried to help him smooth out the roller-coaster inflections of New York, but I didn't want him to lose the huskiness because when he had his arms around me and talked into my ear, that voice did things to me.

Once I remembered how I'd clothed my favorite doll and thought, "Am I doing it all over again with a man?" Why couldn't there be enough smart men in the world so there'd be one for each smart woman?

I made up excuses not to see Nick for a week. He kept phoning me. Finally he said, "What's the matter, ain't I smart enough for you?"

"I'm sure you'll be very successful," I said.

"Hey teach," he said, imitating Dead End Kids from the movies, "ain't I learning to be classy fast enough?"

"You make me sound like a snob."

"Sure you're a snob. I love it. You want me to wear spats when I make love to you, I'll wear spats. I'll wear a jockstrap on my head, okay?"

"Okay, okay," I said. There were no ideal men. "Tomorrow?"

"Sure tomorrow. But today's today. How about today and tomorrow and the day after, too?"

"You're greedy."

"You bet your sweet ass I'm greedy. What are you, a nun? The last time—"

"Come on over." I remembered the expression Bette Davis had in some movie when she was saying yes like she was surrendering a country.

I never had a hangup about pleasure. My excuse to myself was that Nick gave me pleasure. I didn't have the experience to know that some men, when the contract is signed, stop selling.

Nick eased through NYU by charming the teachers the way he charmed me. He learned facts to pass exams. But it was all a means to an end, graduation, and the diploma was all the satisfaction he got out of it. In high school, my favorite teacher, Miss Gladys as we called her because her last name made us laugh, told me there was a new field, working with retarded children in private schools, that could give me more joy than teaching ordinary children because each step was such a triumph. I'd found what I was meant to do, and it was an easy field to get a job in because people, despite their pretensions, are contemptuous of the retarded, as if their condition were voluntary. As Nick said, "You want to teach stupid kids instead of smart kids, that's your lookout. Just so's I can tell people you're a teacher period, it's okay."

For a while Nick talked about this parcel and that parcel, so I thought he'd fixed his business attention on real estate.

"Look, Mary, get off it. I like doing deals. I don't care if it's land or—"

"Larceny?"

He came up real close and pinched my lips together with his fingers. "Sometimes," he said, "you talk out of turn."

On Sundays he could shine as a cook as some Italian men do.

I asked him, "How would you like to own a really elegant restaurant some day that people from far away would come to because the food was so good?"

Nick laughed. "The hours are murder. Besides, who wants to cook what you can't eat?" He put his arms around me. "I'd love to cook you."

I think Nick skipped in and out of what he called "projects" so nobody would think he was finally into a field he'd stay with. Then one day I was short twenty dollars for something I longed to buy and Nick said, "I'll lend it to you."

The look in his eyes chilled me.

"It's okay," I said, "I'll manage."

"Take it," Nick said. "I won't charge interest."

I'd never heard of friends or family even thinking of charging interest, and I couldn't understand why Nick had said that until I met Aldo Manucci, the Bronx Medici. I learned that moneylending was the family business, and Nick had just been pretending to be interested in various other things so that when the inevitable happened it would seem that he had made a choice.

His father sold some debts to him to get him started. I didn't know you could sell a debt. And since Nick couldn't pay in cash, his father sold him the debts on credit and charged him interest, but not as much as Nick collected from the customers. My friends had become teachers, and engineers and doctors, their work had content, but moneylending?

"Tell your friends I'm a banker," Nick said. "That way you wouldn't be ashamed."

"Oh, Nick," I said, "you're misunderstanding me."

"I got you perfect. You go for the show. I mean like the marble pillars in banks, you know what they're made of? Cement. Covered by a fake layer of marble so people like you will be comfortable about doing business with those solid people behind all that marble. I'll tell you something maybe you don't want to hear, but this country was built by people who took smart risks. Bankers ought to be run out of the country because the only risks they take are stupid risks."

Nick's fervor was erotic. I didn't have to hear what he was saying.

"Mary, banks fight with each other to lend money to businesses that could get along without it, and they turn their backs on the starter-uppers, the people who made business possible. I've seen smart businessmen whose asses have been kissed for years by bankers suddenly hit a snag, a bad deal, something, and the same gray-suit guys are touching the edge of their eyeglasses as if they can't really see you. The guys they turn away are the ones who show up at my father's, hate steaming out of their ears about how banks treated them. So they use my father's money to get back on their feet, terrific, and then what do they do? They go back to their fair-weather friends with the fake marble pillars. Guys like my father ought to get medals for what they do to save businessmen."

"Doesn't your father charge more interest than the banks?"

"Sure," Nick said. "Doesn't a lawyer who takes a case on contingency charge more because if he doesn't win he doesn't get paid? My father takes risks banks won't take."

Shylock was the word I needed to shake out of my head. "Don't people like your father use, well, men who put pressure on borrowers if they don't repay on time?"

"What do you expect him to do, report the delinquents to Dun and Bradstreet? If he didn't get his money back from the people who owed him, there'd be no more to lend the next guy the banks turn their back on."

Thugs was what I thought. "Why are you glaring at me, Nick?"

"I'm not glaring. I'm looking. Are you ashamed of me?"

"I'm not ashamed of anything you do," I said.

I'd lied before. Everyone does. But that was my first important lie. Was being a shylock a vocation? My father, who had that wonderful store, once said to me, "Marry a shoemaker, somebody who makes something. Marry a farmer who makes food. Marry a carpenter who makes houses. Don't marry a man who makes nothing, a businessman." Was he disparaging himself, a storekeeper and a businessman? You can't skip centuries and go back to everybody making something. Even then there were men who put deals together, got the ships going to the Indies. Besides, my father was a reacher, he didn't really want me to marry a workingman. Didn't the "businessmen" he scorned by the way he pronounced the word, didn't they make things? My father was as unrealistic as the dropouts who want to live on barter. Wasn't the important thing that a man enjoyed what he did for a living? Wasn't Nick proud of something that rubbed me the wrong way for the wrong reasons?

Maybe this is all hindsight. At that age what I knew was that I was happy when he telephoned, happy when he took me out, and happiest when eventually he made love to me and it blinded me the way that first blast at Los Alamos blinded the onlookers.

At the wedding, my father met his father. "In the old country," my father said to me, "we would have met earlier. He eats with his fingers."

On the airplane to St. Thomas, where we spent our honeymoon, Nick said, "My old man joked to me about your old man's pointy-toed shoes." We laughed a lot over the imperfect world of our elders.

You might say that in due course we realized my father's dream. Nick and I had a boy and a girl, blond and not at all Italian-looking, and by the time Nick made his first million and won the respect of both fathers, he made love to me only once a month or so, perfunctorily, or in the middle of the night in response to some physical urge, you couldn't call it lovemaking, and I realized what every wife realizes when her husband comes home very late with half-baked excuses ready to sleep. When I finally was able to talk to him about the other women, to ask what had happened with us, he said that if I didn't like the way things were I could take a lover as long as the man didn't come to the house or meet the children.

Nick

It was time for me to say the thing that always cleared the air. "Mr. Riller, I'm listening to you to find out if I can make money on this deal."

Riller coughed into his fist. "Mr. Manucci," he said, "most of my investors make money most of the time."

"Not on this turkey. You said you raised only twenty-two percent. Somebody knows something."

"In my judgment, it's the best play I've come across in more than ten years."

"Maybe something's happened to your judgment, Mr. Riller. My rule is I get mine, win or lose."

Hochman the lawyer decided it was time to earn a living. He said, "What is your proposal, Mr. Manucci?"

"Okay," I said. "You gentlemen comfortable? Here's the way I see this."

Riller crossed his legs, trying to look relaxed, but he looked to me like a smoker who just gave up smoking.

"According to this memo—this is your memo, Mr. Hochman, isn't it?"

"The facts in it are mine," said Riller.

"I don't really care whose, this is what you're selling me, right? This budget for the production is five fifty out of which you've raised one hundred twenty-one thousand, leaving me to supply the missing seventy-eight percent, or four hundred and thirty thousand or so."

"Correct," Hochman said. "Actually it comes to four hundred twenty-nine thousand dollars exactly."

"Wrong. I think Mr. Riller's budget is too low. It should be six fifty." I was enjoying this.

I could hear Riller breathing ten feet away. He said, "I can't renegotiate with those who've already invested on the basis of a five fifty budget."

"You won't need to," I said.

"Besides," Riller added, "I plan budgets carefully. We don't need the extra hundred."

"Ah," I said. "The production doesn't need it, but I do. What happens is I lend the production five hundred and twenty-nine thousand and at closing you give me a hundred back in cash. That's my management fee."

"Management fee?"

"I'm managing to get your show on the road, ain't I? On the five twenty-nine, I'm not charging street vigorish, which is six for five. I'm charging—"

Hochman butted in. "What's six for five?"

"Twenty percent a week," I said.

"That's illegal," said Hochman.

"Sure it's illegal. I said I'm not charging that. You need Q-tips for your ears? I'm charging on a per annum basis, prime plus six, just like a factoring division of whatever bank you do business with, very fair."

"I can't pay interest out of the budget," Riller said.

"Oh, I know that. It'll have to come out of your share of the general partnership, which will be forty-nine percent because the other fifty-one percent is my payoff if the play works."

I could see Hochman straining to keep from going into his briefcase for his calculator. Riller leaned back like a real gentleman and did it in his head.

Riller's face got formal. "Mr. Manucci," he said, "let me be sure I understand. As a limited partner, you get what you'd normally get, seventy-eight percent of fifty percent, the rest going to the other investors. But in addition, you would be getting fifty-one percent of my half plus a payback of the whole five twenty-nine, including the hundred thousand I paid as a management fee? Even if the play is a smash, what's left might not be worth the candle."

Carefully, like tightening my finger on a trigger but not pulling it, I said, "I didn't realize you were ready to ditch the play."

Riller clasped his hands together like a kid making a London bridge. Maybe his left hand and right hand were teaming up to hold each other from doing something they shouldn't do.

"Mr. Manucci," he finally said.

I said, "Yes," to help him along.

"I can't abandon the production because I can't return the money already invested. It's been spent. And I've committed to expenses well beyond that."

"How well?"

"At least two hundred thousand dollars."

"Which you don't have?"

He nodded, so I said to his Mr. Hochman, "When Mr. Riller spent the investors' dough before the partnership was officially complete, that wasn't exactly legal, was it, Mr. Hochman?"

What could either of them say? I moved forward in my chair so my face could be closer to Riller's face and I talked real low as if what I was saying was a secret. "Mr. Hochman will tell you that using escrow funds is a criminal offense, the kind you go to jail for. If you don't raise the balance, the Manhattan district attorney, considering how famous you are, he'd get a reelection headline taking you to the grand jury, wouldn't he? More coffee?"

Riller said, "No coffee."

Hochman said, "No coffee."

This was my play, not his. I leaned over toward Riller. "I don't want you to feel uncomfortable about any decision you make. It's got to be an absolutely free decision on your part."

He looked over at Hochman.

I said, "It's still your choice. You can walk out of here, we'll shake hands, remain friends, no harm done."

When I'm at this stage of a negotiation I think someday this guy whose nuts I'm squeezing is going to want revenge. But the only casualty rate in my business is from competitors, not from the public. The public learns to eat and swallow real good.

"Mr. Manucci," Riller said, "I'll put my cards on the table."

Listen to that Hebe, cards on the table! He's got his guts on the table.

"Please do," I said.

"It must be clear by now," Riller said, "that I must have the money and I haven't been able to get it elsewhere. I need the four twenty-nine."

"Five twenty-nine," I reminded him, "You haven't put anything on the table that wasn't there. I knew your situation like a road map before you walked in. I don't waste time on cold calls."

For a second, when Riller grabbed the side of the coffee table, I thought he was going to upend it. My mistake. He controlled himself real good, so in a sweet voice I said, "I can understand how you feel. A man with your reputation wouldn't back out of this production even if he could."

Riller actually cracked a smile. It was like we were both looking at the truth and saying yeah, that's the way it is.

"Getting angry," I said, "doesn't do anybody any good."

He said, "I'm not angry."

"Good," I said, "because I'm going to need a little security to make sure I get my principal back. I know you're famous. Famous isn't collateral. Don't worry, I'm not asking to hold your wife on my farm upstate."

I laughed, waiting for him to laugh a little too.

I said, "Mr. Hochman, I assume Mr. Riller has used all of his cash assets?"

Riller took the ball. "Yes."

"Any equity in your house?"

"Maybe four hundred thousand."

"I'll take a second on that."

"Second?"

"Mortgage."

Riller said, "That's out of the question!"

"The way I figure it, your house is already in jeopardy. What about your stocks?"

"I've borrowed against them already."

"Municipals? A man who's made what you've made over the years must have municipals."

"I can't be left totally without resources if the production doesn't work."

"I'm lending you money, not giving it to you, and I got to be sure to get it back."

"The only municipal I've got is for sixty thousand and it doesn't mature for four years."

"That's okay, I'll just take an assignment of it. I know it's your rainy-day money, Mr. Riller. This is your rainy day."

I know Riller had his hands on his knees to keep the shake from showing. I looked at his hands so he would know I knew he was nervous.

"Don't you worry about resources," I said. "If the production works, maybe you won't be rich, but you'll be out of trouble. Tell you what. I'll hire you as general manager for my next production, how's that? We have a deal. It's nice to do business with you, Ben. Call me Nick from now on." I stood up so we could shake hands on it.

Riller stood up, too, but the color in his face was high red.

His lawyer says to him, "What's up, Ben?"

Riller says, "Mr. Manucci, you've had a lot of experience in business."

"You bet."

"Then you must have learned that a deal is good only if it's good for both sides."

"Oh, sure, I agree with you," I say. "This deal gets you off the hook with your play and puts me on the hook for a lot of dough. We're even steven."

"Like hell we are. You aren't risking a penny. If the play doesn't work, you've got everything I own as security. That isn't business."

"It's the price of money."

"It's extortion."

I turned to his mouthpiece and said, "Mr. Hochman, I get an earache from a word like *extortion*. You are guests in my office. If Mr. Riller is uncomfortable with the terms, take him and his play shit somewhere else."

"Now just a minute," Hochman says. "I'm sure we can—"

Riller's hand on his arm stopped him. "Enough."

This king of Broadway, this low-grade nothing, wasting my time. Who the hell does he think he is? "Fuck you, Riller. Go and don't come back. And take your goddamn lawyer with you."

BOOK II

Louie Riller

They all say the only person Ben listens to is his father. He hears me, but does he listen? He didn't listen when I was alive, why should now be different? These days, who listens to a father anyhow?

When Ben needs seed money for a production he finds a rich man with temporary insanity. He hurries home to tell Jane he's found a savior. What he's found is a stalking horse to bring other investors in. He forgets that when he was a *pisher* of twelve I took him over to the mirror in the bathroom and said, "Ben, look, there is your savior. Are you listening to me?"

"Pop," he said, "lend me your razor."

A twelve-year-old boy doesn't listen. You're driving, you see a stop sign, you stop. Life is full of signs that Ben ignores. Except once.

When Ben was sixteen, I came into his room and saw him with a whole bunch of pages.

"That's a long letter you're writing," I said.

"It's not a letter, Pop."

"Oh?" I said.

"It's, uh, a play," he said.

"Like on Broadway?"

"Just one act, Pop."

I moved closer so I could see the pages on the desk.

"In poetry?" I asked.

"In verse."

"I shouldn't have disturbed you."

"It's okay, Pop," he said. "I was just about finished for tonight."

At the door I stopped to look back at him. My voice came out hoarse. "I'm so proud," I said.

I let too much time go by before I asked him, "How's the play coming?"

"It's coming," he lied.

"Who have you shown it to?"

"Ezra."

"And what did he say?"

"He said, 'It ain't Shakespeare.' "

"Not everything has to be Shakespeare. Did he say it was good?"

Ben turned to face me. "He said you can always show it to Louie, he'll think it's good."

"Why didn't you?"

"Didn't what?"

"Show it to me."

"Because Ezra thinks he's a born critic. I told him to tell me the faults and I'll rewrite it. You know what he said, Pop? He said, 'You've got the mind of a salesman, Benny boy. Why don't you write something commercial?' "

"Boys are mean."

"That's right."

"You should have been deaf better than to listen. Ezra has too much influence over you."

"You always say he's terrific this, terrific that."

"Doesn't matter. For you he shouldn't be a stop sign."

"I don't know what you're talking about, Pop."

"Yes, you do."

To my dying day Ben never showed me what he wrote. Instead he became a producer of other people's plays.

* * *

One Saturday night, before going out on a date, Ben said, "Pop, how about you and me going for a walk tomorrow morning?"

"Sure," I said as he's running out the door. "What time by you is morning?"

"How about noon?" he shouts.

God knows what time he got home. At noon I peeked into Ben's room. He didn't look like someone ready to wake up.

"Hello!" I said.

I waited. Ben forced one eye half open. "Is it morning?"

"How about afternoon?" I said. "A pessimist shortens his life by sleeping late because he doesn't expect life to be much good."

His half-open eye looked around for the alarm clock. He yawned like a young hippopotamus, untangled himself from the top sheet, stood swaying, said, "Okay," and like a blind man staggered past me to the bathroom. I could hear the firefighter's stream, the flush, and then the shower full force.

When he came into the kitchen, both eyes open, I was still digesting my newspaper. "I give the war one more year," I said.

"Yes, General."

The bagel, cut in half two hours ago, now went half on my plate, half on his. I shoved over the cream cheese and poured some of my cocoa into his cup. Ten minutes later we headed for Van Cortlandt Park.

They say I walk fast for a short man. The truth is I have never been able to make myself walk slow.

I put my arm through Ben's. "I think you should stop growing," I said with a laugh. "You're ten inches taller than me."

"I think I've stopped, Pop."

"Thank you." I could see he was embarrassed having my arm through his, so I took it away. I said, "I want to congratulate you for not persecuting your fingernails anymore. You have nice hands now."

"Mom says they're like yours."

I could feel color in my face.

"You know," I said, "when I hear other parents, you think their kids are enemies. You think maybe we're different?"

No reaction.

"I'll bet one thing," I said.

"What?"

"Hitler's father never went for a walk in the park with his son."

I'm not sure Ben heard me. He was fumbling in his pocket. Out came a foil-wrapped package smaller than a box of cough drops. Ben put out his hand with the package on it as if he hoped that I would take it instead of his actually handing it to me, as if that would be less embarrassing.

"What is that?" I said.

"Happy birthday," he said.

"Is that what it is?"

We sat on a park bench for the ritual of package opening.

"You shouldn't have done it," I said.

"How do you know what I shouldn't before you know what it is?" Ben said.

"Only jewelry comes in a box like that. You shouldn't bring jewelry to a jeweler."

"It isn't that kind."

Inside the snap-top box were round cuff links with black onyx insets.

"They're not real gold," Ben said quickly, "just gold filled."

"I'll use them as paperweights. For small pieces of paper." Ben didn't laugh. I said, "I don't have any shirts with French cuffs."

Ben's cheeks's flushed. "Mom's getting you a going-out shirt."

"Your face is red. Are you feeling okay?"

"I wasn't supposed to say anything."

"I won't tell."

How could Ben know that I didn't want shirts with French cuffs because that was what the professor in Chicago always wore, the one who was after Zipporah.

"It doesn't matter," I said. "I appreciate the present." I slid the box into my pocket.

"I thought maybe we'd go bowling this afternoon," Ben said.

"Your mother thinks bowling is for blue-collar types."

"Tell her we're going to play golf."

I smiled. "I tried bowling once in Chicago and kept getting the ball into the gutter. Besides, Aldo Manucci is expecting me."

How was I to know that even then Manucci was for Ben the worst word in the world? Did he invite me to go bowling so that I wouldn't think of going to Manucci's on my birthday?

"Hey, Pop," he said, "no business on your birthday, okay?"

"I go to pay my respect, not for business."

"Respect?"

"Respect."

"He's a shylock, Pop."

My brain couldn't keep my mouth from talking. "Don't you call him that. Not in front of me. Never."

"You said he makes everybody pay through the nose."

"Only once, when I was angry."

"Please don't go there today, Pop. Please?"

I took his chin in my hand and turned his face. "Look me in the eye, Ben. Mr. Manucci is my friend, do you understand that?"

I let go of his face as if I'd made a mistake taking it from him and was now putting it back where it belonged.

"Get up. Let's walk," I said. "I'll think better."

After a while, I said, "Do I talk about your friends?"

"No."

"You think that I watch your friends with my brain turned off? Larry Markowitz, a human snail growing up to be a bigger snail, what's the attraction?"

"He lives next door," Ben said.

"Suppose the Devil lived next door, would you make friends with him because he lived next door? Your friend Linton, what's his name, Boris?"

"Morris."

"Okay, Morris. Maybe he can't help having a face full of pimples, but does he have to dress like a pimple? Does he have to talk imitation James Cagney? Why do you spend time with him?"

"It's hard to avoid him."

"Hard is no reason. It's hard to be honest. It's hard to make a living. It's hard to keep love going. Easy is the Devil's game. Hard belongs to God. I don't tell you to avoid Morris. I ask you why you don't and you give me the world's worst excuse. Where did you go with Frances last night?"

"We went to see a double feature," Ben said.

"I won't ask you which, just in case you're lying. Your mother thinks that girl is bad for you."

Am I doing this because he called Manucci a shylock?

"She's a pretty girl," I said. "Your mother may be wrong. I'm not knocking all your friends. Ezra's a fine boy."

"I thought he was terrific."

"A fine, terrific boy."

"You'd rather have him for a son."

"Oh ho," I said. "Like an animal you want to pee a circle around me so nobody else can come into your territory? I tell you something, Mr. Seventeen, for walking and for talking and for love, the more you share, the more you have. Anyway, look at that, a Good Humor truck. Who eats ice cream before lunch?"

And so I bought two ice cream bars. Handing one to Ben, I said, "This should be the worst sin you ever commit."

As we circled home, Ben's eyes had the sadness of a boy who had failed in his mission. Manucci was still on my Sunday agenda.

Finally Ben said, "Is Mr. Manucci a real friend?"

"I'll tell you." I stooped to pick up a discarded Crackerjack box. Ben followed me to the nearest trash can. I dropped the box in and turned to face him. "A real friend," I said, "is someone you can call at three o'clock in the morning and say 'Come' and he'll come without asking why. Aldo Manucci is a friend once removed. He'd wake somebody else to come running to me. In business you can delegate, in friendship you can't. When I visit him on Sundays to pay respect, it is because we have the next best thing to a good friendship, a relationship in which he knows what I am and I know what he is, he knows what I want and I know what he wants. You know he's Italian, he has a very large family."

"I know."

"I am the official jeweler for that family. Whenever there's a new baby, I supply the baby ring and the cross."

"Mom says he doesn't pay you."

"What does she know about business? Of course he doesn't pay me for those things. They are presents. What he has done for me, there aren't enough presents in this world to make up for it. When we moved to New York from Chicago, the banks here wouldn't talk to me. Aldo Manucci asked me questions for five minutes and gave me a loan, a small one with plenty of vigorish."

"Vigorish?"

"Interest. When I repaid it, I got better terms for the next loan. He didn't squeeze me because we had begun a relationship."

"Pop, he didn't squeeze you because he wanted to keep the pinky rings and crosses coming."

"That came later. You are much too cynical, Mr. Seventeen. You don't remember you went with me once?"

Ben nodded.

"The front room was full of people waiting, like for a king."

"I hated it."

"He took us out of turn. You remember, he took anisette out of the cupboard and offered it to you, too? When I said I'd hurry because of the people waiting, he said, 'That's just business. They can wait.' And when it came time for me to sign the book for the money, he said, 'Louie, you don't need to sign.' That was for your benefit. To show we were friends."

"You pay him interest."

"That's how he makes a living."

"Interest plus presents."

"Together they don't add up to half of what he charges others."

"What makes you so special?"

I looked at Ben. At that age, they are all the same.

"When you were younger, I told you stories. When Manucci uncles and cousins get together on Sundays for spaghetti around the long dining-room table, I am the only outsider. With their ears sticking out they listen to my stories. Manucci and I both have something to give. Ours isn't a one-way street. Ben, you have to know."

"What?"

"I made one really horrible business mistake. It looked like I was going to lose absolutely everything if I didn't get a big loan fast. Manucci had a lot of loans out at the time. He couldn't come up with enough to save my business. So he called in a bank—he hated banks—and took a mortgage on his house so that I could have the money to save the business."

I gave it a minute.

"Ben, that mortgage was harder than a friend coming in the middle of the night."

"Maybe I was wrong about Mr. Manucci, Pop."

"I don't want you to get the wrong idea, Ben," I said. "The biggest danger in life is other people's money."

"I hear you."

"Like a deaf man you hear me."

"I hear you, Pop."

After a minute, I said, "I'm sorry." I added, "You know, Ben, despite a little difference here and there between you and me, I like who you are becoming. It's good to be ambitious. Only remember, the nearer you get to the front of the line, the more people with knives can see your back."

"I can take care of myself."

"I hope so. I wish I could live long enough to see how you will be on your own."

"You will, Pop."

"That's not for you to decide."

Out of sight of other people, I put my arm around Ben. "Mama's probably wondering where we are by now. Ben, two things make a man a *mensch*. You've got to have a good attitude to the failings of others. And you have to remember that strong people sometimes have strong problems. You must stay in touch with reality. On the ocean of life, it's the only dry land."

"I'm not sure I understand what you're trying to tell me, Pop."

"The truth is, Ben, people take hostages. Sometimes the hostage they take is themselves."

· · · · · 8

Louie

Of course I'm a wanderer! Moses wandered, Columbus wandered, should I have rotted in the old country? Should I have stayed in my *shtetl,* a subject not only of the czar but of every Cossack who wanted a Jew to beat? You don't need to be an Einstein to know that nothing plus nothing equals nothing. I got out because in Russia the future is for others. If I'd stayed, would I have met a woman like Zipporah from a big city like Kiev? Would this woman and I have produced an impresario like Ben?

Any time in the past four thousand years you ask a Jew what he wants, he says a son, by which he means a future for his name. But—pinch your nose—the Lord God Almighty Who blessed our people with a certain amount of brains and the *chutzpah* to use them, be careful of Him. If He offers you a chair, look before you sit down. God is the world's most experienced practical joker. Don't take my word for it, visit the sideshow of a circus and you'll see how God plays tricks on human beings. He's been playing Red Sea games since the beginning of time, which is a warning to our enemies. Better watch out because we've played with the Best and we're still here!

On me personally God played two dirty tricks. In 1914 when I finally managed my escape from the czar's army and got by crook and hook to Windsor in Canada, and then over the border to Detroit, I learned that my brother Mendel, who sneaked into America before me, changed our name from Razelson to Riller. Who Riller? What Riller? What am I to do, go around with a name different from my own brother? And so even before I have a son, I have lost my name.

Dirty trick two is that in the Golden Land I met a woman who was a queen compared to most of the women in this world, a lady named Zipporah, educated, tall, a beauty among beauties, and she says yes to me. Crazy! Who said a man five-feet-two can't reach up into heaven and pluck himself a star? Did God try to stop me? No, He encouraged me, part of His game! Harold was a son I couldn't have hoped for in my dreams, a blond like his mother, at six months his arms and thighs begin to be strong like a Cossack's yet he has the brains of Maimonides, what more could a Jew want? To make a living, not to have to borrow money, to bring up a family in peace, to be let alone by the Dirty Tricks Department. When God struck Egypt with the plagues, the worst was of course taking their firstborn. Dear God, I am not an Egyptian, can't You tell? Though I am something of a social democrat, I still believe in You. With Your help, I wanted in this country to be a small winner, and what did You do? You snatched away my firstborn like Hauptmann took the Lindbergh baby! When Harold was three, anyone could see he might become a Nobel Prize winner. You, Creator of the World, didn't You have enough Death that you needed my three-year-old?

Comment by Zipporah
■■ ■■ ■■

Louie, you're running away with yourself as you did all your life long. You're inventing more than God did.

If you'd had an education, you'd have learned to respect facts. You changed your name for a very practical reason. You didn't want any more than your brother Mendel did to be picked up by the Immigration Service and sent back to Russia. The name Razelson never meant anything to anyone in the old country. Nothing was taken away from you. And Harold was lost not because of some spiteful trick of the Almighty but because doctors had not yet invented a cure for nephritis. Louie, if you had a tenth of an ounce of science in you, you'd know God doesn't have time to pay attention to you. You talk to yourself. Be glad it isn't the Middle Ages anymore, you'd have been stoned as a lunatic! You had from me Ben, a son who lived, who is recognized in restaurants, who knows all the big stars, who became the biggest man on Broadway since Ziegfeld. Count your blessings, Louie, count your blessings.

Louie

I am not going to get involved in an exchange with that woman. Something has to come either from books or from life. Books were her department. Life was mine. To me, born poorest of the poor, food is a feast. To her it is a meal to prepare. To me the sun is the warmth of the universe. To her it is something that gives you freckles. Even the one thing on which I thought Zipporah and I agreed best, making love to each other, is to me heaven on earth and to her something to do quietly so the children shouldn't hear.

Zipporah won a gold medal for scholarship from the same czar who would have spit on me. A woman of breeding who at twenty-two was Superintendent of Evening Schools in Kiev. A royal woman, admired not only by her relatives but by mine, too. A woman who, if you listen to her, made only one mistake, marrying down.

Meaning me, who was born in a small village in Russia called Zhitomir in the year 1892. When I was eight years old, my father slipped on a muddy street in front of an oxcart and was so badly trampled that all the Jews of the village except his children prayed that God would relieve him of his pain and accept him in heaven. Those days God was not so accepting when it came to Russian Jews, and my father lingered for a month until He finally paid attention to a special promise made by the Rabbi.

As soon as the period of mourning was over, my mother, whose womb had been strong enough to produce eight children but whose lungs were weak, told me that I, like all but my youngest sister, would have to leave school and take whatever work the good people of the village found for us. And so as an eight-year-old I was apprenticed to Schmerl the carpenter, who put a bowl of food in front of me twice a day and tossed me an occasional kopeck.

Schmerl's place of work was a converted barn. In the loft, he stored the finished pieces of his work, mainly chairs—for Schmerl was beyond doubt the best maker of chairs within the distance that a man and his cart, pulled by a horse, could travel to buy four chairs from Schmerl and return to his home the same day.

You who sit on chairs all the time, how often do you think that someone actually made out of wood the piece of furniture that cradles your bottom? Schmerl taught me to respect a chair as you would a painting, to really *see* it. Mind you, Schmerl's were not chairs of the sort you'd find in a fancy department store. They were made of rough wood, smoothed so they would be without splinters, and stuck together at the joints not with fancy dowels but with a wood glue of Schmerl's own formula that held the pieces together like Samson. People would notice one of those chairs and say, "I see you have a Schmerl" and not, "I see you have a chair."

I was short for my age and Schmerl sometimes needled me. "I wonder if you, little *pupik,* have the strength to saw a piece of wood in two?"

I bent my arm to show the muscle. "My father, God rest his soul," I said, "let me chop wood."

Schmerl thought I was exaggerating, that my father probably had let me *watch* him striking a log with an ax, but never mind. Schmerl showed me how to saw through wood at the place he had marked with a crayon.

I cut my first piece of wood exactly along the mark. Schmerl, though he believed sentiment interfered with discipline, allowed himself to muss my hair in recognition.

As the days went by, Schmerl had to notice that I did what I was told in less time and with a better eye for the marked line than one would expect of an apprentice, but he also noticed, God help me, that between pieces of wood, my attention would drift.

"Are you daydreaming, boy?"

"Oh, Schmerl," I answered, "please forgive me. My mind flew to heaven, where I was showing my father the work I did today."

Well, what could Schmerl say? His voice, usually harsh, was like an embarrassed whisper. "Get on with it, there's a lot of wood to saw." He must have thought that my father had deserted me at too young an age.

"Schmerl," I said, trying to comfort him, "when I have a son, I'm going to wait until he's grown up before I die."

"That's God's business, not yours," Schmerl said, but I noticed that after turning back to his work, he wiped the corners of his eyes with his sleeve.

Of course Schmerl had done my family a great favor in taking me in as an apprentice. And so I felt guilty that when I had sawed three or four lengths of wood to the right size, I would sometimes without thinking lift the saw with my right hand and run it back and forth an inch or so above the crook of my left arm as if it were a violin. How could I explain to Schmerl that my ambition to be a poet was impossible now that I no longer went to school, but perhaps one day I could realize my other ambition of playing the violin.

In time I hoped that I could have people come to hear me play the violin the way people came from many *viorsts* away to buy chairs from Schmerl. Though the few kopecks Schmerl gave me went to my mother and not to violin lessons, I did not give up hope.

I don't want sympathy. What happened when I was eight was my father's tragedy, he was the one robbed of life. I may not have had some of the *chatchkes* that other boys had, but in my heart burned a blacksmith's fire and what went on in my head made me richer than the czarevitch in Petrograd. Two years' schooling is not enough for getting along in the modern world, but I had learned the secret! Much of the world is hidden in books. At night I read by an oil lamp, living through every experience as if it was mine. Also, I noticed most people let their brains rest behind their eyes, but I watched carefully how people said things so I could learn why they said them. With such knowledge, I felt, I didn't need to remain an orphan in Zhitomir, I could go anywhere in this world, to Europe, to China, to the top of Mount Ararat, even to America.

Comment by Zipporah
▪▪ ▪▪ ▪▪

I used to tell Louie that when we met everybody must have been sitting down because it was only when he came to call on me the first time did I realize how short he was. It was my responsibility as an educated woman to pretend that a man's height wasn't important, just his mind.

I was sharing a small apartment in Chicago with two other young women who had already gone out for Saturday evening. I invited Louie to sit in the living room and offered him tea.

"I'm taking two courses at Loyola," I told him.

"I envy you," he said. "My school was Schmerl and life."

How do you talk to a man who hasn't been to a high school much less a university? "Why don't we go to a movie?" I said. The movies in 1922 were pretty terrible, but what should I discuss with him, that I wanted to see O'Neill's *Anna Christie* when the touring company came to Chicago?

"I'll make a movie for you right here," he said, sitting down next to me on the couch. "Have you ever been to the Grand Canyon?"

I shrugged. Why should I admit to him I'd never been out of Chicago since I'd arrived in America a year earlier? I hadn't met a single Jew from the old country who had seen the Grand Canyon.

"The Grand Canyon," Louie said, "is an improvement on the rainbow. The orange is burned brown by the sun. The rock is so many layers of gray it is like a gray rainbow. The whole canyon is like a great big *V* sliced out of the earth by the side of God's hand. And at the bottom is this river, wilder than anything I ever saw in Russia. Close your eyes. Imagine we are on a raft at the bottom of the canyon. The water is as cold as a Siberian winter, the rocks are like Cossacks waiting to kill you."

I could take care of myself. I closed my eyes.

"I have to steer the raft away from the giant rocks, can you see them? Don't open your eyes!"

For his sake I saw them with my eyes closed. Usually men took me to a museum or a concert.

"The sun," he said, "is turning red because its skin is on fire. It begins to sink behind the cliffs."

I could feel his weight getting up from the couch.

"Don't open your eyes," he warned.

I could tell he had turned off one of the lights. "We must reach the shore before it gets dark," he said. "You'll have to paddle just as I am. Are you paddling, Zipporah?"

What should I say to this man? "Yes, I'm paddling."

"With all your strength?"

"With all my strength." Crazy?

"Oh my God," he said, "the sun is gone. We must reach the shore!"

I felt a moment's alarm. He had turned off the last light. I could feel his weight on the couch beside me again. I opened my eyes. The room was in darkness.

"We made it," he said. "You're a good paddler."

I said, "Don't tell me you've been to the Grand Canyon."

"Never," Louie said, "but it was as good as the movies, wasn't it?"

This unschooled young man, I had to admit, had managed at the beginning of our first date to get us sitting in the dark on a couch. And that wasn't everything.

"Would you mind if I kissed your ankle?" he asked.

"My ankle?"

"That's what I said."

"Why would you want to do that?" I said.

"I didn't say I'd do that, I just wanted to know if you'd mind. Would you?"

"I don't think you should be kissing my ankle," I said.

"On moral grounds or sanitary grounds?"

"My ankle is as clean as the rest of me," I said quickly.

"Would you mind if I kissed your back just below the left shoulder blade?"

"Through the dress?" Crazy, yes?

"Please answer my question, and then I will answer any questions of yours. Would you mind if I kissed your back just below the right shoulder blade?"

"I thought you said left?"

"First the right, then the left," he said. "I don't want to be unfair to either side. You are very beautiful, Zipporah."

"Thank you, but why are you talking about my ankle and my shoulder blades?"

"You would prefer that I talked about your breasts or hips?"

I had a strange feeling from this Louie. He hadn't once touched me, yet I couldn't deny a breath of arousal. "Can we turn the light on?" I asked.

"The sun's gone down."

And so we sat in the dark for two hours, talking about life in the old country, and he told me about Schmerl. I mentioned the trouble of getting to Loyola by streetcar and learned he owned a new automobile, he must be on the verge of being rich, and I thought maybe he'd been trying to save money by not taking me to the movies. It turned out he'd read Gorky in Russian and Galsworthy's *The Forsythe Saga* in English, and Sholom Aleichem in Yiddish for the third time, all this year.

"I eat books," he said, "like a camel drinks water. I store them in my hump for the time when I might be poor again."

"You can always go to the library," I said.

"Not the same. I write in the margins. Besides, if I like a book, I want to see it occasionally on a shelf, to be reminded."

"Did you find out about the Grand Canyon from one of your books?"

"No, from a movie," he said, laughing, and my apartment sharers came home and found us sitting in the dark talking and they never believed that we hadn't touched each other that night. You see, my roommates were nice, ordinary people to whom you could not explain that the Colorado River could happen in someone's head or that you could fall in love with a man who was five feet two, and who, despite grave faults I was yet to learn about, became a human being so extraordinary that at his death the funeral chapel was filled to overflowing with men and women, Gentiles, Jews, and all of them could have been said to admire and respect his brains and hands and imagination more than anyone else they had ever called friend. What was his magic? Can I, who am supposed to be educated, explain why I married him instead of the professor?

The professor was a fine-looking man of normal height. Louie was four inches shorter than I was. It took me years to get used to walking in the street with a man who had to look slightly up to smile at me. But that smile was something. I spent much of our married life trying to fight off the other women who wanted to share Louie. He threw sparks of energy—they said he had wit, charisma—that when he talked to you, not just me, but them, and everybody, you felt refreshed, like after love.

And a talker? To our friends, to our children, our children's friends, businesspeople, the plumber, customers, the Manuccis. You could put Louie in front of the League of Nations to talk on any subject that came into his head and you'd think I married the most talented *mensch* who'd ever charmed his way illegally from Russia to America. Who do you think I was, a little girl who couldn't see anything but the golden tongue? I always wondered how Louie knew to make such expert love to a woman if he'd never been a woman himself. In bed afterwards, I was ready to believe God-knows-what to keep that man coming to my bed instead of somebody else's.

Louie

Zipporah used to say that my sense of humor was my number one troublemaker. I tell you, if it hadn't been for my sense of humor, I'd never even have met Zipporah. The biggest opportunity of my life came in 1914 when I was yanked by my ears into Czar Nicholas's army, which, as you know, consisted mainly of peasants. They had to have a piece of hay tied to their left foot and a piece of straw to the right foot so they could learn to march to the commands of "Hayfoot, strawfoot."

At the end of my second week of training, while forty of the czar's subjects were flat on their *pupiks* on the firing range learning to hit a target, the peasant on my left, confused by the instructions, asked me which target he was supposed to shoot at. "Thirty-five," I whispered in his ear. The man nodded gratefully. You see, I thought, a *zhid* can sometimes be useful. It turned out that the man lying on my right was also mixed-up and asked me what number target he was supposed to be shooting at. "Thirty-five," I whispered.

"Shut up!" yelled the sergeant, who then distributed five bullets to each man.

According to the sergeant, as I squeezed off each of my shots I was supposed to be thinking of the enemy. What enemy? My enemies were all around me in the same uniform I had on!

Though each of us had only five bullets, when the shooting was over, thirteen holes were found in my target, number thirty-five. Targets thirty-four and thirty-six were untouched. The sergeant, after a question here and a question there, figured out what had happened. In front of all the peasants, he yelled at me like a Cossack, giving the fellows to the right and left of me permission, once they got a hold of me in the barracks, to make the little *zhid* pay for his prank in a way he would never forget.

Naturally, as the end of the day came closer, I was terrified. Some of these peasants had experience tormenting Jews. I could see them whispering to each other, glancing at me, planning, rubbing their hands together. Think, I told myself, or you are not long for this world. That gave me an idea.

We shlepped back to the wooden building that served as our home. The others, of course, headed first for the latrine at one end of the building because they were as obedient to their bladders as to the sergeant. I ran inside, rolled my few things into a blanket, and took off like a bandit, my bladder full to bursting. I didn't stop to pee until a sufficient number of *viorsts* separated me from the camp. As you can see, the czar's army lacked a piece of equipment as essential to any human environment as air, a sense of humor. In an army run by someone like myself, my target with too many holes would have been accepted as a sign of leadership and I would have been immediately promoted to noncommissioned officer! In fact, in my fantasies of the time, if I and not Rasputin had been the czar's adviser, the Romanovs would still be ruling Russia and all the problems that beset the world, from Siberian camps to threats of world annihilation, might not have occurred, all for want of advice from a little Jew with a sense of humor.

And so, unrecognized by Mother Russia, I found myself doing what refugees the world over have done before and since. I voted with my feet, which, though aching, took me by slow and difficult steps through Poland, Germany, and France, and finally to a coffin-size place in steerage on a boat whose destination was Canada.

Coming to America was like going to a movie somebody said was really good. You're not sure what to expect, and not knowing sprinkles pepper on the excitement. Everywhere you went you met young people who lived in different cities than their fathers lived in, and had better jobs. They seemed to have the kind of spirit that drives the engine of a man the way gasoline drives a Studebaker. Do you realize how wonderful it felt to be twenty-two years old and in the promised land?

I made contact with my brother Mendel, and through him my other relatives and landsmen. I even got a little used to my new fake name of Riller. God would have to figure out all over again who I was.

I decided it was time to do what I had always wanted to do. I went to see a music teacher, a man of seventy named Meyerson, who spoke to me with the authority of a rabbi.

"You have a charming personality, young man, but I won't give you violin lessons on credit. You are too old. By the time you can really play, you'll be thirty, ancient, and who will feed you in the meantime? And who says that you'll be able to achieve what you want even then? For every fiddler who makes it to the concert hall, three hundred play in small bands for bar mitzvahs."

Twenty-two is too old to study music? The man must be cracked!

"Please," I said, pleading.

"No," he answered.

"You ought to go back to the old country," I shouted at him. "You have no hope!"

Meyerson showed me the door, so I had to find another door, this one up three flights in a tenement, led by a young lady I had made happy on Saturday night. From inside the apartment we could hear the sound of scales being played on a piano. She rang the bell. It was answered by a man so tall he had to stoop to see us clearly. Quickly the young lady said, "Mr. Banderoff, this is Louis Riller, who wants to learn the violin."

"I don't teach violin anymore," Mr. Banderoff said. "Only piano has a future. And you should never interrupt me in the middle of a lesson," he concluded, starting to close the door.

"I'll pay for the lessons," I said loudly so that he'd hear me before the door closed. "I'll pay real good."

Mr. Banderoff, whom God had made a head taller than me, stared down. "I am an artist," he said. "My opinions are not for sale. The violin is finished. Piano is the thing. You should have started when you were eight years old."

"I just came here," I pleaded. "When I was eight I had to work as a carpenter in the old country."

"Then work as a carpenter here," Banderoff said with finality.

As we were going slowly down the tenement steps, the young lady squeezed my hand.

"It's no use," I said.

"Kiss me," she said, meaning to cheer me up, "no one is looking."

"This hallway smells of pee," I said. What I really meant was my mouth had the taste of gall.

Though I didn't come here to be an American Schmerl, I had to do something, so I went to see a retired master carpenter named Irving Teitelbaum and told him my story, maybe dressing it up here and there. Teitelbaum, a nice man who had pictures of his grandchildren all over his living room, said, "In America chairs are made in factories. Fine chairs are made by cabinetmakers. These are high artisans who need ten years' apprenticeship and need to love wood as if it were a woman. Besides, you're too old to start now. Don't you need to make a living?"

Frankly, in a way I was relieved to find my pursuit of carpentry discouraged because I knew I did not love wood as if it were a woman.

A wise man on the boat had said to me: The way to be happy is to be in the company of happy people; the way to get rich is to be with people who are already rich. Wanting to be both, it suddenly came to me that only the rich decorated themselves like gypsies, only their bracelets were of gold and platinum, studded with rubies and sapphires, and the rings on their fingers held real diamonds for all the world to envy.

I, who had learned that the electricity for getting ahead went through what the Americans called "contacts," got in touch with a diamond dealer I had befriended named Max Regenwitz, who liked the way I told stories of the old country. Max knew a jeweler named Zalatnick, who didn't keep a store but made the jewelry himself, with apprentices he trained. And so I got dressed up in clothes I borrowed from Hillel, another friend who was as short as I was, and presented myself in front of the security window inside the door of J. ZALATNICK, FINE JEWELRY MANUFACTURING, TRADE ONLY, on the eighth floor of a high office building in downtown Detroit.

The receptionist-secretary behind the security window was a homely woman of thirty or so. When she looked up, I smiled at her as if she were a great beauty I was seeing for the first time. She blushed and said, "Yes?," her voice cracking slightly.

"I am always glad to hear yes," I said to her, leaning my elbows on the sill. "It is such a sweet sound compared to no."

"Can I help you?"

"I hope so. I am here to see Mr. Zalatnick."

"Do you have an appointment?"

"I think Mr. Zalatnick will see me."

"I see you," a gruff face suddenly said from behind the security window. The hand belonging to the face was resting protectively on the shoulder of the young woman. "What do you want?"

"Our mutual friend Max Regenwitz suggested that we should meet."

"Max? Why didn't he phone? Come in, come in." Zalatnick pushed a buzzer somewhere and the door next to the security window un-latched. I went through, carefully closing the door behind me, and followed Zalatnick's chubby waddle into a tiny office in the back. Glancing into the main room, I saw the backs of ten or twelve men huddled over workbenches, loupes in their eyes, working on small objects clasped in vises.

"Where do you know Max from?" Zalatnick asked.

"From Zhitomir," I said.

"You speak pretty good English for a greenhorn," Zalatnick said. "You here for a job?"

I held my hands out, palms down, in front of Zalatnick.

"What's that?" said Zalatnick, puzzled.

"Max said you needed workers with steady hands."

"I don't have time to teach greenhorns anymore. I need people with experience."

"How does a fellow get experience unless someone brilliant teaches him?"

"Flattery don't work with me," Zalatnick said.

I looked straight into Zalatnick's conscience. "I wasn't referring to you, Mr. Zalatnick. I was talking about someone with foresight."

Zalatnick stared back at me, but I wouldn't drop my gaze. Finally, Zalatnick looked away.

I said, "I'd like to try your penny test."

"Oh ho," Zalatnick said, "Max told you. All right, I guess you win, come inside."

Zalatnick led me into the shop not as if I was a fellow looking for a job but as if I was a friend of a friend. I was sure the men in the shop could smell the difference.

Zalatnick perched himself on one of the high stools, gestured for me to take the adjoining empty one. I noticed some of the men glancing over in my direction. One of them had a snicker on his face.

"The routine," Zalatnick said, "is this. You take this saw, it's very delicate, and you cut Lincoln's head out of a penny. If you break the saw blade, finished. If Lincoln's head has an extra bump when it's out, flunk. If a piece of Lincoln gets left behind in the penny, good-bye. I have to warn you, nine out of ten can't do it."

"How do you get the saw blade through the penny to start cutting?" I asked.

"I'll drill a hole for you over here," Zalatnick said, heading for the small drill press.

"Please," I said. "My penny." I handed a brand new copper coin to Zalatnick. "I'd like to practice once on my own penny."

Zalatnick looked at me. I guess it was the first time a greenhorn had suggested practicing on his own coin.

"Be my guest," Zalatnick said. "Ruin yours instead of mine." He drilled a hole in my penny right near Lincoln's nose. He loosened the saw blade, put it through the hole, then retightened the blade.

I went to work, carefully trying to carve out Lincoln's face and my future.

After ten minutes, Zalatnick came back from his workbench to see how I was making out. "Ready for the test?" he asked me.

"A second," I said, deep in concentration. A moment later the Lincoln head fell out of the penny.

"Practice over?" Zalatnick asked, a penny in his hand. Then he noticed the Lincoln head on the bench. He picked it up and examined it under an eye loupe. A moment later he picked up the frame of the penny's remains and rubbed it between his thumb and forefinger. "You've never done this before?"

"Never," I said.

The men were now staring at me openly.

"Pay attention to your work," bellowed Zalatnick, then gestured for me to follow him into the privacy of his office.

"You've got a lot of confidence," Zalatnick said. "And a steady hand."

"Thank you," I said, my right hand in my pocket feeling the brand new cut-out penny and Lincoln head Max had provided me with to substitute for the other one if the work hadn't gone right. Truthfully I was very glad I didn't have to use my backup penny. Now I could keep it as a souvenir of a crime I didn't commit.

"I'll teach you twenty minutes each morning if you come in twenty minutes to eight, before the men. You get carfare and lunch money. When you produce stuff I can sell, you'll get a dollar an hour to start. That's a lot of money."

I nodded.

"I'll provide you with a loan apron," Zalatnick said. "When you're making money, you buy your own."

I nodded again.

"Okay?" Zalatnick concluded, standing. "Come in Monday."

"I'd like to borrow a saw and two blades," I said, "for practice over the weekend."

Zalatnick must have thought, Boy this is an ambitious *pisher*. "If you break a blade, you pay for it."

"Of course," I said.

"One more thing," Zalatnick said, nodding toward the homely young woman. "She's mine."

I practiced all day Saturday and Sunday. When I finished with the drilled pennies, I cut into undrilled ones and tried all kinds of experiments for the fun of it, making Lincoln look bald or putting a bump on Lincoln's nose. By Monday morning at seven forty, I handled the delicate saw as if it were an extension of my own hand.

"Some apprentice!" Zalatnick told Max the following week. "He's as good as Moshe, who's been with me for three years!"

"Then start paying him," Max said.

And so within a year, I was making out of metal a leaf so real-looking an onlooker could fool himself for half a second into believing it was from a tree. And within two years, as anyone who knew me could have predicted, I had parted company with Zalatnick and set up a shop in Chicago. Within months I had seven apprentices of my own. My apprentices worked as hard as I did. We all wanted to be perfect. Soon my shop of master workmen had a Saturday morning lineup of customers who, in those wild days of the twenties, had money to spend as if there was no tomorrow. Tomorrow, meaning 1929, was still a few years off.

But whatever my hands did for metal, they did more for the ladies that I met, and to be quick about it, though I might have taken up with any of three dozen beauties in Chicago, I eventually settled in to live in sin with a tall, and it was said royal-looking, beauty from Kiev, a properly educated woman who carried herself like a queen, and who joined with a carpenter's apprentice from Zhitomir to effect God's will.

God's will, it turned out, was that I and the queen from Kiev, Zipporah, should share an apartment on Kedzie Avenue for a wonderful year, and then, satisfied that our backgrounds mattered less than the common ground of a mattress holding two contented lovers tangled in a good night's aftersleep, we agreed, amidst much kissing and relief of our friends, to get married.

Comment by Zipporah
▮▮ ▮▮ ▮▮

Marriage? Forever? How could an educated woman marry a man who left school at the age of eight? Do I look like a housekeeper who'd tie herself to the tail of her husband's kite? I could fly by myself. I was tall and fair-skinned. Louie was almost as dark as an Egyptian, half a foot shorter than I was, a man who couldn't tell blue from green unless I went with him to pick his clothes. Did I want children from him? True, he did have a magnificent head of curled soft hair, and strong hands that touched like velvet when he wanted to. My skin sabotaged me. It cried out for his touch. All right, so I lived openly with him for a year, but marry?

My father, who I brought over from the old country on my earnings as a teacher, was a six-foot, straight-backed giant with a full red-blond beard, who, if he hadn't dressed in traditional black, you'd never have thought was a Jew. A month after he came he was already playing touch football in the park on Sundays with the *goyim*, who couldn't understand how a man of that age could learn to throw and catch the strange-shaped ball as if he'd been doing it all his life, or why he didn't trip over the tails of his long black coat.

One Sunday, after watching my father play, I sat with him on the park bench and he asked the question I knew sooner or later would come.

"Zipporah, when are you and Louie getting married?"

"I don't know."

"It seems to me," he said, "you are already married."

I recited my reservations. I told him the professor—he knew all about that, too—would be a better match. My father, who came from the same village on the outskirts of Kiev as I did, where matchmakers arranged everything, shook his head. "Love is better." Just like that.

So I married Louie, my father beaming as if I were marrying Gilbert Roland instead of Charlie Chaplin, that other little fellow who made us all laugh. And I had from him Harold and a year later Ben, and like everybody else we all became part of Louis Riller's audience.

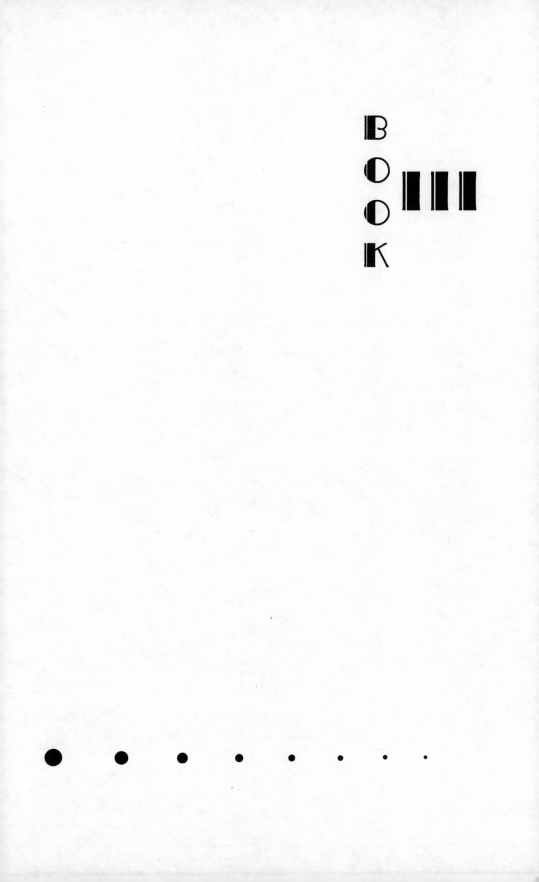

BOOK III

Ben

As the cab pulled up in front of my office building, Ezra said, "Why don't I come up with you? Maybe we can figure a way to deal with Manucci."

I shook my head.

"Two heads are better than one," Ezra said.

"If you had two heads, Ezra, you could double your hourly charge."

"I'm glad to see you can still joke."

I got out of the cab and did a little quick-step on the sidewalk.

Ezra rolled down the window of the taxi. "Put your hat on the sidewalk, maybe someone will throw something in."

"You know I never wear a hat."

"Maybe *that's* our problem."

I watched the cab pull away. Ezra was looking out the back window, but the voice I heard wasn't Ezra's.

Ben, negotiating is not surrendering.

Manucci didn't give an inch, Pop.

Manucci's offered over four hundred thousand dollars to save the show, that isn't an inch?

He wants everything I've got as collateral.

What are you going to do, Ben?

Find Manucci's short hairs and pull.

I never fought with his father.

Maybe you should have.

Hey, I was just beginning to enjoy the argument, where did he go? The only person in sight was a young black messenger riding his bike up onto the sidewalk with a bump. "Hey, whacko," he shouted, "out of the way." All I was doing was watching him chain the bicycle to a lamppost, when he said, "Touch this bike, mister, and I'll cut your balls off."

I let the messenger go into the revolving door first. He pushed it so hard the wing behind me hit my back. He waltzed straight into the elevator, saw me, and darted his arm out to hold the door open. "I'll wait for the next one," I said.

"Whacko," said the messenger.

There was only the one elevator.

I watched the overhead indicator light two, three, four, and stop. My floor. This kid, I said to myself, is a messenger, not a mugger. Manucci's the mugger.

When the elevator returned, I took it to the fourth floor. I stepped out, looked left, looked right, nobody.

Straight ahead were the black-outlined gold letters on my office door. What I read wasn't written there: NICK MANUCCI PRESENTS BEN RILLER'S PRODUCTIONS.

Inside, Beloved Charlotte took her eyes off the package the messenger was handing to her. "Jane called," she said. "Alex wants to see you. You look terrible, Ben."

"Thanks," I said, staring at the messenger staring at me. "What's he want?"

"Somebody's got to sign for the package," said the messenger.

Charlotte said, "It's a script from Bertha. She said she was messengering it over. Shall I buzz Alex to come in or do you want to wait till you're in a better mood?"

I closed the door of my office. The hat tree behind the door was useless, not just for me. I can't remember when somebody hung a hat there. My finger hit the intercom. "Charlotte, have someone get rid of my hat tree."

Not a word.

I opened the door. "Didn't you hear me?"

"I heard you. I think you better see Alex."

"If you know what he's going to talk to me about, why don't you tell me and save him the trip."

"I'm here," said Alex, a skeleton rattling coins as he came down the hall from his office into the reception area.

Theatrical producers don't have chief financial officers with MBA's. If a bookkeeper is with you long enough, you call him your accountant. Mine, Alex the Pencil, is an owl of a man, who keeps one eyelid half shut not because of an affliction but because there is much in this world he is not prepared to see. Alex lives alone with his high blood pressure. His life takes place within the four walls of his office, where I usually go to see him so that he can then say to Charlotte, "You see, Charlotte, *he* comes to *me*."

"Ben," Alex said in his sandpaper voice, "I sent you a note."

"Come on in. Sit," I said, pointing to the high-backed leather chair behind my desk.

Alex flashed me one of his *you're crazy again* looks and did as he was told.

"Ben, we need to talk."

"I gather."

"Ben, I don't feel comfortable sitting here."

Next to the hat rack was an ancient bentwood chair. I picked it up and placed it in front of the desk with its back to Alex so that I could sit astride it and rest my folded arms. "I read your note, Alex."

"Ben, your liquidity stinks. You get hit by a truck this week, you're going to leave Jane and the kids with a lot of headaches."

"You driving a truck this week, Alex?"

Alex let out an experienced sigh. "Ben, I wish I earned what a truck driver earns."

"This isn't the time to pitch for a raise, Alex."

"I know that better than you do. The only thing I'm pitching is damage control. What I was trying to say before you cut me off is that I can turn most of my assets into cash and you can't. You want to sell your house? You want to sell your Matisse? You want to sell the gold cuff links Helen Hayes gave you? If Jane had to sell your assets as part of an estate, you know how people take advantage."

"Jane is smart."

"Then how come she married a play producer? It has got to be the lousiest business on earth. People in other businesses don't have to go begging for new investors every single season. In other businesses you test market. Here, your whole investment is at risk before your first out-of-town audience puts their asses into their seats. Even if they all applaud like crazy, if they cheer like they're having a community orgasm, they don't have one bit of influence on a bunch of critics in New York who are going to decide whether the production lives or dies. The more successful you are, the more they hate you. You call that a business?"

I was about to answer him when Alex said, "Let me finish. This business got a handicap invented by the Devil. You know what it is?"

I said nothing.

"It's love, that's what it is. I ask you about a new play, you say you love it. You know what happens to people in love, they go nuts. They float like crazies up in the air without an engine and without a parachute. All right, people fall in love once, twice in a lifetime, you fall in love every goddamn season. In other businesses people *like* their products, but love? In other businesses you manage a group of people for years, things work smoother when you get to know each other. In this *mishegoss* every production means a new mob of faces, new actors, a new director, a new stage manager, and they all want you to love them like you love the play. Then comes out-of-town, and everybody's sure you picked the wrong play, the wrong actor, the wrong something, and you can't go near your hotel-room window because someone will push you out. That's love? That's business? That's an asylum, and everybody expects you to be the doctor who comes around with a fix of hope that you need more than they do."

"Finished?"

"Finished." Alex handed me a folded sheet of paper across the desk.

"What's this?" I said.

Alex cantilevered himself up. "I'm a human being with one fifty-five over a hundred. I don't need any more threats from bookkeepers who want their money yesterday." He pointed at the folded sheet of paper in my hand. "You don't have to open that. I'm not one of your writers. It's just two words, *I resign,* and my name."

Ben, if Alex leaves, Charlotte will leave, then Jane will leave.

"Shut up!" I said.

Alex took a step back. "That's no way to talk to me, Ben, not after all these years."

"I wasn't talking to you."

The top half of the Pencil's body leaned back as if he didn't want to breathe the same air I was breathing. "Then who are you talking to?

You got a woman hiding in the closet, Ben? I'm the only one in this room."

Ben, stop him from leaving.

"Are you okay, Ben? Where are you looking? Look at me. Maybe you better sit down. I didn't mean to shock you. I assumed you could guess I had enough."

I let myself down into my high-backed chair. Alex put the bentwood back in its place and sat down in the Naugahyde chair alongside my desk.

I said, "How come I never fired you, Alex?"

Alex picked up the daggerlike letter opener from my desk. For a moment I thought he was going to stab me with it but he was only pointing it at me for emphasis. "Because you're surrounded by asskissers and I tell you the truth."

"Then how come even before the play goes out of town you're ready to bury me?"

"Because you're better off dead. Insurance is cash, and cash is what you don't have. Don't reach into your pocket, your forty dollars mad money will get you a taxi from here to Hoboken. Have you forgotten we owe Grayson the final payment on the set of a play you closed four months ago? His bitchy bookkeeper calls me at home."

"Why doesn't she call you here?"

"Because I duck calls, just like you do."

"Tell what's-her-name to call me. Charlotte is very good with people who misbehave about money."

"So am I. Grayson's not misbehaving. You're eleven months overdue on that payment." Alex expelled another of his calamitous sighs.

"What is it?" I said.

He shook his skinny head barely an inch side to side. "Do I have to say it out loud?"

"You're not supposed to keep things from me, Alex."

"I don't want to hurt you, Ben."

Whatever he was holding back colored his face.

"Out with it," I said.

"I can't make payroll."

I stood up. "Son of a bitch, we had a deal. We always reserve payroll no matter what!"

"Don't jump on me, Ben. We got served with papers on the costumes. If they didn't withdraw the filing, you'd be all over the newspapers. The only way I could shut Bixler up was to settle with him."

"By giving him some of the payroll? Are you crazy?"

"I had to, Ben. I know what the papers do to you and Jane when they find something. I was relying on the money from Martinson."

"It was due this week."

"Yeah. I called. We're not getting it this week or next week or the week after. Martinson's filed for chapter eleven."

"Shit."

"That's exactly what I said."

"Hold my paycheck."

"I already figured that. Holding back mine, too. It's the cast I'm frantic about."

"Alex, how can you be concerned about the cast and in the same breath say you're quitting? Take a Kleenex, blow your nose, get on the phone. We can't miss payroll. You're a genius at collecting."

"I've been at it all week, Ben, ever since I learned about Martinson. I guess I'm not a genius anymore. All the money out there seems to be dead or dying."

Money was my father's song. *I put it in the ground and nothing grew from it. In 1929 I took it to a bank, and the bank went to heaven, taking my money with it. Forget money, Ben, do what you like to do. There'll always be a few dollars somewhere.*

Where, Louie? I was listening, and hearing nothing. Everybody hears somebody's voice, though some of us don't have the guts to admit it. I have heard Louie's voice in New York and Hollywood, in the shower and while driving on the open road, and once when I was about to make love to a woman I wasn't in love with. It was for Louie's approval that I set out to conquer the world, not like Alexander the Great, who hated his father, and Genghis Khan, who hated everybody. Alex is right, Broadway is an unmarked minefield in which everybody says they're in love with everyone else.

"Alex, please don't sniffle."

"I'm sorry, Ben."

"What are you sorry about?"

"I should have told you earlier. I was so sure I could come up with something. We always used to." He picked something invisible off his upper lip. "You've got four business days, Ben. Equity is not going to extend."

"Alex, when you first came here—"

"Eighteen years is a long time."

"You're my colleague, not a bookkeeper. You're in charge of my money matters. You're my friend. I trust you."

Alex blew his nose. "I'm used to you spending it first and making it afterward, but I have to tell you, Ben, this flop could kill you now."

"Don't talk flop. We're not even out of town yet. We've got months to the opening."

"Didn't you hear me, Ben, we can't make payroll. The play isn't going to get out of town." Alex slumped into the depths of the Naugahyde chair like a long, skinny balloon deflating.

"I don't want your blood pressure going up over this, Alex. I'll get to work on the payroll right away, first things first."

I despised the deprecating hand I laid on Alex's shoulder. I loathed hearing my voice turn into its Vigor One Mode. "Alex, just for you, I'll produce a hit." Why was I bullshitting this man?

He said, "Take your hand off my shoulder, Ben. I'm older than you are. Even if the play was a hit, you're in so deep, it might only pay for your past sins. To get ahead, you need two hits in a row. Neil Simon plus Neil Simon."

"Alex, because you're a longtime friend, I want you to sleep well. I'll let you in on something."

Alex looked at me with his owl eye.

"Ezra and I have had a talk with somebody important."

"To hell with important, has he got money?"

"Tons."

"How many units is he talking?"

"All of it."

"You wouldn't lie to me, not now, would you, Ben?"

"Scout's honor."

The Pencil looked skeptical. "True?"

"On my life."

"At least you could swear on something worthwhile."

"On your life then."

Alex's wrinkles beamed, a boy rewarded. "How long will it take to get his money in?"

Forever. There's no way I can take Manucci's deal. I said, "Alex, truth time. You haven't taken another job, have you?"

He was as good as the best of actors. He waited a beat before replying. "If I left I'd feel like a coward. I expect to die down the hall, in my chair, in my office. A long time from now."

I held his resignation out to him.

"Throw it in the wastebasket," he said, getting up.

"Thank you, Alex."

"Don't thank me. Just make payroll, do two comedies in a row that your backers will love, and I'll be a happy man forever."

I accompanied him to the door and watched him trek down the long hall to his office, a blur of a lovable man. How had I dared say to him *truth time*. The truth was I'd just sent back a very commercial comedy because the idea of doing another one bored me. Once I'd read Gordon Walzer's *The Best Revenge,* it had opened a door into my past I couldn't close.

• • • • • 10

Louie used to say experience is what enables you to have a guilty conscience when you do something you know is wrong because you've done it before.

I should have sent Walzer's *The Best Revenge* back the day I read it. The bastard had written the kind of play I'd hoped to write. Ardor is bad for business. The professional in me argued: When was verse drama a hot ticket? This is not for theater parties. The scalpers won't line up for it. Let someone else do Walzer's play, off Broadway, on the cheap.

I put the script in my desk drawer.

A month later Charlotte had said, "What did you do with the play Bertha Goodman sent over? Did you take it home?"

"It's right here," I said. "In my desk."

"It's not going to get better lying there. When you want to do a play, you head for the phone like sixty. Bertha's called twice. Why don't you let me return it?"

"My instinct won't let me."

"Instinct? I remember your instinct about Meryl Streep."

* * *

Meryl Streep came to see me on February 14, 1979. All of Broadway knew I was casting the female lead for a play called *Other People*. I had in mind a younger Jane Fonda, or a Diane Keaton type who can hold a live audience in the theater, but nobody suggested Meryl Streep, possibly because she hadn't had the lead in a hit movie yet or been in a noticeable Broadway part, and maybe because she was very pregnant at the time. Charlotte was soft on pregnant women. Or maybe over the decades she had come to recognize the difference between aspiring hopefuls and great actresses on the verge.

When my waving hand offered Meryl Streep one of the upholstered armchairs to sit in, she declined with that self-effacing nod that has become so familiar to us and let herself down into the straight-backed chair in which Charlotte usually took dictation. "It's easier for me," she said.

I was instantly caught up in the details of her face. The individual features were imperfect, but the whole of it was like a reservoir with dangerous unseen cracks. Bette Davis, when young, had seemed like that. What Streep said was, "I apologize for not doing this through my agent or lawyer," she said, "but I *want* to play that part." She said *want* as if it were the apogee of desire and necessity, ordained by the universe and incontrovertible.

Like a klutz I nodded in the direction of her burgeoning midriff. "What about . . . ?"

She smiled a mock-deferential smile that whole world has now seen. "Babies get born," she said. "This one will be before rehearsals start."

I was always a sucker for a woman who exuded authority. I said, "I don't doubt you have the range. Your age is right. But I was hoping to get some of my financing from a studio and you know what they'd say."

Anger flushed her face. "I'm not bankable," she said.

I swear I remember her words exactly. "Mr. Riller, I can't bend my choice of roles to superstition. Paul Newman and Jack Nicholson are damn good actors, but they don't carry a flop. You know Jane Fonda is too old for this part. I want to play it. Tell your studio financiers they can put Betty Boop into the movie version. I'm sure a producer with your experience doesn't have to rely on what pygmies think."

"I can't ask you to read for it," I said.

Meryl Streep stood the way a heavily pregnant woman will, in two motions, out of the chair and then up. "You can ask anyone for anything." She took a slip of paper out of her purse. "I'll expect you to call soon."

When I walked her to the door, I said, "I hope I have a play one day that's got a scene like this in it. You played it to perfection."

You think an impresario doesn't have night sweats?

"What's the matter, Ben?" Jane said, shaking me awake.

I tried to talk.

"Catch your breath first."

"I've caught, I've caught," I said loud enough to wake the kids down the hall.

"What could you have been dreaming?"

"Never mind what I was dreaming, I'll tell you what it meant. Why shouldn't I cast Meryl Streep in *Other People?* She wants to do it. That makes it unanimous. Who cares what the schmucks on the Coast think? I've got enough investors east of there to finance this play twice over. She's perfect for the part."

"Then what are you waiting for?" asked sensible Jane.

So after weeks of churning uncertainty I called the number Streep had given me. The operator referred me to another number. It was her agent's phone. I told him I was ready to offer her what she wanted, the lead in *Other People.*

You know how agents laugh when they are about to twist your balls? He said she'd have to work forty weeks on Broadway in my play to make what she'd been offered for six weeks' work in a new movie. She wasn't available for Broadway. Out there in fucking Hollywood the great actress with the funny name was suddenly bankable.

Alex is right, why does anyone in his right mind get involved in this business?

Jane says it's the turn-on of discovery, the excitement of holding in your hands something that, once it's a hit, everyone wants to be part of it. You take the head of a Fortune Five Hundred company who comes to New York with his wife or his bimbo and what does he want? Seats to a show, even if he has to pay a scalper to get them. Ask him in the secret itch of his soul would he like to trade places, produce a Broadway show? He may build skyscrapers in Houston, but when he hits the Big Apple he wants to build what I build. Even actors who've made it on the Coast say they'd give their left tit or their right ball to star in a Broadway smash. In showbiz it's the top of Everest.

* * *

You want to know what that desire tastes like, listen in. My secretary, Charlotte, has Walzer's agent Bertha Goodman on the line.

"Hello Bertha, Ben Riller here."

I haven't said anything of substance yet, but I'd bet Bertha's blood pressure is fluttering her heart valves. Why is he calling? Does he like the Walzer play?

"Hello, Ben. To what do I owe this?"

She has to be thinking: If he didn't like it, he wouldn't call me, he'd just send it back.

"I've read the Walzer play."

What have I said? Nothing. I haven't committed. I can hear Bertha's breathing on the phone.

"I like it," I say.

The first whiff of success. She's torn between wanting to hear the rest and quivering to call the author and tell him, "Riller likes your play!" Take it from me, the reason she's so anxious to pass on the news is that the electricity she is now receiving becomes voltage she will send straight into the author's heart. Walzer's chest will vibrate like one big tuning fork. My opinion has become transformed into her power. The author was wise enough to seek protection under her wing. Now, with a few words, she has the possibility of changing his life forever.

The first hint that a play *may* get done produces a reaction equivalent to hearing the first three numbers of a six-number lotto jackpot and you've got those three numbers! Dummy, consider the odds of getting the other three! "Riller likes your play," and they all become instant believers: This one will go all the way.

"I'm glad you like it," Bertha Goodman says, pretending studied calm.

"Before I commit," I say, and in the interval before my next words are spoken, Bertha is sliding down an incline toward a precipice as in a dream gone haywire. It isn't definite. "Before I commit, I'd like to meet Walzer, see what he's like."

Bertha swallows air as if she's been underwater for too long. "Of course," she says.

I name a time. She says Walzer will be there. Conversation over. For Bertha Goodman and Gordon Walzer a new life begins.

For a minute I put my feet up on the desk. I've produced seventeen plays and it's still a thrill when the engine starts. Opening night is a long way off. Six hundred gowns accompanied by six hundred tuxedos will be attending your hanging or beatification, and you won't know which until long after midnight when your press agent's spies read the next morning's reviews to him on the telephone. I love it.

I woke up in the middle of the night and found myself having a conversation with God about Meryl Streep. Dear God, I was saying, I'm supposed to be decisive. If I'd said yes to her right then in my office, I wouldn't have had to settle later for an actress who with her whole body couldn't convey what Streep can infuse in an audience by the lifting of one part of her upper lip. With Streep, *Other People* would have run two years. If it had run two years, I'd be beholden to You for my good luck and wouldn't be looking for miracles in the wrong places. I'd have been up to my neck in happiness by this time, getting out a second road show, lining up the rest of the foreign productions, I wouldn't have had time to get involved in *The Best Revenge*—God, are you listening? Show business is a hill of ice, and when you're on top all you see is the little figures climbing up toward you with pickaxes. From now on I promise to look up, not down. Believe me, I'll recognize You.

Maybe I never thanked You enough for giving me fourteen out of seventeen hits. Why are You slamming me with everything in Your arsenal? Is it because I didn't say yes fast enough to Meryl Streep before her picture hit big? How about we do the Meryl Streep interview over again and this time I'll make the right decision as soon as she's in the door? I'm sure You've wanted to do some things over again, how about giving me this one chance?

All right, if You feel You can't set a precedent, how about encouraging me to go forward by, say, letting *The Best Revenge* be a hit. Commercial comedies don't need Your help. Here's a chance for You to invest in what I'm sure You believe in, real quality. What do You say? I've never asked You personally for anything before, be a sport, help me this once. Get me off the hook and I'll put on a revival of Eliot's *Murder in the Cathedral* or, if You prefer, a festival that will make Oberammergau look like amateur night in the sticks. Is it a deal?

I was sitting up in bed, in the dark, Jane fast asleep, waiting for a response, when I heard Louie's voice. *Save your breath,* he said. *It's the Devil who negotiates. God never made a deal with nobody.*

The first time Ezra ever asked to read a play was when I decided to do *The Best Revenge*. "Stick to law journals," I told him. "You don't know fuck about theater."

"I want to read it for libel."

"It's fiction. It's made up. Don't be a pain in the ass."

That's how Ezra gets his way. You give in to get rid of the nuisance, a lawyer's trick.

Two days later he barged in, plunked *The Best Revenge* down on my desk as if it was a stack of subpoenas, and said, "Ben, find another play. There are a million of them out there."

"Ezra," I said, "why don't you divorce Sarah, there're a million better-looking women out there."

"You twist logic like a corkscrew."

I went around to Ezra's side of the desk close enough for him to feel my breath. I said, "I want to do *The Best Revenge* as much as a man wants to do a particular woman he's in love with, even you can understand that. I'm off and running. Don't get in my way this time."

"What do you mean 'this time'?"

"The other time was long ago. I wrote a play, remember?"

"Oh, that."

"You kept me from showing it to Louie."

"You kept it from him, Ben. Not me. Taking on Walzer's play for the wrong reason—or even the right reason—doesn't make it a commercial play. Jumping into something this offbeat isn't like you."

"Bullshit, it's more like me than anything I've ever done."

"The others smacked of success the minute you got your hands on them. This one's fancy. Fancy means upscale. Upscale means problems. All I'm saying is find another play."

"Who's going to do *The Best Revenge* if I don't?"

"Now that is super-idiotic. Social responsibility is something you're supposed to grow out of. Besides, what makes you think you're the only theater maven in New York? If the play's good, someone will do it fine. Maybe someone who is not dependent on other people's money. If it's not done on Broadway, then maybe it'll get done off Broadway, or off off Broadway, or in Minneapolis, and you won't get hurt."

"I'm not a coward, Ezra."

"Neither am I. If I were, I wouldn't have taken you on as a client when Duckworth told you to take your business elsewhere."

"They were charging me for their research time. Why should I pay them for what they don't know? Besides, I liked the idea of hiring you, Ezra."

"Sure, it keeps all the actors, directors, and investors who want me to sue you from hiring me."

"Nobody's suing me."

"I'm not talking today. I'm trying to save your ass tomorrow. I'm talking as a friend, not as a lawyer."

"Ezra, be reasonable for a moment. If another producer does *The Best Revenge* in Siberia, will the first-string critics come?"

"If you did it, they'd come."

"Off Broadway is not my scene."

"But the risk would be so much less!" Ezra said, losing control of his voice.

"Name one," I said.

"One what?"

"One goddamn functioning producer with a brain who can put on a verse drama by a new playwright and make a hit of it."

Ezra didn't say a thing.

"You can't name one," I said, "because there aren't any."

"That's not your responsibility," he said.

"What's your responsibility, Ezra?"

"You," he said.

"That's a great curtain line, Ezra." As I sometimes do with actresses, I smiled the kind of smile that is supposed to cure anything, and held up my middle finger as I went out the door, leaving Ezra in my office.

Why was it that the second I closed the door, I felt a wind tearing at my axis, the mistral inside my chest a premonition that if I took one more step I would tumble into a pure void like a doll in outer space?

Comment by Ezra
■■ ■■ ■■

Very theatrical exit, Ben leaving me stranded in his office.

It was from Louie that Ben got his instinct for theater. When Ben and I were twelve, I went up to the Riller apartment to bring the word that my father, the bastard, had taken off for good this time. All

Louie had said was, "I got two arms," and he put one around me and the other around Ben.

Louie always had messages for Ben, for me, for the world. "If you want to know people," he once said, "find out what causes them a secret shame." When Louie died, Ben and I found his, in a metal box in his dresser, filled with tickets. "Hey, look," Ben said, trying to joke, "he must have seen a lot of movies, look at these stubs." I read the names: Provident Loan, State Street Loan, Milwaukee Loan. Eight hundred thirty-four pawn tickets. And a notebook. The last date on any of the pawn tickets was just a few weeks before the first entry of the notebook: "Manucci, $300, thank God." We were eighteen, still kids. Ben stayed in the bathroom a long time, letting the water run so I wouldn't hear him.

Another time, Louie said, "Boys, of course the Bible was written by sinners. How else would they know?" And about women Louie always wanted the last word. "Boys, you follow your pecker, you've got a schmuck for a guide." And, "If you're lucky like I was and you find a smart woman some day, please don't try to teach her to light matches."

Jane used to be the silencer on Ben's pistol. If he was about to go off half-cocked, she'd find a way to stop him.

"Jane," I said to her on the phone, "Ben's not listening to me. You know this new play of his is in deep trouble."

"Oh, I know. But I also know that if Ben wants to chase whales, Ezra, he'll chase whales."

"He can't afford a mistake now, Jane, his cash position is execrable. He can't risk this kind of gamble, you know that."

"What kind of gamble?"

"How many verse dramas have shown a profit on Broadway in the last fifty years? How many have been produced altogether?"

"Ezra, Ben used scrim imaginatively in the fifties. He dropped all four walls in more productions than anyone else. He hired Crawford when everybody said she couldn't possibly make a comeback at her age. And he's always succeeded."

"Jane, you're overlooking one essential difference. The other times he was somehow able to convince his loyal pack to invest. This time they're not buying in because they look at the script and can't understand it."

"They have no business asking to see scripts. They're investing in his judgment, not theirs. Ezra, when you cross a bridge is it because you've examined every strut yourself or because you have faith in the bridge builder?"

I remembered Louie saying, "Of course there's a difference between men and women. Who ever saw a woman pissing into the wind?"

That's what I was doing.

"Please," I said.

"Please what?"

"Talk to him."

"Ezra, you know better than anyone. The only person Ben listens to is his father."

Ben

When I read *The Best Revenge* the second time I suspected the female lead had been modeled by Gordon Walzer after his common-law wife Pinky. A star I knew slightly, Ruth Welch, immediately came to mind for the part. In my Machiavellian head I suspected that the director I wanted, Mitch Mitchell, would be tempted by Ruth Welch, too.

Mitch was zapped by Walzer's words. And when I mentioned Ruth Welch, Mitch saw right through my attempt at casualness. "Ruth's a brick shithouse with kettledrum lungs," he said, laughing. "She scares most men. Talk to her. If you survive, I'll talk to her."

"One caveat, Mitch. Ruth works a very narrow range."

"Ben, that range is this role. Go for it."

My luck, Ruth Welch was not only in New York but in a play on twofers, its audiences dwindling rapidly. An actress on the rebound, she invited me for a drink at the Waldorf Towers apartment she had subleased, warning me, however, that as soon as her play closed, she was off to her house in Bermuda for a much-needed rest, and I was not to tempt her with any near-term proposition. It was the usual bullshit: Chase me. See if you can catch me.

When I arrived, I started to shake hands but she immediately offered me her cheek, then gave me a hug that hurt. As I sat opposite watching her swirl the ice cubes in her glass, ordering them to melt faster, what I saw was Ruth Welch as a huge female insect with large thighs strong enough to crush a man. If she screamed at orgasm, it had to be an absolute glass-breaker. Perfect for the role.

"Ruth," I said, "you're brilliant in the play," referring to the one whose audience was dwindling, "but the vehicle was a bit Model A, don't you think?"

"When the audiences don't come, I don't look around for someone to blame."

"I'm sure you would rather have been in Colleen Dewhurst's play. It was a perfect vehicle for you."

She seemed to be trying to decide if yes was a good answer to give me. I spared her. "My father used to say that if you take a good look at your neighbor's yard, you'll find that her green grass is plastic outdoor carpeting. But go ahead, look, he would say, she won't see you, she's busy looking at your grass."

Ruth laughed. Of course I'd made that story up. There was no plastic carpeting in Louie's day.

"Is your father someone I should know?" Ruth asked.

"No, he's someone I should know." Again she laughed, and I said, "No one famous. Just a father. Ruth, I have a question." I pulled my chair forward almost close enough for our knees to touch. "What did Duse, Bernhardt, and Vivien Leigh have in common?"

"This a parlor game?"

"Not a game at all, Ruth."

"I can't imagine, except that they were all, in their own ways, number one for their time."

"Ruth," I said, "you're an intelligent woman as well as a remarkable actress. What did Duse, Bernhardt, and Leigh do that you haven't done?"

"Step all over producers," she said.

I provided her with the obligatory smile. "One more guess."

"They're all dead and I haven't died yet," she said, a trace of gray in her voice.

"They," I said, "are in fact immortal to a degree because of something they chose to do that you have not yet chosen to do."

"I'm waiting," she said. Her knee touched mine.

"They all made a point of performing verse drama."

"You're not doing a Shakespeare revival? I'm too old for Juliet," she said, her voice ha-ha-ing.

The ground was mine, the nervousness hers. Time to spring.

"Ruth, I'm planning a contemporary play called *The Best Revenge* that won't have a limited run like Shakespeare. The female lead is a strong, resourceful woman, not an infatuated youngster. She needs a powerful vocal instrument like yours for words that might just out-live us both and give you the vehicle that will make your ultimate position in the theater secure."

She bought time by sipping at her drink. Then she put the glass down hard.

"You come on very strong," she said.

"Not as strong as you come on, Ruth," I said. "You can hold an audience of a thousand. I can only hold one person at a time."

"I wanted to go to Bermuda."

"Bermuda won't sink into the Atlantic waiting for you, but I will if I have to wait a season for you to say yes to the most perfect role ever created for you."

"You'd wait for me?"

I nodded, knowing the Almighty also has to deal with actors.

"Is the script in that envelope?"

"Yes," I said, holding it inches from her hand because I wanted her to reach for it.

The audience entrance to the theater was a row of eight glass doors under the marquee, now locked against intrusion, but through which, each evening of a run, a crowd would funnel toward the ticket taker's inner door, anticipating live actors on a stage. A live play has the power to congeal strangers into a body that laughs not only because of what it sees and hears but because everyone else is laughing too. To the rich unwashed, the theater is a tax-deductible place to take a client or customer. Over the years, while counting the house, I'd learned not to look too closely at the audience.

I passed Fred, the stage doorman, without my usual nod and felt his gaze in my back. I turned to him and said, "Fred, I'm just going to slip in around the back of the house," at which he touched his fingertips to his forehead, a salute for taking notice of his presence. Ezra says I lack the instincts of a democrat. This is not my century.

I circled around to the back of the dark auditorium and lowered myself into a seat in the last row undetected, or so I thought. The cavern, empty of onlookers, was filled with silence from the stage, as Ruth Welch, standing like a watchtower at stage right, barely visible twenty feet from the worklight, said:

I gave you my better years.

My eyes went to Christopher Beebe, standing stage left, as far from Ruth as possible: *You gave no one your better years. Not me and not yourself.*

As he spoke, Christopher, shorter than Ruth by inches, was reinventing himself physically for the confrontation.

Ruth said, *Where is she?*

He: *Strike the mirror.*

She: *I'll find her.*

He: *Strike the mirror.*

She: *I'll kill her.*

He: *Strike the mirror, Margaret, before it, in sweet revenge, strikes you.*

From the fifth row, Mitch yelled, "Okay, take a break. We'll run it through from the top in ten minutes."

He turned in my direction and, though I doubted he could see me clearly in the dark, said, "Hello, Ben."

I like to get in as much as I can of run-throughs without the actors knowing I'm there. The weaker ones try too hard if the producer is in the house. Mitch Mitchell's boy, sitting next to him, must have spied me.

The boy, like a page-turner for a concert pianist, kept Mitch's script always turned to the right page. His thighs were there for Mitch's hand. When you hired Mitch—and who would not want to hire his brilliance—you hired the nameless boy also, his private gofer and concubine who changed with each production. To me they always looked the same, pretty chickens whose eyes let you know even when they were standing that they were on their knees and ready.

Mitch once said to me, "You take sex too seriously, Ben. Cruisers shop for trouble. I like to go to the refrigerator and find what I'm looking for right there, just like you married types."

As Mitch moved sideways to the aisle, the boy skittered out of his way. When Mitch got close, I asked, "How's it going?"

Mitch nodded twice, a response no more serious than my question.

Somewhere in that theater, Louie was saying, *Ben, the actors lie to the director, the director lies to you, you lie to the investors. You deserve each other.*

"There was a three-piece suit looking for you," Mitch said, excavating a calling card from a mass of miscellany in his shirt pocket.

The card said only HARRISON STIMSON. No raised-letter thermography, the real rare thing, engraved from a die. No corporate affiliations. No address. If you didn't know where or how to reach Harrison Stimson, you were not a likely recipient of his card.

"He's coming back," Mitch said. "Trouble?"

"No, no, no," I said. "I wrote to him about *The Best Revenge.*"

"For Christ's sake, just now?"

"No, no. Quite some time ago. I guess he's been away."

"I thought that guy was a heavy in every one of your productions. I thought he had a big piece of this one. Doesn't he?"

I didn't want to be caught.

"Wait a minute," Mitch said. "When you first pitched me, you said Harrison Stimson was in. You called him the cornerstone."

"He disappointed me."

"Ben, sometimes you disappoint me."

"Maybe Stimson is changing his mind. Why else would he be coming by?"

"Sure," Mitch said with the same intonation he'd say *Fuck you.*

"What's eating you, Mitch?"

"Nobody's eating me," Mitch smiled his little joke. "I need that set."

"It's supposed to be ready Friday," I said.

"You talk to Watkins. That son of a bitch told Ruth Welch that he'd stopped building because he hadn't got the second check. The worst any prick can do is tell an actor. You'd better romance Ruth first chance you get. She says she wanted to go to Bermuda and you roped her into this play, Ben. She's a wicked backstage gossip."

"I know."

"We need her at the top of her form."

"Yes, Mitch."

"Please keep Watkins away from the theater."

Watkins, whose firm had built eleven sets for me, was the kind of businessman to whom even old customers were new tricks who needed to pay before they unzipped. When Watkins built a set, he'd never even buy raw materials until your down payment was in. The bastard must have suspected I was a long way from closing the partnership. He wanted to make sure that even if everyone else got stuck, he'd have his.

"Watkins should have been an astronaut," I said. "He'd probably like recycling his urine."

Mitch granted me a tight-lipped smile.

"I'll deal with Watkins," I said.

"Of course," Mitch said, "it's your show."

"It's our show."

"Yeah, yeah. I got five percent of the never-never. You own this thing. Maybe what you own is zip. Maybe less than zip."

"Mitch," I said, "to my knowledge no one has ever replaced you in mid-rehearsal."

"You bet your ass."

He turned away and trotted down the aisle, yelling, "All right, everybody, break's over, let's take it from the top." There were a thousand ways Mitch could have got the message to me nicely, but he's from a different school. If you've got an icepick in your hand, stick it in.

I wasn't going to leave the rehearsal. I was going to stay and see if I couldn't pull Stimson back in. And in the meantime, I was going to watch this next scene and rivet my eyes into the back of Mitch's head so he'd know I was there.

I felt a presence, turned, and there was Harrison Stimson looking like Cordell Hull, ready to shatter lesser people with a cough. I shook his hand and learned that mine had been perspiring.

"Hello, Harrison. Heard you'd been here. Want to grab a taxi with me to the office?"

"With your permission, I'd like to see a bit, Ben. I got your letter. I'd like to help, but I hear funny things about this play."

"Who from?"

A loud voice from stage center interrupted us. It was Jack Feuer, the stage manager. "Quiet, please! We're about to start."

"Come on," I said, touching Stimson's elbow.

"No," he said, sitting.

I slid in next to him.

Ruth Welch was saying: *Who is she, George?*

And Christopher Beebe, turning to her, answered: *A Japanese beetle.*

She: *Cut your clowning, George.*

He: *Her pheromones won't leave me alone.*
Margaret, when you see a beetle on a leaf
that, on closer look, is two beetles on a leaf
you can be sure of three things: the upper one

is male, he is copulating, and as soon as he stops
he will die.
She: *You haven't yet, George.*
He: *Ah, my dear larger-than-life,*
that's why I never stop. Fornication
is a way of living, not just for beetles.
She: *Do you love your ladies?*
He: *I make love to them.*
She: *I said do you love them?*

Christopher came as close as he dared to her, lowering his voice so that we had to strain to hear.

He: *What I do with others has always been*
my means of reaching you.

If there'd been an audience, every couple might feel an elbow's touch.

Stimson got up. I followed him out, with just one backward glance at Mitch hopping up onto the stage to make a point.

Outside, daylight struck our faces.

"The rain's stopped," said Stimson. "Let's walk toward Fifth."

I accompanied him, of course. I could see that his limo driver needed no instructions. Slowly, the stretched blue-black vehicle started after us.

"I liked that last bit," Stimson said. "Quite moving. Bit over the audience's head, don't you think?"

"Better over than under."

Stimson laughed, and his Phi Beta Kappa key moved with his midriff. "Ben," he said, "today crap sells."

"Not to everyone."

"Ben, the *Partisan Review* can't sell advertising because it has only five thousand subscribers. It survives on charity, you know that. A class play in verse can't sell enough tickets to pay for the set. Do it as a hobby, Ben, way off Broadway somewhere, a regional theater."

"I envy you, Harrison," I said. "You never let your taste interfere with your business sense."

"I'd have thought you'd do the same. Cast been paid?"

I nodded.

" 'Course they would be. Equity'd scream. Putting it out of your own pocket, are you?"

"Some."

"The set?"

"I made the down payment. Another's due. I got in touch with you because I'm still some way from closing the partnership and it's getting late. You've made good money with me on eight shows, Harrison. I was counting on your loyalty."

"Always liked your candor, Ben. You're using escrow money, aren't you?"

"Always have unless the money comes in quickly."

"Got releases from your investors, have you?"

I didn't answer.

"Your lawyer lets you spend the money without releases?"

"He works for me, not me for him."

Stimson chuckled.

"Balls. Real balls. You should have been in oil."

"Thanks." I knew he meant it as a compliment.

He'd given some kind of signal I hadn't seen, for the limo pulled up quickly and the driver was out of his seat and holding open the curbside rear door for Stimson.

"Drop you anywhere?" he asked.

"Thanks," I said. "I want to get back to the theater. Will you be thinking it over?"

"Have. Great for cultural improvement, this new one of yours. I don't need the deduction with all the tax credits flowing from new equipment. Think I'll skip, but thanks sincerely for asking me. Enjoyed that bit in the theater. I'll come see the show."

I felt as if the plug had been pulled on the Atlantic Ocean. I stood in the dry waste, drained. "Phone for house seats," I said. "Any time."

Stimson lowered the electric window. "I'll get mine from the brokers," he said. "Or from a friend who's read the reviews. Depends, doesn't it?"

My last chance at putting an investor's money into the partnership pulled away. I watched the limo like hope, making its way to Park Avenue, then turning, lost to sight. Blindly I found my way back to the rehearsal, sat in the dark, not really hearing the lines, waiting for Louie's voice. I was twelve years old, and getting ready for my first magic show for strangers. Louie, watching me rehearse in front of the mirror, said, *The next thing you know you'll be pulling rabbits out of hats.*

All my life, Pop. That's why the hat is empty.

Jane Riller

The day Harrison Stimson turned the faucet off, Ben came home late, his brain boiling. He put his attaché down. It fell over on its side. He left it there. When he hung his topcoat it slipped off the hanger to the closet bottom, over the children's boots. He didn't pick it up. I didn't need a news report to gauge the weather in his head.

I have been credited with intelligence, courtesy, reserve, poise, calm, control, and understanding, when my only act was to keep my mouth shut. Jews conceal their vulnerabilities not by silence but by talking too much. Why is my WASP tongue tied? Father had said, Jane, the cat got your mother's tongue for life. Keep yours. A man in trouble needs a woman's talk.

Silence is safe.

Not this evening.

"Ben," I said at risk, "I feel trapped in Manhattan. Let's drive up to Westchester, maybe dinner at the railroad-car restaurant in Valhalla. Nora will feed the kids. Say yes."

His skulk declared war on everybody.

I came close enough to run my forefinger around the periphery of his ear. "Please?"

He pulled away and headed for the closet, picking his topcoat off the floor. "Why not? Maybe a truck will hit us broadside."

"No trucks on the Bronx River Parkway. Change your mind?"

"I'm not taking my coat off again. Come on."

On the parkway I watched Ben, his gaze forward, both hands on the wheel, looking for an accident.

There was a time when we first started going together that his left hand on the wheel was enough. His right would be on my thigh, and I would feel the vibration of the car in my pubic bone. The ultimate destination of those rides was almost always sex, after dinner, after a Westport opening, or instead of either. On a high of success Ben could be turned on by a whisper.

I put my left hand on his thigh.

"What are you doing, Jane?"

"Remembering."

"Like what?"

"Playing contortionist in the back seat."

The first hint of a smile.

"That light's red," I said quickly.

Ben braked hard. "I saw it," he lied.

I turned, expecting a police car behind us.

"Want to tell me what happened today?"

"Lots."

"Like?"

"Lots of unreturned phone calls."

"And?"

I was famous with Ben for my "ands." You'd have made a terrific psychoanalyst, he once said. You say one word and expect a torrent in return.

The flesh between Ben's brows furrowed.

"Are we in as much trouble as I think we are?" I asked.

He started to say something, stopped.

We were a submarine running silent all the way to the village of Valhalla. Seated in the restaurant, we ordered. Then Ben said, "I've got twenty-two percent of the units sold."

"That's the same as three weeks ago."

"Yep."

I looked for the enthusiasm and energy in his eyes that always carried him from day one to opening night. What I saw were eyes looking down at food in a plate, picking it apart with knife and fork.

"You're not eating."

"I guess not." He looked up, his eyes awash.

"Could you—"

"Could I what?"

"Bring yourself to close the show."

"Before it opens? I've never learned to walk backward."

"Only the cast will know."

"The pigs will wallow in it. The whole fucking world will watch me crash."

Driving home, hurtling through the dark, I could hear his heart. Or was it mine?

"Ben," I said, "are you doing a Louie?"

"A what?"

"Is *Revenge* a way of screwing up your life Louie-style?"

He looked at me as if I were a hated stranger.

I said, "Please keep your eyes on the road."

The light ahead was yellow, then red. Ben drove right through. I glanced behind us. We had the parkway to ourselves.

"Let's be practical," I said. "Stop rehearsals, pay off the set builder for work done, abort the production, cut your losses. It isn't a matter of face. It's common sense. Slow down."

He floored the accelerator.

I said, "Can't we talk this out?"

"Louie was right."

"Right about what?"

"He said if you marry a *shiksa,* it'll be like living in enemy territory the rest of your life."

"Stop hurting yourself, Ben."

"Everybody else is having a go at me, why shouldn't I?"

My father is still living, but less and less. Judge James Charles Endicott Jackson, his "appellations" as he called his full name, that tall, lean, hollow-cheeked man who had made a religion of the law, preached from the head of our dining-room table each evening of my young life.

On the day that I announced I would be leaving the nest in Quincy for what my father called the buzz-factory of Barnard and Columbia, he delivered a warning. "Those New York City people talk with their hands."

I knew what he meant.

When they stood next to their car at the bus station, for a moment I thought my mother was going to leave the Judge's side long enough to come forward and say a few words more than good-bye. But it was only the wind ruffling her dress, not a movement of her body that I saw. I admired her as one would a pioneer farm woman, someone who had lived a life no longer possible. What great and unacknowledged actresses the women of my mother's background were; to avoid shattering the fragile innocence of their spouses, some of them simulated not only their orgasms but their entire lives.

My father, who consecrated my graduation with three thousand dollars in the hope, he said, that I would use it for traveling in Europe —was it to spite him that I went to Greece, Turkey, Yugoslavia, Italy, countries full of people who talked with their hands? I suppose I discovered my sexuality on that trip because some of the idiotic things men say to get you into bed sound better in a foreign language. As for love, that took a long time coming.

At home, we went to bed.

He lay on his side, I on mine.

It was too late at night for pinwheeling talk.

I could hear the faint whirring of the digital clock on the bookcase across the room. We need firm sounds. At home in Quincy, the grandfather clock in the hallway sounded chimes every quarter hour to remind us, if awake, that we were losing life.

I must have dozed. The bed beside me was empty. I flicked the bed light on, afraid I'd trip in the dark.

The stairway down was ablaze with light.

The kitchen was dark.

The living room was dark.

"Ben?"

I heard breathing.

I turned on the overhead light.

"For Christ's sake, turn that thing off, it's blinding me."

Ben was sitting on the blue couch, holding a tumblerful of ice and booze. I turned the rheostat so that the room was barely lit.

"What's that I smell?" I said.

"I smoked a cigarette."

"You don't smoke."

"Now I do. You think I have no business being in the theater anymore?"

"That's not what I said. I said the theater is not a business anymore."

Ben jiggled the ice in his glass.

"I am not the enemy, Ben, come upstairs."

"What am I supposed to do at this stage of my life, package air? I'm entitled to do a play I know is good."

"Of course."

"I mean without having to worry about where every nickel is coming from. Besides."

"Besides what?"

"Stimson wouldn't miss the money for a second."

Ben the hunter is waiting in a blind for me to let a thought fly so he can shoot it down.

"What are your choices?" I asked. "Have you tried London? Your track record—"

"How the fuck do I turn that into money? I've turned over every rock I know except . . ."

"Except what?"

"Manucci. Maybe you're right. Maybe I'm in the same damn trap my father was in. Maybe I ought to take off like Gauguin."

I went to sit beside him. I took his hand. "I love the feel of your skin," I said. "All of it."

"Seducing me won't do either of us a bit of good."

Ben gave me back my hand, saying, "Nobody ever welshed on your father, did they?"

"Ben, this isn't finding a solution," I said.

"When the crash hit, every last son of a bitch who owed my father money welshed."

"Ben," I said, "you love your father more than anyone I ever met. He must have done something right."

"The drapes were taken off the wall by the sheriff's people."

"You told me."

"My cowboy suit was taken to satisfy a claim."

"You told me."

Ben stood up, his eyeballs red. "I was the only white kid in first grade when we moved to Harlem. It was like jumping out of a plane and finding out your father forgot to hook up your parachute."

"Come up to bed, Ben. Please?"

He was looking at the carpet.

"I know how Louie felt," he said, "when the ceiling crashed."

"Remember how long it took—?"

"To what?"

"To finance *Truckline*."

"I should have closed *Truckline*. In rehearsal."

I tried to touch him, but he pulled away.

"Don't start giving me my type of hope," he said. "You can't bullshit a bullshitter. There are two choices. Abandon the play or . . ."

"What?"

"Manucci."

"Ben, you've got a solid history to trade on."

"I've haven't got a fucking thing to trade on. I'm finished." He flung his arm wide, spraying drink and cubes across fifteen feet of room.

I went to get paper towels for the carpet. When I knelt, working at the tufts, he knelt beside me. I tried not to turn, scrubbing away. But I could hear. Ben was sobbing.

The hell with the carpet. I cradled his head. After a while I thought we'd fall asleep that way. The children would find us in the morning.

"Come upstairs," I said.

On the bed, Ben lay on his side, I on mine, an estuary of gloom between us.

I was a very little girl when we had our chimney fire in Quincy. I dreaded another more than my father's wrath. You could retreat from wrath, go up to your room, hide. You couldn't hide from a chimney fire, you had to deal with it. For fires of the heart, we had New England remedies: discretion, tact, propriety, appropriateness, silence. I was schooled to bar visible emotion at any cost.

Was that why I fled New England, my genes crying out for someone like Ben, whose people are less concerned about chimneys than storms in their brains. The thrust of their lives was to overreach themselves. My father would have said to the brothers Wright, Aren't the feet God gave you good enough? I suppose Louie would have said, *I love you. Fly!* Even in death Louie talks to us more than my father who is still alive.

The thought froze in my mind like a thief caught in a flashlight's beam: What must it have been like to have been made love to by Louie? Was I imagining it from Zipporah's point of view, or was that just camouflage for my own curious, suddenly windmilling mind feeling his hands on my skin, his tongue on my skin, his illicit kiss?

Sometime, in the drowning moments between sleep and waking, I felt the interruption of unexpectedness, the touch of one finger at the back of my neck descending tantalizingly down the length of my spine. The finger turned into a familiar hand. Then at the base of my neck it was lips, a flickering snake's tongue between them, traveling the same route slowly. I tried to turn but now two hands were on my shoulders keeping me from interrupting the traveling tongue. I twisted toward him as his fingers, all erotic members now, cruised my inner thigh. His lips exploring my ear found my lips until breath demanded breaking, and he was at my left breast nipple, taut, the right crying out jealously, and then his mouth descended at last to the other eager avid lips. How restive, fretful, anxious, and zealous ardor is. I pulled Ben's body up to split me, the rocking horse rocking as in the surge of the surf, to the apogee, cresting, splaying, sweaty, trembling, exhausted, sailing free.

The bedside phone exploded with a shattering clang.

"This is Sam Glenn," the voice said. "Put Ben on."

"It's two o'clock in the morning!" I said and hung up hard.

Ben was sitting up in bed. "Who was it?"

I put my hand on my lover's hand. "Nothing. Wrong number. Go to sleep." I reached to take the receiver off the hook when the phone's ring resounded. And again. I had to lift the receiver to stop it, and heard his bellow: "Don't you fucking hang up on me, lady. Put the bastard on the line."

Ben said, "It's Sam Glenn, isn't it?"

I nodded and handed Ben the phone.

Ben

I said, "It's the middle of the night, Sam."

"You duck my daytime calls."

"What's so urgent?" My never-changing image of Sam was from high school, the six-foot-four hulk who picked fights and used his stomach for butting.

"You didn't close the partnership, true or false?"

I sat up at the edge of the bed. "You want some additional units?"

"Are you fucking crazy? My money's still in escrow. I want it back."

"The money's spent, Sam."

Jane was now up on one elbow, watching me.

"You listen to me, Ben. You can't spend the first dollar till the last dollar comes in. You'll go to jail for fucking around with those funds."

"Oh, Sam."

"Don't oh-Sam me. You wouldn't last three months in the hoose-gow."

"Sam, we've known each other a helluva long time. I'm sure if we sat down face to face and talked this over you'd understand."

"I doubt it. If the production has used my money, just send me a personal check plus interest from the day of investment. That comes to—"

"I don't have that kind of money anymore, Sam. Look, the middle of the night on the phone is no way to talk. Are you coming to New York anytime soon?"

"I got enough keeping clear of muggers in Chicago. I don't go to New York. I want a no-bullshit answer right now. Are you going to send me a check by Fed Ex or do I do what I have to do?"

"If I take a plane in the morning, Sam . . ."

Jane was shaking her head.

". . . we could have lunch together . . ."

"I don't eat lunch. I'll expect you in my office by eleven o'clock. With a check."

He hung up.

"Call him back," Jane said. "Tell him you can't go."

I lay back on the pillow, my hands under my head, staring at the ceiling. Chicago, once my town, was now enemy turf.

I could hear the clock across the room. "What time is the alarm set for?"

"Seven. Are you going to call him back?"

"Change it to six."

In the fan of moonlight sneaking in between the slats of the blinds, Jane looked like a young woman. "Wasn't there once a time," I said to myself, "when I could talk anybody into anything?"

On the plane I got a magazine from the stewardess. Even the ads seemed unreadable to me that morning. I closed my eyes, retrieved long-stored snapshots of Chicago. My mother's nervous warmth. Homebound by the impenetrable snow. The policemen who always seemed fake to me because of the silly black-and-white checkerboard bands around their caps. Why no snapshot of Louie? Where was he?

I'm right here. Where are you?

On my way to Chicago, Pop.

If you're going to Chicago, why don't you see Anna?

How do you know she's still alive, Pop?

I know.

How did you get on this plane, Pop?

He put his hand on my shoulder, gently. I opened my eyes. It was the stewardess waking me for breakfast.

*   *   *

In O'Hare's bedlam my eyes scouted for a public phone not in use. It was still early for my meeting with Sam.

I dialed information. "Addison, Anna," I said. "I don't know the address."

Maybe information wouldn't have a number for her.

How many Anna Addisons do you think there are in Chicago?

You here, too, Pop?

Where else?

A synthesized voice announced, "The number is . . ."

See. I told you.

Comment by Anna Addison
■■ ■■ ■■

I have two links to the outside world: the grocery boy and the man who delivers for the cleaners. When that phone rang for the first time in two weeks, I thought it was probably a wrong number. Still, I went to answer it with all the eagerness of sixty years ago when Charles and I would phone each other at least once a day. Please don't hang up before I get there.

"Hello, hello," I said quickly.

A man's voice, deep as if from the bottom of some ocean, said, "May I speak to Mrs. Addison, please." His voice seemed surrounded by a lot of Donald Ducks yammering in the background. I had to strain for every word.

"Yes, yes, this is Anna Addison. Who's calling?"

"This is . . . Ben Riller, Louie . . . and Zipporah's . . . son."

Oh, how those names jumped out at me from memory! "Bennie, where are you?"

"At O'Hare. I'm glad information had your number."

"If I could afford it," I said, "my name would be in every city directory in the whole country! What are you doing in Chicago, did somebody die?"

Stupid thing for me to say. It must be thirty-five years since Louie died. Maybe twenty-five since Zipporah followed him. "I guess I should be the next one," I said.

"If I remember you correctly," Ben said, "you'll live forever."

"That kind of lie I like to hear."

"I'm in town," he said, "for a meeting with one of my investors. My return flight's not till five. Can I pay you a visit early this afternoon?"

"Of course." I repeated my address twice so he shouldn't make a mistake.

"It's hard to know the exact time," Ben said. "I'll call when my meeting's over."

"Don't waste money on a call. I'll be here." I saw my hand on the telephone receiver, my knuckles like small doorknobs. I've gotten so thin since Charles died. "I'll make us a lunch," I said.

"Don't go to any trouble. I've got to run now."

When he hung up, I held the receiver to my breast like a gift I didn't want to put down. Do I have a decent dress that fits me? What if I died in the next couple of hours, who would tell Bennie not to come?

Comment by Louie
■■ ■■ ■■

That woman Anna always fussed about the way her hands looked. She used to say that she had the right hands for a woman and I had the right hands for a man, whatever that meant. Right in front of me she used to ask Zipporah things like did her bust look natural with some new brassiere she was wearing. I was tempted to say, How do I know if it looks natural if I don't get to see what the natural looks like?

Some of our friends in Chicago used to think it funny that Zipporah should have a best friend like Anna who wasn't Jewish. In the old country, there was us, and the rest were enemies, but in America, people are people, give them a chance. Our friends thought she was stuffy because she called her husband Charles instead of Charlie. She wasn't. When she talked, her soul steamed out of her eyes. She talked with her breath, like a woman on the verge. I thought of her as someone I should make love to, and I knew she knew, but we were always on good behavior, she for her Charles, and I for Zipporah. That woman, Anna Addison, taught me that whatever pulls a man and a woman together can also jump over the fence of centuries, that the days of Jews marrying only Jews would soon be over. When we met, and a kiss on the cheek in front of Charles and Zipporah was called for, Anna and I were as careful as kids in front of their parents. I never laid a hand on her except in my mind. When we left Chicago, leaving her was for me harder than leaving all those books with the stickers that said EX LIBRIS, LOUIS RILLER. Most of those books I had read. Anna I had not yet read.

Comment by Zipporah
▐█ ▐█ ▐█

Of course I knew that Louie had a crush on her, what wife doesn't know such things? But I loved her more. She was reserved the way I thought only older people were. Outside, her poise made her seem like a live statue, inside, a soft heart beat. If I loved her, why shouldn't Louie, who was flesh and blood? I sometimes imagined them making love together. I don't know when they would have had the opportunity. But in front of me, and Charles the husband sitting there, too, they sometimes talked to each other as if a secret perfume enclosed them both. Sure, the contact of flesh to unmarried flesh is forbidden, but the Devil knows that people do things in public that are more personal than sex in bed.

Comment by Anna Addison
▐█ ▐█ ▐█

My family has been Protestant since Luther. Why do I envy the Catholic widows? Because if their voices are still strong and their manners cleverly deceitful, they can flirt with the priest through the wire mesh, pretending he doesn't know they are in their eighties as I am. They can look forward to ring-around-the-rosie with Mary and Jesus and the Holy Ghost when it's over. What does a Lutheran lady of the same age have if she never had children and her husband is dead? None of the male parishioners of a suitable age are willing to risk more than the frailest friendship out of fear that anything else might require something they couldn't do, when I'd settle for an affectionate kiss.

You realize after a time why the widows with pensions move to Arizona or California or Florida. In Chicago, without a body to get close to during the night, the winters get longer as the antifreeze drains out of your bones. When did I see Bennie Riller last? At Zipporah's funeral, twenty-five years ago! Oh how I miss that woman. I remember her sitting right here beside me. And the truth is I miss her husband more. Louie and I were virgins with each other, yet when did a week pass when I did not imagine his lips on my neck?

In the shower I caught myself singing a song of fifty years ago. Hoping my voice would not betray my age, I called the beauty parlor and asked could they give me a special appointment for a permanent this morning. I meant right away. They said, Sure, come on down, sweetie. Going outside for my appointment, Chicago suddenly looked like the most beautiful city in the universe. Ben is coming, sang the song in my head. Ben is coming.

Ben

Samuel Glenn, Inc., occupied the entire four-teenth floor of the Michigan Tower Building in the Loop. The reception-room chairs were occupied by men and women who tried to avoid looking at each other. Every few minutes a different young woman came in, called out a name, and then escorted whoever responded through a door into a huge room filled with desks and ringing phones like a broker's office.

I picked up *Business Week*. Every story seemed to be about Sam Glenn. I put the magazine down and stared at my fingernails like everybody else.

In high school Mr. Edwards kept Sam on the football team because Mr. Edwards understood that crowds find violence entertaining. Sam was expert at flinging his body against a running linebacker as if he was hoping to break bones in the process of bringing the man down.

While Sam played up his repulsiveness, I detected signs of loneliness. Something simple, like Sam saying, "I'd like to go out with you guys," stuck in my head the way a piece of chewing gum can stick to the sole of your shoe. The more you try to get rid of it, the worse it seems to get. When Sam tried to be friendly, it came across like a threat, and the guys would head in the other direction. I went to the movies with him once and we had to stand until two seats opened up in the last row. Sam said if he sat anywhere else, he'd be blocking someone's view and it would end up in a shouting match. I suspect he was the only male virgin in our class.

I lost contact with Sam until maybe a dozen years later he phoned from Chicago and said he had what he called "a little loose change" and could he invest in one of my plays.

I said, "Sure." To be polite, I asked what he was up to.

"A little of this, a little of that," Sam said.

"I heard you went to law school."

"You heard right, Ben."

"You practice law?"

"Not really. I also got an accounting degree. I don't do that either."

"How much do you want to invest?"

"Twenty-five."

"It comes in units of thirty thousand. Want half?"

"I'll take thirty. Send me the stuff. Nice talking to you, Ben."

He hung up, leaving me feeling like a clerk in a store.

That play made money, but I didn't invite Sam in again. It was easy enough to finance my productions with money from people who didn't go at everything as if it were a contact sport. Then one day I got a phone call from Sam, pushing money at me.

"I'm full up with old investors," I told Sam. "Sorry."

"I lent you two bucks in high school. That makes me your oldest investor."

I gave him his laugh, but not a participation. When too many of my regulars stayed away from *The Best Revenge,* Charlotte dug out my backup list and there was Sam's name. I did my short-form pitch, and Sam said, "Don't do me favors, Ben. If you need my money, say so."

"So," I said, which drew from him something like a snicker.

"Okay," he said. "I'll take two units. That's about what I made the first time. See to it I don't lose it."

I soaked in thought for nearly half an hour in Sam's waiting room before a bird-beaked woman called out my name. I stood.

"Follow me," she said and led the way through a huge room filled with desks occupied by fast-talking people with phones on shoulder rests. Along two walls were glass-walled cubicles in which I could see people from the waiting room getting grilled. I followed the woman to the far corner, where she stepped aside to let me into a cavernous office with half a dozen huge potted plants—*trees,* I thought—sized to Sam, who came from around his large desk with palm extended. I braced myself for a brutal handshake.

"You don't look a day older, Ben. Life must be good to you. I hope you got some sleep after my call."

I noted the photographs of several children on the credenza along one wall.

"Nephews and nieces," Sam said quickly. "My sisters are baby factories. I'm not married."

After the how-was-your-flight prattle, I said, "Sam, I still don't know what you do."

"A little of this, a little of that."

We both laughed.

"I collect money," he said, doodling on the pad in front of him.

"What do you sell, for Christ's sake?"

"Nothing. No investment in inventory. I'm the collection agency."

I wished I hadn't asked.

"Sam," I said, "I'd like to make a deal with you, to have you aboard for all my plays."

"That's real nice, Ben, but we're talking about the play you got both feet in right now. I want out."

"Sam, if you pulled out now, I couldn't invite you into my future shows."

"Bennie, this isn't high school. I invited myself in the first time. You didn't invite me back. You don't like me."

"I have every confidence . . ."

He waited. I didn't finish.

He said, "Did you bring a check like I said?"

"Sam, Mitch Mitchell has given me three hits and no flops. The casting is perfect. *The Best Revenge* is a terrific play. I wish you would have faith and stay. Please."

Sam stopped doodling and put the pencil down. "In this place, Ben, we hear a lot of pleases on the phones. If I listened to words like that we wouldn't be in business. All *please* means is you don't have a bargaining position."

"What do you want?"

"Your personal check. I'm sure you've got a blank in your wallet."

"If you leave your units in, Sam, I'm prepared to give you a side deal of a kind I've never done with anybody. In addition to your share I'll throw in five percent of the producer's share. And I'll give you an airtight right of first refusal on my next five productions."

"If you don't have a blank check, Ben, I can give you one. What's the name of your bank? I can phone and get the account number."

"I came to Chicago because I thought we could talk things over."

"We just did, Ben. I have a young friend in Manhattan, a kid lawyer who's been very helpful privately with some big New York accounts. I can call him right now, while you're here." He buzzed his secretary.

"Sadie," he said, "get me Forty-four in New York."

"Cancel the call," I said, taking out my checkbook.

When I handed him the check, he studied it a moment and said, "You flying back?"

"Not till five. I've got another appointment."

"Mind if I write down the number of where you're going to be?"

Anna Addison

Ben was broad-shouldered like his father but
nearly a head higher. Without touching his bushy hair you could tell
it was soft like Louie's, but the rest of him was more like Zipporah,
the tall way he walked into my apartment, kissing me on both cheeks
as in a French movie, and putting into my hands a small blue package
tied with an elegant silver elastic. On the box was one word: *Peacock's*.

"Go ahead, open it," Ben said.

I lifted the cover. Against the white cotton lay a silver teardrop on
a delicate chain, a girl's engagement present.

"Do you like it?"

"I love it," I said, rubbing my eye with the back of my hand. I
didn't want him to look at my hands. He took them in his as if to say
the bumps didn't matter because the hands were mine.

I had to break loose and go to the bedroom for a handkerchief. I
pulled out the drawer and there beside the neat pile of cotton hand-
kerchiefs was the lace one I used to stuff in my sleeve when Charles
and I went gallivanting. I took that one, of course, and hurried back
to find Ben staring out of the window.

"You remember Chicago?" I said.

"Only the inside of hotel rooms, rehearsal halls, restaurants. You know how it is on business trips."

He never got in touch with me.

"Is something wrong?" Ben asked.

"No, no, no," I said. It takes reaching a certain age to want to connect back with the past before you die. "You remember nothing from when you lived here?" I asked.

He turned from the window, such a good-looking man, such sad eyes.

"I'll help you remember," I said, "as soon as I put up some tea."

Settled over sandwiches and tea, I said, "Would you like to have your tea leaves read?"

"I've never gone to places like that."

"No, no. I meant here. By me. I haven't done it in years."

Ben looked into his cup. "It might show what I don't want to see."

"Ben, I don't need leaves. A man with your gifts has his future in his pocket. All he needs is to remind himself once in a while."

"Thank you, Anna."

"Thank Louie. Thank Zipporah, not me," I said. "You know your parents, we were very close."

"I know."

How could I say to him that they were the first good friends I had who were Jewish, whose feelings glided off the tips of their tongues. They'd say anything in front of me. At first it made me nervous to be around such people. I had to get it through my skull that it was an honor to share instead of to hide. Those two people took the walls off my soul.

"Anna?"

"Yes."

"What do you know about the money?"

"What money?"

"My father was making out very well and suddenly it all vanished."

"There was a depression."

"You came through it okay."

"Charles was a teacher."

"Other people came through it."

"The past is the past. Why think about it now?"

What did I say wrong?

"I think about the past, too," I said. "It wasn't just money. Your brother Harold's nephritis, you must know about that?"

Ben nodded.

"He was what, three years old? In those days there weren't antibiotics. The doctor, I'm trying to remember his name, he used to push hope at your mother. Louie didn't buy it. Once I asked Louie how he could be so sure that Harold would die. He said, 'A Jew is born thinking that every door he opens will reveal some form of the angel of death.' After listening to Louie, I would lie in bed at night praying for Harold."

Ben leaned over. "If it hurts to talk about it, don't," he said.

"More tea?" I asked.

Ben shook his head of hair just like Louie. I wasn't going to tell him that when Charles reached over to console me at night, I pushed his hands away because I was thinking of Louie's hands!

I said, "Your mother and father were like a tribe of two people beaten in war."

"They never got over it."

"They loved you, too," I said.

"You can't compete with the dead," Ben said. "They grow more perfect year by year."

"Do you remember the baby grand piano?" I asked Ben.

"No. Who played the piano?"

"Nobody, Louie said if you want your son to be a mountain climber, you put him in front of a mountain. In those days Louie could afford anything so he bought the piano thinking it would be an inspiration."

"For Harold."

"Don't be ridiculous. For both of you. Do you remember the parquet floors around the Oriental rug? The library—ten thousand books, floor to ceiling everywhere. Some Russian, some in Yiddish, a complete set of Zola signed by Zola if you'd believe, and in English, all of Mark Twain, all of O. Henry. You used to play in that room all the time, opening books as if you could read them."

"I don't remember," Ben said.

"How could you forget a room filled with more books than Einstein could read in a lifetime?"

"You make it sound as if my father were very successful."

"Oh, he was. If you asked your mother, she'd say it was Louie's funny stories that attracted customers. But she knew the truth. Most of the people who bought from Louie hated the fancy atmosphere of the jewelry stores in the Loop, with salesmen who condescended to help you pick something in good taste because obviously you couldn't. In Louie's place it was just a little office half the size of this room, a table, three chairs, and a big safe. People got bargains from Louie. He had so many customers he could pay for the carpets, the piano, for clothes that made your mother look like a queen and you like a prince. Zipporah was always going on about how she could have married some professor, but what professor could have given her all those belongings. And more."

"More?" Ben asked.

There are some things you don't say to a son about his parents, even if the son is over fifty. So I said, "Louis was an interesting person" instead of a good lover, because how would I have known if Zipporah hadn't told me how addicted she was to the touch of his fingers.

Why was Ben staring at the phone? "Are you expecting a call?"

He shook his head. Louie was a liar about such things, too.

Suddenly Ben said to me, "Anna, you could have been an actress."

"Me?" I said. "I can't remember my grocery list, how would I remember a whole play?"

"That's not what I meant," Ben said. "You have such poise. Your back is such a straight line."

"Charles always said I had good posture."

"It's the authority," Ben said. "You could have played a queen."

"You're confusing me with your mother." I felt very uncomfortable with the way Ben was looking at me. I don't mean uncomfortable. I mean too comfortable. What a foolish thought. Quickly I decided I better bring my Charles into the room as a chaperon!

"Charles," I said to Ben, "loved books differently than your father. He would examine the type sizes, measure the margins on the page, figure out the number of words compared to the outside dimensions. He was looking for efficiency. We all get something different out of books, why should I interfere with his pleasure just because he didn't like to read."

I got up and went over to the window, happy to hear Ben chuckling softly behind me. I used to love it when men reacted to my way of putting things.

I pulled the curtains a bit farther apart. Was it to let in more street light, or to dispel an atmosphere that I suddenly thought ridiculous? I am thirty years older than him, he must have a beautiful wife, he is not Louie. I felt a pain, thank God, in my left arm and shoulder, a sign. To change the subject I said the first thing that came to mind: "How did you come to pick the theater, Ben?"

"It picked me."

His face completely changed. He was staring at the telephone again. Why did Bennie, the most successful person I had ever met, suddenly look like his father's ghost? I was about to put my arms around him, when the phone pierced the room with its aggressive, demanding, insistent sound.

Comment by Ben
■ ■ ■

My instinct was to grab the phone. I thought, It's her phone.

"Hello, hello," Anna was saying. "Yes. A minute please."

She held the receiver out for me. "It's for you. A man."

"Yes?" I said into the phone.

"Ben, it's Sam Glenn here. I got some bad news for you. I never deposit a check that might bounce without checking the bank first. Ben, using escrow funds is a crime. Knowingly issuing a bad check is a second crime. You better come back to my office right now."

"Relax, Sam," I said, "I've just closed the partnership with a single investor who's picking up the balance."

"You are a fucking liar, Ben."

"I can't say what I'd like to say, Sam, there's a lady in the room."

"She your investor?"

"No, someone in New York I talked to half an hour ago."

I saw Anna trying to understand my lie.

Sam said, "You better give me his name."

What name?

"I'm waiting."

Go ahead, Louie said, *use it.*

"Manucci," I said.

"Spell it.

I spelled it.

"First name?"

"Arthur." Whole cloth.

"Phone number?"

"Listen, Sam, I just made the deal. Give me three or four days to get the papers signed."

"Is he listed?"

"Must be."

"Manhattan?"

I couldn't hesitate. He'd know I was inventing. "Bronx."

"Hey, Ben, what the fuck is someone with that kind of money doing in the Bronx? You come down to my office."

"I've got to catch the five o'clock out of O'Hare."

"Ben, I'm going to call this Arthur Manucci, just in case he's real. I'll tell him I'm just a friendly fellow investor checking to see who else is in the deal. You'd better not be fucking me over, Bennie. I'm getting my dough back or you're going to jail."

He slammed the phone down so hard I was sure Anna heard it.

"What's the matter, Ben?"

"It's nothing."

"Nothing is nothing. Tell me."

"I'm having a little trouble raising the money to put a play on."

"If you don't raise the money," Anna said, "don't put it on."

There it was, straight and simple, from a woman who knew nothing of business. How could I explain to her that all my life I did things first, then figured out how to pay for whatever I was doing?

I excused myself to go to the bathroom not just because much tea will eventually require it, but because I wanted a moment's thought without Anna's face in front of me.

In Anna's bathroom, an enema bag hung from the shower curtain rod as if it were a permanent fixture for daily use. I committed an unpardonable invasion of privacy. I opened the medicine cabinet and surveyed the bottles and ointments, reading the labels. Codeine for arthritis, charcoal tablets for gas, a diuretic, the rudiments of Anna's aged life. And a razor. Was it Charlie's, kept as a memento? Perhaps she used it. Sometimes answers were simpler than questions. Why didn't I just close the play down? Flush it away. Settle what I could. Slink off till everybody forgot about it, then come back like gangbusters with a comedy smash.

Carefully, I put the seat back down the way I had found it. There was no man in this house anymore. I washed my hands and dried them not on the single towel, but with some tissues from the box, though Anna's problems were not communicable. Perhaps I had heard enough for one day. Louie's problems had been his, mine were mine. Why did

I want to hear more? Besides, Chicago was only a two-and-a-half-hour flight from LaGuardia. I could return. Would that inventory of medicaments keep her alive?

Anna, her eyes searching my expression, asked, "You're not leaving, are you? Your plane is when?"

"Five."

"Plenty of time. Besides, you can't eat and run."

Now or never.

"Anna, what really happened here?"

She was avoiding my eyes.

"What did Louie do that was so wrong?! My mother said he was a thief."

"He wasn't a thief!" Anna cried out.

"She said he stole her life! What was she talking about?"

"In the Depression it wasn't only jewelry. People stopped buying everything. Zipporah and Louie were like bugs in a puddle, flailing every which way trying to stay alive."

"Was he playing the stock market?"

"He didn't invest except in himself."

"In a fool!"

"No, Ben, Louie's so-called devoted customers were the ones who bought stocks on margin. They thought everything would go up forever. What was Louie to do when his customers started pawning their jewelry instead of buying more?"

"Maybe open a grocery store."

"Would you, Ben? Louie had this fantastic plan. His inventory, full of beautiful things he had designed himself, was his secret treasure, waiting only for an upturn in business to be sold. Tomorrow was just around the corner—don't you feel the same way? He was full of plans, schemes, solutions."

"He wasn't an optimist, he was crazy."

"Crazy about you, your mother, your future, while out there were all those animals waiting to take everything away from him because he hadn't finished paying for the gold he had made into jewelry nobody wanted to buy."

"Then the fool did buy on margin."

"Bite your tongue, Ben. Charles and I knew that Louie's debts to refiners and diamond merchants had always been high, but as long as Louie was able to keep his loving customers buying, there was always enough cash to pay a little here and there."

"Charles wasn't a gambler like Louie, was he?"

"No. Maybe that's why I wanted to run away with your father. Who wants to run away with a science teacher? If he could have figured out how to make love without touching he would have done it." Anna put her fingertips to her mouth. "I'm sorry," she said, "I didn't mean to say that. God forgive me."

I took Anna's hands. They felt warm.

"It's okay," I said. "You're right. I'm a gambler like Louie. I live on margin."

"Oh, Ben. Learn from experience."

"Learn how not to be attractive to women like you? Not a chance."

"You talk just like Louie." She took her hands back from me. "Listen Ben, my Charles was a practical man. He advised Louie to remove the diamonds and rubies from the jewelry in his inventory and give them back to his so-called suppliers, or sell them to someone else at a discount and at least pay some of the bills. You know what Louie said? He said, 'A painter can't sell his frames. My frames mean nothing without the stones.' Ben, your father was a great, foolish, wonderful romantic. But I'll tell you something, I hope you're a better business-man. Your lunatic father said, 'I will pay all my debts dollar for dollar if it takes me the rest of my life.' Charles warned Louie what could happen, told him the law gave him a way out. Don't be stubborn, he said. The Depression isn't your fault. You know what Louie said? He said, 'I hate the law.' And by saying that, Ben, he committed you and your mother and himself to the consequences of his pride."

I could hear Louie's voice clearer than ever. *If you think I was a fool, Ben, what will your son think?*

Anna was saying, "I'm sorry my Charles isn't here. He would have liked you."

"I'm sure I would have liked him, Anna."

"Sit down, Ben, standing makes me nervous. Don't run like Louie did."

"I'm not running away to New York, I live there."

"You know what I mean. Running somewhere else. Louie fled Chicago like a man running from the wind. Your mother saw the move to New York as a descent into hell. The expensive furniture he'd bought just two years earlier was sold for next to nothing. Her friends were in Chicago. Her courses were at Loyola, even though they could no longer pay for them. In New York she'd have to start all over again. I told her all these things were less important than Louie making a new start. Zipporah felt I was taking Louie's side, and so she told me her secret."

Anna put a knuckle to her lips and bit it.

"Tell me," I said.

"It isn't God's will that you should know everything."

"You don't know God's will," I said.

She took it like a slap in the face. I tried to take her hands but she wouldn't let me have them.

"Just like Louie," she said. "You want to know everything."

"Only about them. And the professor."

"I can't believe it. She talked about him?"

"Only when they quarreled. He was a weapon."

"I tell you, Louie had no competition."

"Anna? Please. I want to know everything about them."

"Before I die? All right. That's fair." For a moment she turned her back to me as if it would be easier to talk to the wall. "At first, Ben, I thought the professor was somebody your mother made up. After your father went off to New York to look for a job, she told me who he was, a distinguished scholar from the old country who had emigrated at the same time as she had and who, perhaps to follow her, was then teaching at the University of Chicago, his position as secure as Charles's and he was paid a lot more. Your mother—with tears—confessed that she met with the professor alone, first for lunch at a nice little restaurant near his bachelor apartment. It wasn't really a date, she explained, just a meeting, but yes, she had gone up to the apartment afterward. They had talked about the state of the country and the world. The professor was an intelligent man, and your mother, like so many of you Jewish people, was excited by intelligence more than by anything. So when the professor put his hand on her hand, it confused her. The mere thought of infidelity in those days was very exciting. But his hand was clumsy, and the physical feeling made her pull her hand back in a way, she said, that the professor mistook for reproof. She went on to me about how well-read he was, his theories about the world, and so on, and I interrupted her to say, 'Zipporah, you're not telling me how you feel about him.' You know what she answered? 'When you cut an apple in half, the insides turn brown. That's how I feel, in half and rotten. You know what excites the professor more than me? When his worst enemy, another professor in the same field, publishes something new!'

"And so I told her what she knew, that she loved Louie, and she said, 'I don't love what's happened to us. The professor at least has his feet on the ground.' And so I said, 'You're not in love with the professor's feet.' Thank God your mother had a sense of humor. Listen, Ben, enough about the old days. Will your play come to Chicago so I can see it?"

"Why wait? I'll fly you into New York for opening night."

"Oh, I couldn't. I don't have, you know, the right thing to wear."

"My wife will take you where she gets all her gowns."

"I couldn't afford—"

"It'll be on the house."

"You are just like your father. If only Louie and Zipporah were alive to know of your success."

"They know," I said, barely above a whisper.

Comrades, we shook hands.

"Anna, I really have to make my plane."

"I know. I'm so glad you came."

"Me too."

She said, "Give my love to the father of your children."

I kissed her cheek and said, "This has been more important to me than any business trip."

I took her wizened hand in my left hand, turned it palm up with the long lifeline showing, and put my right hand on top of hers, cradling her hand in mine.

"Jews touch," I said. Then I hugged her bosom against me. Louie, who was as tone deaf as I am, sang in my ear. It enriched me to know that with Anna and Zipporah in the same room, Louie must have felt like a king.

I was on the other side of the threshold, the line of demarcation between us, when Anna said, "Your family was the best part of my life."

For a brief moment I memorized her face, then fled down the steps to the street.

BOOK IV

It was the first time I arrived at the office with a Band-Aid on my cheek. "What did you do to yourself?" Charlotte asked.

"Shaving and thinking at the same time."

The tall vase on Charlotte's desk had sprouted three long-stemmed, orange-yellow roses.

"You have another admirer?"

"Another?"

"Other than me."

Her eyes bright with mischief, she said, "It's my birthday."

"Jesus."

"That's in December. Today is mine."

"I forgot."

"No, you didn't." She picked up a slim, white-beribboned box. "I figured you were preoccupied. I bought this for you to give to me."

"I'm embarrassed."

"That'll be the day."

"I truly am. What is it?"

"A slightly fancy pen from Tiffany. I charged it to your account. Thank you, Ben."

I kissed her blushing cheek. "The man who has you, Charlotte, has everything."

Her look denied that. That worm needed to be put back underground. "Any calls?"

"How was Chicago?"

"Centrally located," I said.

"I meant your meeting with Glenn. That's who called."

"This morning?"

"Twice. Very rude man. I told him to try being polite because it was my birthday. He said if you didn't return his call before ten o'clock, your most recent birthday would be your last."

"He actually said that?"

Charlotte pressed a button on the phonemobile. I heard the rewind hiss. She pressed another button, and Sam's voice was saying, "and another thing, sweetie, you tell that Jewboy boss of yours that if I don't hear from him by ten this morning, his last birthday is going to be his last birthday, you got that?"

"Don't erase that tape," I said to Charlotte. "Please get him on the phone and record both sides."

"With pleasure."

By the time Charlotte buzzed me, I was ready. In my most nonchalant manner I said, "You called?"

"Twice. I had some son-of-a-bitch time getting that old man to come to the phone."

"Manucci?"

"Yeah. And his name ain't Arthur. And he's not an investor. He gave me his son's phone. Don't you know who that Nick Manucci is? He said he offered to bankroll your whole production and you turned him down. Are you fucking dumb or what?"

"There are some kind of deals I won't do, Sam."

"Let me tell you something, prick. You owe me mine. If you got a deal that will bale me out you take it."

"You're not running my life, Sam. If I took Manucci's deal, you'd still be in."

"You're getting deaf, Ben. You didn't hear a thing I spoke to you in Chicago. You go kiss this Manucci's ass. When he funds the production, the first check you write is a refund of my piece."

"When I told him how much was in I included yours."

"Well you tell that dago mine what was in is out. I don't care if he takes a few more points off your end, you get me my money. If you don't do a deal with Manucci, sell your wife, but get me my dough or I'll grab every asset you got including your wife's diaphragm."

I slammed the phone down and presented my red-faced self to Charlotte.

"I think I got it all," she said. Instantly, the phone rang. Charlotte's voice, suddenly half an octave higher, sounded as if she were chewing gum. "Carson Chemicals, can I help you?"

She hung up. "It was him."

I laughed and applauded Charlotte's performance.

"Who shall I get first?"

"The guy I want to talk to doesn't have a phone," I said, and retreated to my office.

I looked at the fist I'd made of my hand. I opened it palm up to look at the lifeline.

The best revenge was the play's revenge on me. That play was what Louie had once expected of me. Even if it ran for a year, would my share be enough to cover Manucci's take? What if interest rates soared and I couldn't meet the payments? Manucci will grab my house.

You won't lose it.

Hey, Pop, Manucci wants a lien on it.

You lean on him. Think of a way.

I need some cards.

Hear me out, Ben.

I've got a headache.

You'll have a bigger headache if you don't listen. How many times did I tell you that if you don't want people to pick on you, walk as if you're taller than they are.

How did a shrimp like you get by, Pop?

With women, charm.

With men?

By letting them know I don't give an eye for an eye, I give two for one. I'm not interested in revenge, I'm interested in prevention.

Then how come a mountain of trouble fell on you?

My father didn't stay around to talk to me. All I care is you come out all right. I made old Manucci need me. You've got to make young Manucci need you.

How the hell am I supposed to do that?

Every man's got trouble. Find out what his trouble is. Then make it worse in a way that you can make it better.

Ezra would say that isn't cricket.

You tell your friend that Americans don't play cricket. They play baseball.

Hardball.

You got it, Ben.

You think your way could have stopped Hitler, Pop?

Funny you should ask. I sometimes dreamed that I could talk each of the six million to put up a buck apiece. In the 1930s you could have bought every Mafia hit man here and in Sicily a thousand times over for that kind of money. I'd offer the jackpot to whoever knocked Hitler off first. Believe me, they would have lined up for the job.

You're a tough man, Pop.

Ben, if I didn't teach you to play tough, I failed.

"You didn't fail," I said out loud.

"Talking to me?" Charlotte asked. "Where've you been?"

I opened my eyes.

"It's okay," said Charlotte. "I won't tell." She slid mail into my in box.

"Any of that good news?"

She shook her head.

"Looks like we'll have to make some of our own," I said. "Get Steve Nissof on the phone. And don't look at me that way."

"Oh, Mr. Riller," Nissof said, in a tone that acknowledged an honor. Maybe he hadn't heard about the trouble I was in. "What can I do for you?"

"Depends."

"Give me the name."

"I'd rather see you in person."

"I could make time tomorrow."

"How about right now? Where's your office?"

He gave me the address.

"I'll be there in fifteen minutes tops."

He'd charge more for an emergency. So what? There was zero time to spare.

* * *

Getting a cab in New York quickly always gives me a rush of triumph. I got in. The driver didn't say a word. That isn't reticence. It means he doesn't speak English as well as the drivers who speak it badly. I had to repeat the address twice and, in pidgin, told him how to get there. I didn't want to look up and find myself crossing one of Manhattan's bridges into another borough.

I persuaded myself to sit back in the seat. I'd never been to Nissof's office. He'd come to mine or we'd talked on the phone.

His address turned out to be one of those partially remodeled ancient office buildings. The front had been sandblasted clean only to slightly above eye level. The rest of it was New York gray.

Inside the lobby, the elevator starter, who looked like he had survived the Spanish-American War, tiredly held out a sign-in clipboard, which I waved away.

"It's rules," he said, his voice a mixture of fatigue and rust. I scrawled *Al Pacino*. The man didn't look. He waved me toward the elevators.

The two self-service elevators had new, imitation bronze doors. I stepped into the one with the doors open and pushed seven. The creak of machinery made me think some mechanical giant with a hernia was trying to haul the elevator up on a single, frayed rope. Miraculously it reached the seventh floor. I stepped out and the doors immediately groaned to a close, abandoning me.

I faced an array of frosted glass doors. Number 704 was halfway down the hall. All it said was STEPHEN NISSOF. I wasn't the only producer on Broadway who used him to check out potential investors if they suspected dirty money.

The doorknob didn't turn. The sound of a chair scraping came from inside. I rapped on the glass.

"Coming, coming," said a voice. Nissof, a tall, skinny man with freckles, had to open two deadbolts to let me in.

Arrayed against a wall was a row of steel filing cabinets, gray, beige, and brown, each with a vertical bar lock. The waiting area looked as if no one had ever waited there. "It's a real pleasure to have you here, Mr. Riller," he said, nodding me into the inner office. He gestured to a wooden chair and took refuge behind a desk that must have been secondhand before he owned it. Fortified by a yellow pad and pen, he said, "Name?"

"Nick Manucci."

Nissof put his pen down. "That's a name I don't have to look into."

"Bad news?"

"Stay away from him."

"Too late, Steve. He's buying a big share."

"In what?"

"My new play."

"The dog?" He coughed into his hand. "I'm sorry."

"Steve, we've been doing business a long time. Your opinion about plays is not why I'm here."

"I was just kind of repeating. The word's around. I didn't mean anything personal." He poised his pen again. "What do you want on Manucci?"

"His short hairs."

Nissof didn't move.

"How's business?" I asked. "Not too good?"

"What kind of short hairs?"

"Income tax filings. Audits in progress. Women. Wife's boyfriends. Kids on dope."

"I can do income tax. Have to pay out so it costs you more. Women won't do you any good, his wife knows. I wouldn't play tiddlywinks with Manucci. If you want to play hardball, it'll cost."

"How much?"

"Five thousand and no attribution."

"How will I know it's worth it?"

"Mr. Riller, you didn't get where you are being Santa Claus. Have I given you your money's worth in the past?"

"Sure, Steve, at three hundred per name."

"You don't want to find out if Manucci's money is clean. You want to negotiate better terms, right?"

"I sometimes forget you were a lawyer."

"Don't get unpleasant, Mr. Riller. I am a lawyer. I practice more than some guys who still have their licenses. You want to play hardball with Manucci, my retainer is five thousand. That's backstage only. Your lawyer has to play out front. Deal?"

Where to get the five thousand?

"I need to know more," I said.

Nissof smiled. "Seeing's we done a lot, I trust you." He leaned forward on his elbows. "You got the five grand, don't you?"

"Of course," I said.

"Ever hear the name Barone?"

"Lends money to actors."

"Biggest shylock operation in New York State. Manucci's a pimple on his ass."

"I know Manucci's family. I don't know anything about Barone."

Nissof laughed. "I wasn't suggesting Barone as a substitute investor. He wouldn't get into anything as lunatic as play production. You asked about short hairs. Barone is Manucci's short hair. Barone hates him. Five thousand gets you a meeting with Barone."

"What good would that do me?"

"Let me finish. A meeting with Barone and a script. I'll write the script. You know what to do with a script, don't you?" Nissof laughed again. "I'll call you."

I stood up and put my hand out to Nissof.

"Cash," he said. "No checks."

"Nondeductible."

"Tough."

"Okay, cash."

He shook my outstretched hand. "What'd you do to your cheek," he said as if noticing the Band-Aid for the first time.

"My barber tried to cut my throat and missed."

"You won't have to worry about things like that if this goes wrong," Nissof said. "You won't have to worry about anything any-more."

· · · · · 17

Nick

Forget what somebody else told you, I'm telling you a lawyer is a soldier. His job is to go out and kill the enemy. You wind him up, point him in the right direction, and get the hell out of the way. All the rest is bullshit.

My lawyer was a friend from school, Dino Palmieri. First, he was clean, which was good for my business when I started up. You don't need guilt by association from the wrong lawyer. Second, Dino did a good job on my loan agreements, mortgages, crap like that. Then I get hit with trouble. Twice I lent money to Golub, a beer distributor on Long Island. The second time, when it's due he twiddles me. We have a big argument in his office, he calls the cops to throw me out, you believe that? Worse, he throws a lawsuit at me for three times what I lent him on the grounds that I am interfering with his business.

Dino arranges a settlement conference in Golub's lawyer's office. I don't want to be in the same room with Golub, it's too tempting to reach across the table and grab him by his neck. Dino estimates what it's going to cost to fight this case, I swallow and agree to the conference, and what I see there makes my eyes bug out. This distributor has got a lawyer so short you wouldn't be able to see him if he sat behind a desk. And he's Yul Brynner bald. But when he shakes your hand you know this dude could squeeze an apple into apple juice. Golub's half-size lawyer is named Bert Rivers, and every time Dino opens his mouth, this lawyer pisses into it. In ten minutes, I wouldn't want to be represented by Dino if he was my brother. I want this Bert Rivers.

The meeting breaks so we can each talk privately about settlement money. For Dino, I got only one question. "How come you so fucking scared of Rivers?"

"His reputation is he doesn't lose too often."

"And you're scared shitless of his reputation, is that it?"

"Hey," Dino says. "Easy, Nick."

"You expect to get paid, win or lose, right? How about you only get paid if you win? Don't answer me."

I walk back into the conference with a check in my hand. "Golub," I say to the distributor, "the way I see it is if we let these two lawyers fight it out in court, mine is going to get money he's not worth, anybody can see that, and yours is going to get money from you every month for how many years it takes, and then you're going to find out that N.M. Enterprises, Inc., which is what you're suing, is only one of eleven corporations I got, and by coincidence, N.M. Enterprises doesn't own enough assets to keep these lawyers in toilet paper. This check is for ten G's, drawn on one of my companies that has ten G's. I can tear it up or hand it over to you and you give me a release and that's it."

I start to tear the check, just a quarter inch, and Golub is standing, saying, "You've got a deal."

The first thing I do when we're out of the building is say, "Good-bye, Dino."

He says, "Don't you want to talk about this?"

"Why? You going to pay me for my speech in there? I can't afford you, Dino. You're fired. As of yesterday."

The second thing I do is arrange for someone I know to do a little night work in Golub's offices. I tell him not to bother with the bookkeeper's cash box, to go straight to Golub's office and I tell him two places to look. A guy who runs his business the way Golub does has to keep a lot of cash handy. I tell my guy whatever's in there, I want exactly ten G's, not a penny more or less. I want Golub to know. I pay my guy two G's, which is less than what Dino would have cost me. Then I call Golub. I'm hanging on a long time, but he takes the call. I say, "This is a friendly call, Golub. I don't think you should keep cash around the office. In fact, I don't think you ought to carry it because who knows what happens in the streets these days. Don't you agree?"

"I'm listening," is all he says.

"About your loan, with the vigorish to date, you know what that comes to?"

"I can figure."

"Can you figure you start paying that down like five G's a week minimum?"

I hang up before he can say anything because under the circumstances the only acceptable answer is yes.

The third thing I do is call Bert Rivers.

"I shouldn't be talking to you," Rivers says. "I should only speak to your attorney."

"I'm afraid I don't have an attorney anymore, Mr. Rivers, because I fired him and I'm expecting to hire you. You don't have a conflict of interest anymore because Mr. Golub and I settled our case, right?"

"I'm not so sure."

"I'd like to tell you why I'm sure."

In his office Rivers interviewed me like a machine gun—how did I make my money, did I know the New York State laws on usury, how many times did I get sued, how many times did I get threatened, how often did I threaten somebody else? I made zero impression until I told him my office was in the Seagram.

"Is that right?" he said.

"What kind of retainer do you get?"

"Money," he said.

I gave him the ha-ha. "How much?"

"I believe," he said, looking me straight in the eye, "you would take a lot of my time."

"Hey," I said, "I never sued nobody in my life. I never been arrested. I just want the paperwork done on time, good advice, and your phone number just in case ever, you understand?"

"I'm sorry, Mr. Manucci," he said, "genuinely sorry."

Genuinely shit. You ever hear of a one-man law shop that turns down business? There's got to be a reason he isn't jumping into my lap.

"Is it Golub?" I asked. "That conflict-of-interest stuff?"

"Not really. I'll see you to the door," he said.

"I can find my way out," I said.

I walk back to my office bumping into people, steaming. That shitkicker turns *me* down? My old man always said to look for dirt in a man's laundry basket. I had my usual check run on Mr. Highfalutin Rivers, same as I do when a new customer wants heavy money. Two days later Gorgeous hands me a four-page memo I could have kissed. Mrs. Rivers number one and number two left him because he's got race-track disease? And guess who his bank was? You got it, Barone!

I'm sorry, Mr. Manucci, genuinely sorry. In a pig's ass he turns me down. Twenty percent a week vigorish kills you quick. That's when Barone looks to see what else you got besides money. Barone isn't stupid. Inside a couple of weeks he does what all the psychiatrists in New York put together couldn't do. He cures Rivers of gambling by putting out four words to the bookies: No credit to Rivers. This city ever wants to stop all drug traffic real cheap all they got to do is pay the right price to Barone and give him five weeks to clean up Queens and Harlem and three days extra for Wall Street. Only any politician got the guts to go to Barone better have another job waiting as soon as the smear starts.

When Barone gets a guy like Rivers up against the wall, he doesn't break Rivers's legs, he uses them.

I remember five, six, seven years ago, when that gorilla bought out the independents in his territory, one by fucking one. The guys Barone couldn't buy, he ran out. When he said he wanted to see me, I said, "Sure. In my office. Alone." He came all right, looked around blinking like he was above ground for the first time in his life.

"Some office," he said.

"What's on your mind?" I said, as if I didn't know.

So he told me. And I told him to go take a flying fuck. At the door, right in front of my secretary, he said, "Soon as your old man six feet down, somebody's going to send you to keep him company."

I told her, "Write that down. What you heard him say. Take it to a notary. I want an affidavit that you heard his threat."

I heard Barone went nuts in front of his boys, screaming, "How come I got to work out of restaurants, lofts, when that little shit Manucci got an office like a king?" My guy phoned me, laughing so hard I could hardly make out what he was saying. He said the boys tried to quiet Barone down, saying, "Boss, the Feds can't bug you if you move around."

Barone's problem was I had figured out how to get away with what he couldn't get away with. I was a businessman. He would always be a hood.

I never don't lock my car in parking lots. One day three four years ago I came out of the barber shop and saw someone sitting in my front passenger seat.

I've got a good smeller for trouble. I started walking away when the guy inside my car rolled the window down and said, "Mr. Manucci, Mr. B. would like to have a short discussion with you."

I knew two guys who'd been summoned to "discussions with Barone." Along the Belt Parkway the tall grass will hide a body, but not for long.

"Where?" I said, thinking maybe this is a chance to get a finger to Barone again.

"There's a little restaurant near Mosholu, you know, near Montefiore, the Italian Garden."

"Sure," I said. "I know the place."

The door on the driver's side was still locked. He reached across and opened it for me. I slid in, wondering if he'd checked the glove compartment and discovered the .38. I wasn't about to find out with him sitting right in front of it. Besides, I had something else in mind. Barone had taken the initiative, but this was going to be my show.

"You're driving slowly," the man said after a while.

"You in a hurry?" I asked.

"Maybe Mr. Barone is in a hurry."

"I'm a slow driver," I said, my eyes searching. I spotted the cruising police car about four blocks away, headed toward us. The man saw it, too. He didn't react. What's a police car?

I let the left wheels go over the double yellow line a bit. Then a bit more as we got closer. I wanted them to notice me. Then when we were half a block apart I turned just enough into the oncoming lane to cause the police car to brake.

"What the fuck are you doing?" the man said, stretching his cords.

I stopped a couple of feet between my radiator and theirs. Both cops came out at once, the tall one reaching my window just as I rolled it down.

"Thank you," I said to the cop. "I wanted to get your attention.

This man . . ." I jerked a thumb in the direction of my visitor, "broke into my automobile in a parking lot and was abducting me."

They made us both get out and put our hands against the roof of the car. I could see the anger boiling in the man's face. The cop frisked me, found nothing. The shorter cop patted the man down and, surprise, he had a gun in a holster under his arm. "You have a permit for this?" the cop asked. "I want to phone my lawyer," the man said as the cuffs were snapped on him. The cop was deaf. He pushed the hood's head down as he shoved him into the back of the police car.

"We'll need a statement from you," the cop said to me. "Follow us to the station house."

On the way I reached into the glove compartment and put the gun in my pocket in case the car was searched.

Barone phoned me at my office. My girl told him I was out. He called a second time and said, "Tell Mr. Manucci one of my people saw him come into the building a little while ago so he ain't out." Okay, I took the call.

Barone said, "I don't understand you, Nick. What'd you do to my fellow?"

"I didn't do anything," I said. "I just introduced him to some local law-enforcement people. If you want to talk to me I'm always happy to see you in my office, alone. Would you like to make an appointment?"

"This was going to be a friendly meeting," Barone said. "I was going to make you two offers. I buy all your outstandings for five hundred percent of face. You can retire rich for a few years or you can come in with us on a percentage of everything. How do you think about something like that?"

"Mr. Barone," I said, "my father didn't like the idea of working for somebody else. He said he was no good as an employee because he didn't know how to take orders. And I'm like him, no feeling for organization. I've got a long-term lease in the Seagram. Though I have to tell you, Barone, five hundred of face is pretty damn generous."

"Thank you. I thought you might say no, so I have a smaller proposition, a little business we could do, all right? As you know, Nick—it's okay I call you Nick, right?—I been putting together pieces in a certain eight-square-block area in Woodside, right, almost perfect except for a small piece of property the size of a hat, a candy store with three apartments up above, that somebody else owns, you know what I'm talking about?"

"That piece is owned by one of my companies, Mr. Barone," I said. "I thought you knew that."

I'd seen what he was doing in Woodside and I bought that small parcel overnight. He hadn't played fast enough. The rest would be no good to him unless he got my piece.

Barone said, "I know you get a lot of real pleasure out of that candy store, Nick, but I thought you might get more pleasure if I paid you two fifty for it."

"I have a better idea, Mr. Barone. Why don't I give you five hundred for your parcels?"

He hung up so hard my eardrum hummed. I could have kissed the telephone. It was as if a whole church choir was singing all around me. Oh God, how I loved screwing Barone to the wall! I walked a foot off the ground.

When I told the old man, I expected him to say, "Wonderful! Wonderful!"

What he said was "That's not the last time you hear from Barone, Nick."

"Better offer for my parcel? I still won't take it."

"Barone not stupid. He wait for you to make mistake."

I didn't think Barone had the patience to wait three four years.

I picked up the phone and said to Rivers's secretary, "Sweetie, this is Nick Manucci. Put Mr. Rivers on."

In two seconds she's back. "Mr. Rivers is busy."

"Tell him Barone sent me."

I heard her breathing but that's all.

"Sweetie, don't sit on your twat. Tell him what I said."

The next thing I heard is Rivers saying, "Mr. Manucci, what you said to my secretary has got her very upset."

"Did she give you my message?"

"I have someone in my office."

"Well, step out of your office into her office 'cause I am going to have the rest of our conversation now."

That tough son-of-a-bitch lawyer's got Barone's nutcracker on his balls. Somebody stupid would have said to me, "Who's Barone?" or something like that. Rivers is not stupid. When he gets back on, he said, "What's this about Barone?"

"Mr. Rivers," I said to him, "this is my offer. I'll pay you a retainer, rain or shine, two grand a week."

He coughed. He didn't have a cold. He had a pineapple up his ass he couldn't get rid of.

"I'm not kidding," I said to him. "You use my two grand to pay Barone back and in no time—three years tops—you're free and clear."

He did the cough again. I'm polite. I said to him, "You take care of your cold, Mr. Rivers."

"I don't have a cold. I'm thinking."

So I said, "Let me help. You can live on what you get from your other clients. You can forget Barone. Your new wife—you do have a new wife, right?"

"As a matter of fact I do."

"Well, she'll sure appreciate not having to worry about Barone. And I'll appreciate being your number-one client. That makes two people who'll appreciate you who may not be appreciating you right now."

It's time for Rivers to say something, so I shut up and concentrate on finishing my doodle, which is a tic-tac-toe I always win.

"You're an interesting negotiator, Mr. Manucci. I thought you handled the Golub matter beautifully."

"We have a deal?"

"I'll come over to your office." He sounds like I just let him out of jail.

"We don't need a meeting. We just had it. You want me to pay Barone direct? He'll know it's from you, but he won't know it's me that's paying it."

He's thinking. I don't want him to strain himself, so I said, "This way you won't have to think about income tax."

I figure by this time Rivers wants to kiss my ass. "You can draw up a piece of paper," I said.

"I'd just as soon not have it in writing. You're a gentleman, Mr. Manucci, I trust you."

What am I going to say? "Terrific. You're retained. The first payment gets to Barone on Friday." I don't want him thanking me, so I said good-bye and hung up. What I'm thinking is Hey, Papa Manucci, when I walked in there Rivers was working for Barone—now he's working for me!

Ben

I arrived at the office late. Charlotte said, "That Chicago man called."

"Did you tell him everything's under control?"

"He didn't want to talk to me. He wants to talk to you."

"Tell him I've got a strep throat."

"Your check-up man called, too."

"Who?"

"Steve Nissof. He said it was urgent."

"Why didn't you call me at home?"

"I did. Jane said you were still asleep, that you'd had a rough night."

"She should have awakened me."

"She said she'd leave a note."

"I didn't see a note."

"I'll get him," said Charlotte, dialing.

"I hurry my ass off," Nissof said, "then I can't get you."

"I'm sorry."

"Well, Mr. Riller, you're lucky. You got yourself a deal."

"When do I see Barone?"

"You don't have to. I offered him three thousand to light a little fire. You should have heard him yell. Three thousand is tipping money! But when I said the fire was to be under Nick Manucci, hey man! If Barone didn't have a habit of taking money, he might have done this for nothing."

"You didn't tell him the job was for me?"

"Absolutely not. You should have heard him on the subject of Manucci. Our timing was perfect. Apparently Manucci screwed him out of some collateral just a couple of days ago. What you've got to do first, Mr. Riller, is get me my five thousand. I only get two grand out of the deal."

I felt a squirrel in my chest. "I hope this isn't going to involve anything physical."

Nissof said, "Manucci was squeezing your nuts, wasn't he?"

I didn't say anything.

"Now look, Mr. Riller," Nissof went on. "It's done. No backing off. A phone handshake with Barone is made in concrete, understand? I can't welsh on him, which means you can't welsh on me. When do I get the dough?"

"Soon."

"How soon?"

I reached Jane at her office. "I'm in the middle of a meeting, Ben." I could feel the hesitation in her voice. "Can I get back to you later?"

"No. Get rid of them. Excuse yourself. I've got to come up with five grand cash today. The only place I know that's got it is your account at Chemical."

We never discussed her business account. All I knew was that some part of it produced interest that showed up on our joint tax return. Judging by the interest, it had to have over five thousand in it.

All Jane said was no.

I know she put her hand over the mouthpiece, but I could still hear her say something to whoever was in her office. When she got back on, I said, "You want me to beg?"

"Will you tell me what you're doing with it?"

"I'd rather you didn't know."

"Ben, be careful."

I should have been careful a long time ago.

She waited at least ten seconds for me to say something. I was suddenly afraid that she might hang up. "Jane?"

"I'll bring it over lunchtime," she said. "I want you to tell me what this is all about." She hung up.

I looked up at the ceiling. Was I expecting to find Louie there? Louie wasn't anywhere.

• • • • • 19

Mary

Don't ever complain about nothing happening because that's when something happens.

When I came out to prune the roses along the walk I noticed the leaves of the linden tree in front of the Baldridge house across the street dropping a speckled net of shadows across an unfamiliar dark green car. I could make out two men in the front seat.

Nick was very strict about rules. I hurried inside, still holding the pruning shears, and phoned Alice Baldridge.

"I hope I'm not getting you at a bad time, Alice."

"No, no, fine," she said. "What's up?"

"Does that green Caddy in front of your place . . . are those people coming to visit you?"

"I'm not expecting anyone, Mary. But if it's a nice car, maybe I should invite them in."

She's a joker, Alice. I thanked her and dialed the police as I was supposed to.

"This is Mrs. Manucci, Cedar Drive East."

"Yes, Mrs. Manucci."

"There's an unfamiliar car with two men in it parked across the street."

"Maybe they're waiting for someone, Mrs. Manucci."

"I checked with Mrs. Baldridge. She isn't expecting anyone."

The policeman sighed. "Can you see what kind of car it is?"

"Green Cadillac."

"Did you note the license number?"

"Can't see it unless I go out into the street."

"Never mind, Mrs. Manucci. We'll check it out for you."

When we moved to the suburbs I told Nick I wanted a place where the cops were friendly like in Minnesota. Nick grew up in New York City. He couldn't imagine a place where the cops were friendly.

From the bedroom window upstairs I had a clear view of the street. I saw the patrol car come around the corner and pull up alongside the Cadillac. I could see someone on the passenger side rolling the window down.

The policeman didn't get out of his car. The man in the Caddy was saying something. I guess the policeman then said something. When the police car pulled away, and a few seconds later the Caddy went, too, I went back down to my roses, relieved. The man I had my first affair with, Gary, drove a Cadillac.

He used to come to the house because I hated the idea of motel rooms. The kids were in school, Nick never ever came home in the daytime, so it was safe. Doing it in your own bedroom was exciting in itself because Nick said never bring a man home. Gary came here twice a week until someone told him who Nick was. He asked me point blank, "Is that who your husband is?" I told him yes that was Nick, and he never came back.

Doing the roses gives me peace like nothing else. Nick never touches them. Even the forsythia, the first color we get in this neighborhood, I don't let it grow scraggly, I give it shape. And fertilize it plenty so the yellow is the yellowest yellow you've ever seen.

Would you believe it was a poli-sci teacher who taught me to see color? Mr. Milford, the one great teacher I ever had, used to say *Distinguish color carefully and you'll learn to distinguish carefully in other things.* He'd say *yellow can be a dozen different yellows,* by which he meant from the palest ivory which isn't really yellow, to the lemon-dark of these forsythia. *What color are roses?* he would say, and we would chant back *red, pink, white, yellow,* and he'd say *Go on* and we'd yell our new choices: *peach, orange, lavender,* and someone would say *Who ever saw a lavender rose?* and it was I who said *Angel Face is lavender.* And then Mr. Milford would say *What color is the human race?* and we'd say *white, black, brown, yellow* and he'd say *Go on* and we'd have to say *tan, pink, rust, ocher, blue-black, café-au-lait.* Mr. Milford said you have to be precise, you have to be clear, you have to make distinctions.

A noise made me look up quick.

My heart skittered when I saw the same dark green Cadillac drive up and stop on my side of the street this time. The nerve, after being chased by the police!

This time the man on the passenger side got out, and the driver took off. I glanced across the street to see if by any chance Alice was looking out of an upstairs window. Nobody.

The man lifted the hook on our gate at the end of the driveway, let himself in, and put the hook back in place. He was dressed in a striped business suit but didn't look like a businessman. Maybe it was his complexion, dark like the southern Italians my father used to have such strong feelings about.

As he came closer, he took his hat off and held it against his chest in a way I hadn't seen since the old movies.

"Mrs. Manucci," he said. "I just tried to phone you from the drugstore to let you know I was coming, but nobody answered the phone in the house." He smiled. "I guess that's 'cause you were out here."

He was letting me know he knew no one else was home.

"My name is Angelo."

I waited for a last name.

"I need to talk to you. Just for a couple of minutes, okay?"

If I went inside to call the police, would he try to stop me? What would I tell the police, that he was trespassing?

"I don't get involved in my husband's business matters," I said.

"Sure, sure," Angelo said, "but this is different. Can we go inside to talk?"

"We can talk right here."

"If you don't mind people seeing us . . ."

"Please tell me what you want."

"I'm sorry if I frightened you before, Mrs. Manucci. I only wanted to get a message to Nick."

"You could phone him at his office."

"Not really. Mrs. Manucci, I represent some businesspeople who gave a big loan to one of the regular customers. The collateral on that loan was a very expensive computer setup. You know what collateral is, Mrs. Manucci."

"Yes. Of course."

"Well, when we turned down a request for more money from the same party because he didn't have any more collateral, your husband lent him some and took a second mortgage on the computers."

"I'm not sure I understand."

"Maybe you don't have to." Angelo took out a packet of cigarettes, looked at it, put it back. "I don't smoke anymore," he said with a little laugh. "I shouldn't be carrying them. The problem, Mrs. Manucci, is that your husband had the computers loaded on a truck two days ago and moved them to Canada. That's our collateral, Mrs. Manucci, he had no business moving it out of our reach. If he wants to compete with us on loans, that's okay, but what he just did doesn't get done without causing a lot of harm. Please tell Nick that you and the kids would really like to have those computers returned right away."

He put his hat back on. "That's all you have to remember, Mrs. Manucci, to have the computers returned, okay?"

"Where can he reach you?"

"He doesn't reach us. He just returns the computers." He went back out into the street, and almost immediately the dark green Cadillac was there picking him up.

I ran into the house to call Nick, but the phone was already ringing. It was Alice Baldridge.

"That car came back. Are you okay, Mary?"

"Sure, sure, I'm okay, it was just some businessmen looking for Nick."

"I was hoping you'd be okay. I didn't think they'd come back after the police car came by. Were they Americans?" Alice asked.

"I don't know," I lied.

"The man who talked to you, he didn't look American to me. We never used to have cars just sitting there in the street before."

"Before what?"

"I didn't mean anything, Mary."

"I've got to call Nick, Alice, I'll talk to you later." I hung up without waiting for her good-bye.

Comment by Aldo Manucci
■■ ■■ ■■

Long time ago I told Mary, "If you have baby, you tell Nick first, if Nick in trouble, you tell me first." I teach Nick how to wipe his nose, wipe his ass, do business. I tell him never cross anybody. God take you soon enough, don't meet him halfway. When Mary call me, she talk to Nick already. I call Nick. "What make you do stupid thing like that? You got enough customers."

"They wouldn't give him another loan," Nick said. "That makes him a free agent."

"He still owes them. He's their customer."

"Look, Pop, I'm handling it. Please?"

"Nick, you handle it, that's why you got trouble. They know their business. If they won't give a guy a second mortgage, how come you do?"

"Papa, that computer setup is worth eighteen times what they lent the guy."

"Bigshot, you think you're ahead of Barone because you got possession of collateral? You got possession of nuts! If they get to you, it's your fault you're dead. Mary's a smart wife, but the world eats widows. Why you take the collateral to Canada?"

For a minute Nick said nothing. He's making up a lie.

"Don't lie to me, Nick."

"I found out this customer was looking for another loan on top of mine. He was offering the computers as collateral, a third mortgage, without telling them about my loan. I had to protect my loan, didn't I?"

"What about Barone's loan? He come first. You mad 'cause somebody try to do to you what you do to Barone."

"The guy said Barone's people never went to his place like I did. They did it all on paper. I never thought Barone would find out."

"I told you not to lie, Nick. You want give Barone the finger. You want him find out you took his collateral."

"Hey, Papa . . ."

"Nick, hear me good. Return it."

"I can't."

"What you mean?" Nick got me scared now, I tell you.

"The truck was impounded in Canada."

"Mary, Mother of God. Get it back."

"I'm trying. My man up there says it could take three, four weeks."

"Nick, they kill people, you know that."

"I'm not afraid of them, Papa. I can take care of myself."

"I don't give good goddamn about yourself, you hear what the man say to Mary? He said, 'You and the kids want to have computers returned right away.' He was talking going after them not you, *stupido*. You want the disgrace of a man who loses his wife and kids because of a business mistake?"

"They don't do things like that anymore, Papa."

"What you know? You know where Morelli's wife went? Into the supermarket, disappear. You think she run away to Mexico with a boyfriend? Nothing has changed. Use your brains. Get that truck out of Canada, you hear me?"

• • • • • 20

Nick

I got off the phone, blam, instant headache like someone's put a spike in my dome. If I lived to eighty and my old man was
a hundred, he'd still be telling me do this, do that. Don't people know
when they're dead?

So the collateral was driven up to Canada, it's just one mistake, not
the end of the world.

The intercom buzzed. My headache didn't need phone calls. It
buzzed again. I got on and said, "What the fuck are you bothering me
for? If I wanted to pick up, I'd pick up."

Nothing. She said nothing. Then she said, "It's Bert Rivers."

So I said, "I'm sorry I yelled. I got this terrific headache."

"It's okay," she said. "Shall I tell Mr. Rivers you'll call him back?"

"No, no. Put him on."

I said, "What's up, Bert, besides your pecker?"

"Hochman called me twice today. Riller's lawyer."

"I know, I know."

"You got him. He's ready to sign."

"Bert?"

"Yeah?" he says.

"You tell Hochman to forget it."

"You crazy?"

"I got too much on my mind," I said.

"You said it was a terrific deal for you."

"I know, I know." So I told Bert what's happened.

For a couple of seconds all I could hear was my wristwatch. Then Bert said, "Why didn't you talk to me before you moved that truck to Canada?"

"You always said I shouldn't ask your advice on anything that might not be legal."

"Where's Mary and the kids?"

"At home."

I could hear his breathing, which means Bert is thinking, which is what I pay him for. He's not one of those that runs off at the mouth with the first thing that comes to his mind.

Finally he said, "Sit tight. Don't leave your office. Don't let anybody in. Don't talk to anybody. I'll be right over."

Bert Rivers

Jesus, I thought in the cab on the way to the Seagram Building, why Barone?

Nancy warned a long time back, "Why are you taking Nick Manucci on as a client?" Could I tell her because he's helping get Barone off my back? She'd have left me if she'd known how much I still owed Barone, which he could ask for any time, all of it, or "Do me a big favor, Bert." I've seen some of his big favors.

I told Nancy, "Nick's not like Barone, he's a very successful businessman, he can afford to deal with me as if I were a Chinese doctor, pay me a big retainer just for keeping him well." So Nancy said, "You don't want to get involved with the mob again," and I had to sit her down and explain that Manucci had nothing to do with them, that what he did wasn't criminal, that he carefully stayed within the usury laws, etcetera. And now look.

I got shown in right away and Nick pumped my hand as if I'd already done something to save him.

"Take it easy," I told him. "I don't have a life raft. I need all the facts. Let's sit down."

I sat down but Nick kept pacing like one of those caged cats in the Bronx Zoo.

"You should keep one of those indoor bicycles on a stand in here to burn off energy," I said. "You'll get a headache doing what you're doing."

"I got the headache. I'm trying to think."

"How long would it take to get the computers back?"

That got Nick to sit down. I have to give him credit. His voice was pretty calm, considering the circumstances.

I began to see the problem. I didn't blame the Canadians. They probably inspected this particular truck by a fluke. There wasn't even any cover-up cargo, just this computer setup in crates. The driver didn't have a bill of lading that meant anything, it was the kind of thing that might fool a state trooper but not a customs inspector. All the Canadians can think is some American company sold these computers to some Canadian company for an illegal enterprise. The driver is a poor liar so he's held, the truck and its contents impounded.

"You realize I can't practice in Canada," I told Nick.

"Why the hell not?"

"I can advise somebody, suggest things, but we'll need to hire a Canadian lawyer. I know one in Toronto, went to McGill and Yale Law, has contacts, which is probably more important, but in something like this, I don't know. We need to buy time. Maybe I can reach Barone personally, by phone I mean."

"What are you going to say to him?"

"I don't want to rehearse it, Nick."

Nick riffled through his small tan leather address book for a phone number I had in my memory as if it were my birthdate.

"You shouldn't keep names like that in your book, Nick," I said.

If I could calm Barone down, buy some time, I'd earn my retainer ten times over.

Nick wrote the number down for me. "If I kept it somewhere else I wouldn't know how to find it when I needed it," Nick said.

I said, "I want to make this call in privacy."

"Don't promise him anything I can't deliver."

"Don't you worry. The only thing you can deliver that can stop him are the computers."

"Use my office. I'll go down the hall."

"Thanks," I said. He's going to listen in on the conversation. Well, if it hurts Nick's feelings to hear what I've got to say, it's not my fault. I dialed the number. A woman answered. I asked to speak to Mr. Barone. She didn't ask me who I was. A man got on.

"Who wants to talk to Barone?"

"My name is Bertram Rivers. I'm Nick Manucci's attorney." He must have covered up the mouthpiece. I couldn't make out what was being said. Then a different, deeper man's voice got on.

"What can I do for you, Mr. Rivers?" It wasn't Barone's voice.

"I'd like to talk to Mr. Barone."

"Just talk."

"My client, Nick Manucci, did a very stupid thing."

"Just a minute."

Then an older male voice with an accent I recognized got on the horn. "This is Barone."

He's smart, I thought. He'll figure out that somebody might be listening in. He won't tip that he knows me.

"My name is Bert Rivers, Mr. Barone. I'm Nick Manucci's lawyer. I was saying that Nick did a very stupid thing about the collateral. It'll take a few weeks to get the collateral back from Canada, so I have a constructive suggestion."

"Mr. River, I give you a suggestion. Your client, he committed suicide, you know what I mean? Why don't you find a place to put the body?"

Was he doing that because of Nick or because I was working for the enemy? It was like trying to negotiate with an IRS agent. The other fellow has no reason to be reasonable.

"My suggestion, Mr. Barone, is that my client, as a sign of good faith, buy your loan, pay you in cash the hundred thousand that the computer owner borrowed plus any accumulated interest. In other words, you would be satisfied as to the loan, how's that?"

"In our business my customers are my customers. You can't buy their loans from me. Those people come back again and again, you understand?"

"Mr. Barone, how about twenty percent above the principal plus the interest just because my client did the wrong thing, how's that?"

"Mr. River, if an independent works around my territory but don't bother me, I don't bother them. Old man Manucci never gave me a day's trouble. This Nick, what he did, is just not done. If I accept your offer, every independent will know that if he gets caught doing business with my customers, all he has to do is pay me back. Pretty soon they're all over my turf. I know I'm going to get those computers back sooner or later. If I got them back today, Manucci would still be in the worst trouble in his life. His life, understand? And since we never talked before, Mr. River, I save you some trouble. Don't hide him. I'll find him. Here, there, another country. Doesn't matter. You tell Nick Manucci he's dead."

Barone hung up.

Nick came in the door. By his expression I could tell he had been listening on an extension.

"I'm glad you heard it from his mouth," I said. "It saves me repeating it."

"What do you mean, Bert?"

"Come on, Nick. You're in too much trouble to pretend. You pick up that phone and tell Mary to pack a bag as soon as the kids are home from school, lock the house up tight, and go to her sister's."

"She doesn't have a sister, Bert. It's me who's got a sister."

"Your sister got a family?"

"Sure, sure, I told you once. A big house in Forest Hills."

"Her husband have any connection with your business?"

"Are you kidding? He's some kind of engineer."

"Tell her to take the kids there. Tell her to pack some clothes and get out of the house real fast. I'll use another phone to call Hochman. I want him to bring Riller over here."

"What the hell's wrong with you, Bert? I told you I haven't got time for that project now."

"Nick, you've got two choices. Fire me or listen to me. Which?"

Nick knew how efficient Barone's people could be.

"I'm listening," he said.

"I'm not going to walk around with you in public because sometime in the next few days Barone's people are going to let loose and I don't want to be standing next to you when it happens. But I do want Ben Riller standing next to you, sitting next to you, walking with you, riding with you till the computers get returned, and Barone cools off enough for me to come back to him with another proposition."

"What the hell good does it do me if Riller gets it too?"

"Nick, Riller is the best known producer in the theater. He gets photographed in restaurants, coming out of the opera, he's surrounded by well-known actors and actresses, and you're going to be photographed with him, in fact you and Mary are going to be photographed with Riller and his wife, you're going to double-date everywhere, and Riller's PR people are going to see to it that you're going to be as well known as he is. Do you follow? Do you want me to give you a list of the famous people who've rubbed the mob the wrong way who are alive because they're famous? You're an independent and you didn't want any publicity for the same reasons Barone doesn't want publicity. The safest place for you to be in the next few weeks is in the biggest limelight money can buy. And the way to get there is to become Riller's visible partner in this play. If you want to stay alive."

"Do I have time to think about it?" Nick asked.

"One minute."

Nick said. "Call Hochman."

Ezra

Ben and I arrived at Nick Manucci's office to find
the impressive outer doors deadbolt-locked. I rapped on the thick
wood with my knuckles till they hurt.

Ben spotted a dime-sized doorbell on the right jamb and pressed it
with his forefinger.

We heard the sound of feet and then a woman's voice saying,
"Who is it?"

Before either of us could answer, a gruff male voice demanded to
know who we were.

You never know how loud to speak when you're trying to be heard
on the other side of a thick door. With a chest full of air I announced,
"Hochman and Riller."

"Not a terrific name for a dance team," Ben said.

A man in suspenders passing us in the hall laughed.

The door opened a crack. We were being looked at.

The woman's voice said, "It's them. It's okay."

I heard the deadbolt being turned. The huge wood slab swung
open.

"Good morning, Miss Atherton," Ben said cheerily.

Miss Atherton, happy because Ben had remembered her name,

smiled us in. The ox-shouldered heavy standing behind her needed a shave. Ben put out his hand to him. "I'm Ben Riller. How do you do?"

The heavy looked like he was about to flunk an exam. "Dja do," he said, then quickly double-bolted the huge doors behind us. Were we being locked in?

"Someone's being locked out," said Ben the mind reader.

Miss Atherton hurried through the security portal to tell Manucci we'd arrived.

The heavy, without a word, closed himself into a side office from which emanated the voices of other men with imperfect locution. Manucci's collectors? His army?

We settled into the expensive black leather of the reception-room couch.

Miss Atherton reappeared, motioned for us to join her at the security portal. She held her hand out for Ben's metal objects, then mine. We passed through and got our stuff back just as a low-set, bald pit-bull of a man trotted out of Manucci's office. "Hi, gentlemen, I'm Bert Rivers. You're Hochman," he said to me, shaking my hand, then Ben's, saying, "I know your face from the newspapers, Mr. Riller. It's a privilege."

"I thought Mr. Manucci lost interest in our situation," I said.

"Not . . . at . . . all," Rivers said, punching each word like a preacher. "Mr. Manucci's attention was deflected by some business bother, you know how it is."

Bert Rivers's smile consisted of withdrawing his lips so that his teeth showed. When Ben first snitched to Louie that I intended to become a lawyer, Louie said, "There are lawyers who mend and lawyers who bend. Which kind are you going to be, Ezra?" Before I could answer, he'd said, "My dear Ezra, when you play chess with the Devil, remember whatever it is he has is catching."

Manucci came out of his office to shake hands. I could swear his tan had yellowed.

"We will have to speak in confidence," he said, motioning us in.

What the hell was going on?

"Please be seated."

We sat.

Manucci said, "There's a man—" and Rivers cut him off.

"Excuse me," Rivers said. "I'd like to put things in a way that will clarify matters for Mr. Hochman." He leaned toward me as if

Manucci and Ben weren't in the room. "Mr. Manucci is having a bit of a problem with a certain business rival, a Mr. Barone, you may have heard of him?"

I was shaking my head when Ben said, "I've heard of him. He lends money to actors."

"He lends money to lots of people. Unfortunately, Mr. Barone has a bad temper," Rivers said. "He's not the kind of person Mr. Manucci likes to deal with, you understand, but Mr. Barone seems very insistent right now on wanting to deal with Mr. Manucci. Until this blows over . . ."

I said, "Can you fill us in a little as to the nature of the dispute between Mr. Barone and Mr. Manucci?"

"It may not be pertinent, but of course," Rivers said.

He told us some garbage about collateral that vanished up into Canada as if it was a big fuss over nothing.

Why was Ben amused?

"Let me put it this way, gentlemen," Rivers said. "I believe the best kind of business is reciprocal."

"I know how you can help Mr. Riller," I said. "How can we help you?"

Rivers cleared his throat. "Mr. Riller is a well-known man. He is famous to lots of people. Mr. Manucci is not."

I glanced at Ben's face.

Then Rivers said, "If by any chance—and I don't mean chance, I mean by prearrangement—Mr. Riller and Mr. Manucci were seen a great deal together in public places, especially if their being together made news in gossip columns, Mr. Manucci would overnight be in the public eye."

I said, "I didn't know that a man in Mr. Manucci's business wants to be in the public eye."

"Mr. Manucci would rather be in the public eye than in some marksman's gunsight. I trust you understand."

"Less and less."

Ben said, "It's simple. Whatever the dispute between Messrs. Manucci and Barone, Mr. Barone is probably just whacko enough to have someone take a potshot at Mr. Manucci."

Rivers nodded. Manucci nodded.

"Well then," Ben continued as if I were the dumb boy being lectured to, "if Mr. Manucci is in the limelight he's less likely to become a target. It's a given."

"Given by who?" I said. "You want to walk around with a target? You came here for an investment, not to put your life on the line."

Rivers put an avuncular hand on my kneecap. "Mr. Hochman, everyone knows that Barone may be crazy, but he's not a nut. He'd never let his people take someone out with photographers and reporters around. A photograph of someone shooting someone else is the best proof of a crime you can get. There isn't a soldier works for Barone who wouldn't become a snitch under the right circumstances. For instance, the D.A. nicely gives him a choice: he can live in a ten-foot cage until he's too far gone to bang his old lady or he can snitch on whoever ordered the hit. Or the D.A. can throw out some ideas, like who might bang his old lady for him while he rots in the slammer . . . or he can spend a few minutes snitching and do minimum time. I tell you something, Mr. Hochman, you don't need to be an acupuncturist to know that every human body has got pressure points all over. Find the right one, and bingo. If a snitch helped convict Barone, he could go into a witness protection program and start his crooked little life all over on government welfare. Barone would end up in the pen with fifteen guys he's fucked over the years, excuse my expression. If someone like you or me gets unlucky with the law, Mr. Hochman, we end up in some place like Lompoc, getting tan. If Barone gets put away, his wife could start dusting off her widow's weeds."

"Gentlemen," I said, "I must consult with Mr. Riller." I motioned Ben to follow me to a far corner of the room. "What do we want from these gangsters?" I whispered.

"Money," said Ben.

"It's too risky."

"Theater is risky."

"They don't shoot at you."

"Ez," he said, "you forget."

"Forget what? That you're mortal?"

"What Louie said. Death isn't risky. It's life that's a risk. Let's hear their deal."

Manucci and Rivers were staring at us.

"Mr. Hochman," Rivers said, raising his voice from across the room. "If Mr. Riller is willing to go public with Mr. Manucci, come hear our proposition."

I glanced at Ben. This isn't a play, Ben, I wanted to say, it's your life.

"We propose," Rivers said, narrowing the gap between us, "to draw two agreements. One based on Mr. Manucci's original offer with full collateral protection for his investment. The second will be a straight investment on the normal terms that any one buying a piece of a play gets."

"At full risk?" Ben asked.

"Yep." It was the first word Manucci said out loud.

The four of us were now standing in a circle. "The whole amount needed to close the partnership?" I asked.

"Of course," Rivers said. "Contract one, the original proposal, with all supplementary agreements, goes into a safe deposit in escrow. You and I, as attorneys, will be co-custodians of the box. If Mr. Riller and Mr. Manucci work together amicably during the next several weeks until the Barone problem is solved, Mr. Riller has got himself the money he needs free and clear of any obligation. If Mr. Riller reneges at any stage, deal one in the safe deposit box gets activated. If you'd like to discuss this with your client privately, Mr. Hochman, Mr. Manucci and I will be happy to step into another office. Take your time."

Being left in Manucci's office felt like being in someone's bedroom.

Rivers put his head back in. "Mr. Manucci wants me to assure you that the room is not bugged," he said, and disappeared.

I said, "You *like* the idea of living dangerously?"

"How the fuck do you think I'm living now? You think what I'm going through is life-enhancing? Manucci's deal sounds a lot better than running off to Tahiti."

"Not if Barone's people have a go at Manucci while you're sitting together in a restaurant."

Ben looked at me and I saw his strong resemblance to Louie. It had always been there. I hadn't always noticed it.

I said, "Business is one thing. Risking your ass is another. If I were you, Ben, I wouldn't do it."

"You are not me, Ezra. I don't intend to take him to restaurants in the Village. And nobody's going to go after him in Sardi's or the Four Seasons. Before you get yourself worked up, Ezra, I have two questions. First, can you fix the escrow deal so that it doesn't get activated by mistake?"

"I'll propose a two-signature box," I said. "It'll take both of us present to get the bank to open it. I'll also send a sealed letter on the arrangement, signed by Rivers and myself, to the Bar Association. Rivers isn't going to do anything to jeopardize his practice."

"Ezra, I think you're naïve."

"Then get yourself another lawyer. Escrow is escrow. What's question two?"

"What if Manucci gets the collateral returned from Canada and Barone decides to knock off Manucci as a lesson to others?"

Less than five seconds later the door opened and they both came back in, Rivers talking.

"I want to add a point to our proposal. The safe deposit will be a joint box, requiring two signatures and two keys, one for each attorney."

"You said the room wasn't bugged."

Rivers laughed. "As for the other point, though Mr. Manucci has never been associated with the likes of Barone, he understands their mentality very well. He tells me that Barone is very angry now, and will still be angry after the collateral arrives back from Canada, but Mr. Manucci, who acknowledges his mistake, intends to send via a certain route an apology that all of Barone's associates will learn about, thus satisfying Barone's concern about control of his territory."

I started to interrupt, but Ben put his hand on my arm and said, "Hear him out, Ezra."

"Thank you," said Rivers. "To continue. Mr. Manucci has a certain real-estate investment in Queens that has made Barone nervous for several years. It is Mr. Manucci's intention, even before the collateral arrives back from Canada, to pass title on that property to Barone, on certain conditions. I want to assure you gentlemen that Mr. Manucci has things completely under control." Rivers looked at Ben. "For the sake of your show," he said, "we should come to a decision quickly."

"Time *is* a factor," I said, feeling like an idiot. Ben didn't want my advice.

"We'll leave you alone to discuss things," said Rivers.

"Why don't Mr. Riller and I just wander down the hall."

When we were out of the room, Ben pointed me in the direction of a door marked MEN. He went in, came back out. "No one in here."

I followed Ben in. He was at the urinal. "I'll wait till you're finished," I said.

"Ezra, I can talk and piss at the same time. I want you to see this from my point of view. Sam Glenn is quite capable of taking me to law on breaking escrow. All I need is a trial on criminal charges. I'd never be able to function on Broadway again. And think of Jane and the kids."

"I am thinking of them, Ben. That's why I don't want your life on the line."

I took advantage of the second urinal.

Ben said, "I don't think anything will happen."

"You know something I don't know?"

"Yes."

"You own a bulletproof vest?"

"No."

"You want to do this deal?"

"I don't want the humiliation."

"Of the deal?"

"Of not doing the deal and facing all the rest. Letting the cast go, being chased by everyone the show owes money to, the investors, their lawyers, the SEC, you name it. This is a one-stop solution. Like the war, Ezra, remember? All that can happen is getting shot at."

Ben laughed the laugh of a man who had made up his mind. I envied him.

"Well," Rivers said when we returned. "Deal?"

I looked at Ben, giving him one last time to back out.

He nodded his assent.

"We accept," I said.

"That's terrific," said Manucci. "Mr. Riller, I'd like to invite you and your wife to have dinner with me and my wife at any restaurant of your choice tonight."

"Our deal is you and me," Ben said, "not our wives."

"I want this to look social," Manucci said, "not only business. I'm sure you understand."

"I want my wife left out."

"Mr. Riller, if you're in trouble, isn't she in trouble? If you get out of trouble, doesn't she get out of trouble? Wouldn't she want to be part of the solution?"

Ben was pale. The deal was going to blow.

Just then the office door opened, and Miss Atherton stood there, her hand lifted nervously to her cheek. "I told you to lock the front door," Manucci said.

"It's locked," she said, coming close enough to whisper to him. We were all watching Manucci's expression. He gave us nothing, went over to his desk to answer the phone call.

"What is it?" Rivers asked Miss Atherton.

She shook her head. "He'll have to tell you."

Manucci's voice on the phone was formal as he announced his name to the person on the other end of the line.

When he was through, he spoke to all of us. "That was the police chief of my village. My house has been on fire for nearly an hour."

"Is it under control?" Rivers asked.

"Nothing's under control. If Mary'd stayed home, it wouldn't have happened."

"Nick," Rivers said, "if Mary'd been home something worse might have happened."

"Jesus," Manucci said. "That son of a bitch. I've got to get up there fast."

Rivers's hand was hard on Manucci's arm. "No, Nick. If Barone had that fire set, he's got people up there waiting for you."

I couldn't believe how calm Rivers sounded. "Nick," he said, "I'll go get Mary and drive her down from your sister's if you'll give me directions." Then he turned to Ben and said, "If you and your wife will join the Manuccis here, say in two hours, I'll have a limo ready, and it'll stay with you for the evening. I'll reserve in your name, Mr. Riller, if that's all right?"

Comment by Ben
▌▌ ▌▌ ▌▌

I'm in the middle of a meeting and guess whose voice buzzes my ear like a hornet.

Look what you've done. His home's burned.

Pop, it was Barone, not me.

You practically hired Barone to do this.

I hired Nissof.

You push the first domino, you are responsible for all that fall.

Manucci was trying to take my home as security. I was following your advice. Fighting back.

Don't pass the blame to me, Ben. I said give him some trouble you can take away. What will Aldo say? He sent you to Nick for help. It'll be on your head if anything happens to his son.

You got it wrong, Pop. I'm putting myself in the line of fire to save him.

You mean to save your show. Ben, listen to me, God's big trick is a pendulum. He's the big theatrical expert, not you.

What do you mean?

Look at what He's staging now.

Ezra was pulling at my elbow. "Do we or don't we?"

"We do."

Rivers was saying, "I'll phone you at the restaurant, Nick, and let you know where the limo should go after you drop the Rillers off at their place. I'll meet you in my car and take you to a hotel." Then he turned back to me, saying, "I think that tomorrow you'll want to bring Mr. Manucci around to meet the director and the cast and perhaps watch a rehearsal since he's now the principal investor, yes?"

I wish Ezra had Rivers's balls.

"I can't hear you," Rivers said.

I would have to learn to say yes for a while.

"Yes," I said.

"Good," Rivers said. "Mr. Hochman and I can attend to the drawing of the papers first thing tomorrow morning. Meanwhile, I'd better see about that fire." He let out a breath like he'd been holding it in. "Okay now, let's all shake hands on the deal."

I thought of railroad cars in which surrenders were signed. Didn't they always shake hands?

I shook Manucci's hand.

The two lawyers shook hands.

Then Rivers shook my hand, and Manucci shook Ezra's.

I noticed that neither of the lawyers shook hands with his own client.

Jane

Ben came home hyper, deranged, flying. "I did it, I did it," he said, grabbing my hands and trying to swing me like a kid. "Actually, it was your five thousand that did it, thank you," he said, kissing me on the cheek, then on the other cheek, and trying to find my mouth in between. "One pebble and I got a landslide going!"

"Ben, what the hell are you talking about?"

"Get dressed," he shouted, "we're going out to dinner with Nick Manucci and his wife. We've got *The Best Revenge* fully financed on a straight investment deal!"

"What happened to the other deal?" I asked.

"We socialize publicly with the Manuccis for a couple of weeks and it gets torn up."

Ben laid it all out.

"You don't look happy," he said.

"You're risking your life," I said. "And mine."

"Don't be a spoilsport."

"This isn't a sport, Ben. Those are dangerous people."

"Didn't I risk my life with you?"

"I didn't have people chasing me."

"You should have had dozens of people chasing you." His warm

175

hands held both of mine. "Manucci's not all bad," he said. "You'll see."

"What in heaven's name will we talk about?"

"Revenge," Ben said. "His and mine," and he burst out laughing like the madman I once in a while still loved.

"How am I supposed to believe what you tell me?"

"You believe the weather reports on the radio," Ben said, "you'll believe anything."

I knew he would lead me to the bedroom. The light was on, the drapes were open. There was an acre of glass for people to look through. He didn't care. Like the gypsies who fornicated in the cattle cars on the way to the gas chambers, we made love in full public view.

Mary

y sister-in-law Connie is a perfectionist. Her
macramé is perfect. Her petitpoint is faultless. Her crocheting is im-
peccable. Her Sunday dinners are unsurpassed. Connie is also the
world's best grown-up babysitter when she swoops down on our
house. But if her husband Sean is to be believed, in sex she'll never be
a contender.

When I called Connie to say could I drop over to her place, she
said, "Sure, sure, wait'll you see the afghan I'm crocheting," but when
I showed up with all three kids and suitcases, understandably she
seemed surprised.

Quickly I said, "I hope it's okay. It might be overnight."

"Sure," she said, her "sure" less sure than it was before.

"It's very temporary," I said. "We could go to a hotel."

Connie was immediately all over my kids, hugging and kissing.
"With my spare bedrooms, what do you need a hotel for?" And then
pulling me aside said, "You and Nick fighting?"

I assured her we weren't.

"Then what's up?" she said.

"Later," I said, and held a finger to my lips and glanced at the
children.

I assumed Connie's problem about us arriving with suitcases was her chronic toothache over the way Sean acted with me. According to Connie, he doesn't treat me like a sister-in-law, he treats me like a woman. He pats me on the fanny in front of her, he kisses me on the earlobe instead of the cheek, that sort of thing. She once said to me she didn't know how I stood Nick's fooling around, she wouldn't let Sean do that for one second with another woman.

I hope Connie is never surprised the way most wives are at one time or another. It would blow her immaculate world apart. Clean floors call for a clean husband and to Connie sex is dirt.

Once Nick and I were there for a Sunday visit, the main event a showing of Connie's latest, a wall hanging she had painstakingly crafted for over a year that was supposed to have been inspired by a color photo of French renaissance tapestries she clipped out of a maga-zine. It was Queens Boulevard gauche. After a moment's admiration, I excused myself and said I needed to catch something on PBS. Nick, a good guy to his sister, stayed to hear all about the fine points of imitating art.

Sean drifted downstairs and found me sitting on the playroom couch in front of the TV. It was a long couch, but Sean sat down so close his right thigh was touching my left thigh and straight out, no cue, no reason, described their sex life in four words. "Connie just lies there."

Was I supposed to say I'd give Connie lessons?

Then he said, "You and me, we've always got along, Mary."

"Sure." What was I supposed to say?

"If Nick doesn't always make you happy . . ."

"Stop right there, Sean."

". . . maybe I could."

I started to get up from the couch, and only then did I see what Sean was doing.

"Are you crazy?" I said. I headed for the stairs, and Sean the fast engineer was instantly behind me letting me feel in my backside what I saw. I turned around and said, "Sean, you're a nice guy, but this family is Italian. Connie's Italian, Nick's Italian, I'm Italian, you've got to be real careful because Italians get upset very easily about family intrusions."

He echoed "Intrusions?" as if he'd never heard the word before. "It isn't incest, Mary," he said. "You and I aren't related."

I was already up the stairs.

Sean had crossed a line it wasn't easy to retreat back over. And I had crossed a line by my curt dismissal of his pass. What was I supposed to do, keep family relations intact by patting Sean's thing on the head and saying now be a nice boy and stay where you belong?

If I played with Sean, it'd be to send a message to Nick. He wouldn't care about me. He'd care enough about his ego to kill Sean.

I'm glad Sean wasn't home when I arrived with the suitcases. What do I do if he comes into my bedroom at night? I went over to the door. No lock.

I was lying back on the bed alongside my not-quite-unpacked suitcase when I heard the phone ringing somewhere in the house and then a knock on my door, Connie stage-whispering, "It's Nick, for you."

Nick's voice was all gravelly.

"Mary," he said. "I don't have time for a lot of explanation. I want for you to get dolled up fast. Bert Rivers is picking you up. We're having dinner at the Four Seasons."

"With Bert Rivers?"

"Mary, I haven't got time to hang on the phone. Bert's just driving you into town because I can't. We're having dinner with a man named Ben Riller and his wife."

"The producer?"

"That's the guy."

"You thinking of becoming an actor, Nick?"

"I haven't got time for jokes, Mary. Please." He disconnected, but that *please* hung in the air.

"Trouble?" Connie asked.

"I've got to get dressed to go into town, Connie. Nick's got a meeting he wants me to be part of. At the Four Seasons, can you imagine?"

"Oooh, are you lucky."

"Do you mind? About the kids, I mean?"

"No, no, you just go and have a good time." She looked relieved. Because I wouldn't be around when Sean came home?

There was a lot to do in a hurry. Connie got the kids settled in front of the TV while I saw what I could make of myself with what I'd brought, not having counted on needing real dress-up clothes. Nick always jokes about the black dress I take whenever we go on a trip, saying I'm just like the other Italian ladies, always ready for a funeral. I'm going to shove that joke right in his face because that black dress plus pearls, plus pumps and a bracelet and the mirror tells me I'll do for the Four Seasons.

I was checking my hair when Connie came up behind me and said, "You look terrific, Mary," and I thanked her just as the front doorbell rang, the timing was that close.

"This is Nick's lawyer, Mr. Bert Rivers," I said very affirmatively. "My sister-in-law, Connie."

"How do you do?" is all Bert said.

I saw Connie's eyes thinking this could be a story, that Bert was taking her sister-in-law out, so I whispered to her, "If I was cheating, Connie, I'd pick a taller one."

You can't joke with Connie. She took it as confirmation, not denial.

Premature matron Connie stood in the doorway of her large house, watching her sister-in-law drive off in sin with the funny-looking man, but she wasn't going to spoil things between our families by not waving bye-bye to us. I waved back from the car and thought, Connie, don't just lie there.

I felt good about how I'd looked in the mirror. With Bert Rivers driving his Eldorado along Queens Boulevard, I wanted to hang a sign out saying the short, bald man in a not very dressy business suit is not my date, he's just driving the car. My date, I thought flying, was not Nick Manucci, it was that man I'd seen on TV and in the papers, Ben Riller.

That's who was bicycling around in my brain when Bert said, "Mary, I have some not so good news. I want you to remain calm."

Nick's been killed.

"There's been a problem at your home."

"Nick's there?"

"No, Nick's in his office."

"He's okay?"

"Sure. It's the house." He looked at me for just a second. "There's been a fire," he said. "A bad fire. It may still be burning."

I can't believe it. We were just there four, five hours ago?

"I don't know the facts yet, Mary, but Nick had a call from the police chief. It was a real conflagration, very fast. His guess was that it was set, some combustible, probably gasoline."

Something was rushing around in my ears.

"By the time someone turned in an alarm it must have been a beaut."

"On purpose?"

Bert nodded.

"Yes or no?" I said.

His voice was a croak. "Yes."

"That man who came around with the message for Nick, is that it?"

"Or someone else from the organization."

I guess it was *organization* that got me going. You know how you hear your husband is seeing other women and your first reaction is you don't believe it. It's like that with the mob. You hate what you see in the movies and on television, it makes it sound like all people of Italian extraction are in it somehow—which is a lie against my parents and people like them—and then you remember what's-his-name who later got killed in Columbus Circle in a mob of thousands of people, how he got on television and said there was no mob, it was all a fabrication, and his own death proved the lie, but you felt your husband, whatever he did, he wasn't one of them. But if you're insisting he isn't, aren't you admitting they are? And it's like waking up to the fact that your husband really is seeing other women, but you still don't believe until you find the woman's scarf in his car and you can't alibi yourself anymore. It exists. And they do things like this, set fires, kill people.

Bert said, "I'm sorry to have been the bearer of bad news."

If I tried to talk, maybe the words wouldn't come out. "I'm thinking of moving back to Minnesota," I said. "With the kids."

"I'm sure you'll want to talk this over with Nick," Bert said.

"Fuck Nick."

"Excuse me?"

"Nick didn't need a second mortgage on those computers to make a living. He didn't need to rub Barone's face in something for the excitement."

I wanted to tell Bert to drive to the house instead of to Nick's office. It's like hearing about a death. You want to see the body before you really believe it.

Bert said, "Your husband is a remarkable man, Mary. He's really taking this all very well."

"His wife isn't taking it so well," I said.

"It's harder for women."

You bet your ass, Mr. Rivers. "Actually," I said, "having taught retarded children for quite a few years, I've developed a pretty tough skin, Bert."

"I didn't know that."

"With those children," I said, "it was always a case of trying to improve. I don't consider a threatening visit from a hoodlum a potential improvement."

"They're trying to get to Nick because he's got guts."

I've got guts, Bert. I'm married to him.

I said, "I don't like the business my husband is in."

I shouldn't have said it out loud. Not to his lawyer. I've been so careful all these years, thinking but not saying.

"Nick's a respected businessman."

"Respected by whom? The people he lends money to at those rates? Don't they call that usury?"

Bert gave a little laugh, and turned away from traffic long enough to give me the smile that went with the laugh.

"That's a common misinterpretation, Mary. We don't like words like *usury*. It's the price of Nick's product, which is money. Another businessman wants to accomplish something he needs cash for, he doesn't have cash, Nick provides a product, that's all it is."

"Whenever my father needed tide-over money for his business," I said, "he went to the bank, and he was usually able to get what he needed at decent interest. All the women I know, their husbands borrow from banks. Why don't the people Nick deals with go to banks?"

"I think your husband treats his clients much nicer than banks would treat those same clients. When he makes sure that the collateral covers his risk, he's being prudent for your sake, really, and the kids, to make sure your family capital increases at a rate greater than the inflation rate. He's a smart man, Nick, and a good man."

Smart? Good? You take him to bed, Bert, just once. You see how smart he is. You see how good he is.

"I'm glad to be working for him," Bert said.

I'm working for him, too. He doesn't understand reciprocity. He makes each private transaction a deal, tat for tit.

"I didn't hear you, Mary. It's all that traffic noise."

"I wasn't saying anything."

When those retarded children learned something new they were so grateful they kissed your hands. You wanted to kiss them instead because you were grateful. That's what marriage should be like. When Nick took me to Bermuda, I thought he was through with the other women, and I warmed to him again for one week, and then we were home again, back in business.

I could be grateful for one thing. Bert wasn't talking anymore. What I was thinking was that Nick sought Barone like a gypsy moth goes after the lure, he's found the excitement he's looking for: death.

"I know you must be upset," Bert said, turning his head away from the traffic toward me. "This is just temporary, Mary. Nick's got a plan for cooling Barone off."

I know Nick better than you do, Bert. He wants to win and so does Barone. They can't both win.

"Mary, all we need to remember is that we need to be seen in public for a while."

"We?"

"I meant you and Nick."

These lawyers move us around like actors on a stage. I won't need lawyers in Minnesota. Two years ago, when I took the kids to Minnesota for a week, my mother talked to me like a mother and I broke down and cried. She said to me I was rich in money, poor in heart.

"Mary is unhappy," she told my father.

My father's response was simple. "Leave him, Mary. People get divorces all the time now, even Catholics."

"He'd kill me," I said.

"Don't be silly, Mary," my father said. "This is the twentieth century."

I remembered Mr. Milford, whose lectures were always jammed with kids from other classes. He said the twentieth century could be explained through place names, the Somme, Guernica, Lubyanka, Auschwitz, Babi Yar, Hiroshima. We students, with our lives before us, took him on, said he was too one-sided, cynical, too old. "What about Freud and Einstein, what about Picasso, what about computers?" we said, sure of ourselves. And Mr. Milford, with that marvelous, lost voice would say, "You judge a century not by its knowledge but by its acts."

A good teacher leaves a tattoo on your brain. Long after I saw Mr. Milford for the last time, the place names continued their march of definition. My Lai, Budapest, Munich, Lod, Belfast.

I would take the children back to Minnesota. Away from the twentieth century.

· · · · · 25

Mary

Nick had taken me to the Four Seasons only once, on our tenth anniversary. I tried to keep from looking around the enormous, high-ceilinged room like a tourist. But I was one, wasn't I, in places like this?

Nick introduced me to Benjamin Riller, impresario.

"How do you do?" he said.

I do, I do.

His face had what my father called character. He was holding his hand out to shake mine. It was just a hand, firm, warm, but it was as if I could feel it between my legs. I should have married a man like that.

I had to pull my hand away from his or I would have left it there. I had to take my eyes away from his, too, so I could say hello to his wife and defuse.

"My name is Mary," I said to her.

"Jane," she said. I tried to keep my eyes on her eyes. How could a person look so intelligent without talking? I had to look at her clothes. At her body. I wished I could see it all, naked, right now, next to mine, both of us looking in the mirror.

"What a charming dress," she said.

Drop dead. I smiled and slipped into my place on the banquette.

The captain, preparing the way for his tip, introduced the waiter and waitress as if we had just hired them. Those two did their number, lifted unused plates and replaced them with other plates we wouldn't use. Mr. Milford would have said what makes the buying of excess delicious is the knowledge that most other people can't afford it.

"Hey, where are you?" Nick said to me nicely, not loud.

"Do they know about the house?" I asked.

"Ben was with me when the police chief called," Nick said.

Mrs. Riller said to Mr. Riller, "What about the house?"

I could see he wished the subject hadn't come up.

"They had a fire," he said to his wife. "A bad one."

"I'm so sorry," she said.

I guess I was realizing that for me that house had gone down a long time ago except, maybe, for the garden. I wondered if the firemen had ruined the garden.

"Take a sip of your drink," Nick said. "You'll feel better."

Once I was back in Minnesota, settled, I could meet somebody else. Someone who doesn't cut his toenails in the kitchen on Sunday mornings. Someone who works at something I can respect. Work defines a person. Ben Riller did exciting things in the theater. You weren't likely to meet someone like him in Minnesota.

I suddenly thought: Mr. Milford, how do I define myself to myself?

They were talking about the house, commiserating with me. Pay attention, I told myself, but what I saw was Jane Riller putting her drink away. Was she nervous? If I were married to this Riller, I wouldn't be nervous. I wouldn't want anything interfering with anything. I guess Nick would say she was a lady compared to me. He's always comparing, like kids do about batting averages. *A yellower yellow.*

Just then the flashbulb went off, blinding me. Everything was white. Then gray. The photographer retreated.

It must be that racket where they bring out proofs. If you say no, they tear up the pictures of you right in front of your face.

"They're not going to sell us pictures at the Four Seasons?" I asked.

"They're not," Mrs. Riller said.

We were busy with these miniature scallops in butter-and-herb sauce, the smallest bay scallops I'd ever seen, when Mr. Riller spotted this older gentleman sitting at a nearby table, a man with nearly white hair and a trimmed mustache who looked like he'd been secretary of state. Before I knew it Riller was table-hopping and bringing this really fine gentleman over to us and saying, "This is Harrison Stimson, Mary Manucci, Nick Manucci, you know my wife Jane, of course?"

"Of course," Harrison Stimson said. Mr. Stimson shook hands all around as if he wished he were wearing gloves.

"Harrison," Ben Riller said to no one in particular, "has been one of my staunchest investors over the years."

"Oh," said Nick, "you in this new one, too?"

Mr. Stimson's eyes shifted in Ben's direction. "I'm afraid not," he said without looking at Nick.

That's when Mr. Riller said, "My friend Harrison missed out on *The Best Revenge*. It will interest you to know, Harrison, that Nick here has picked up the balance of the units."

Mr. Stimson said, "I'm sure Mr. Manucci will profit from his investment with you." Bang, the damn photographer let loose another flash. I hadn't even noticed him coming up to the table. Mr. Stimson looked like someone had belched. He whispered to Ben Riller, who called the captain over. The captain danced off on whatever errand Mr. Riller had sent him on.

"So nice to meet you," Mr. Stimson said to no one in particular, certainly not to me, and then he got walked back to his table by Mr. Riller.

We were busy talking about nothing when Mr. Riller and the captain returned to the table from different directions and you could see the captain would have preferred to talk to Mr. Riller privately, and finally had to say in a way we could all hear, "I told the photographer not to bother you, sir, but he says he was hired by Mr. Rivers, who works for Mr. Manucci."

Comment by Nick Manucci
▮▮ ▮▮ ▮▮

When I was a kid in the street, the first thing I learned was control the face. Don't let anyone ever see you're bothered.

I did a deal with a Japanese businessman once. He was in New York for a few weeks. Rich as he was, he got himself into some kind of money jam, very temporary, and there must have been a little dirt connected with it because he got steered to the Seagram Building. I'll never forget the control on his face, he needed ten thousand yesterday, he was nowhere near Tokyo, he couldn't get at his own money without questions being asked, but when he showed up you'd think he'd come on a social visit.

I looked for a bead of sweat just below the hairline or over the lip. Nothing, just the frozen face. I asked him what kind of security he could provide, and this Oriental cucumber takes a small purple pouch the size of a half dollar out of the watch pocket of his vest and tumbles out into his palm five diamonds that must have been thirty, forty karats. I'm not a pawn shop, but if a guy who isn't an American walks into a New York pawn shop, he isn't going to get ten thousand for one week for anything. I don't want to disturb his cool so I was very careful when I said, "May I see your airline ticket, please?"

He took the ticket out of his breast pocket and it checked out okay, Japan Air Lines, first class back to Tokyo in ten days.

"May I see your passport please?"

He hesitated.

"Please," I repeated.

He handed it over. I put the passport and the ticket in my safe along with the diamonds because I wouldn't appreciate his going anywhere without my knowing it, and he didn't twitch a muscle in his face as he said, "Very well, Mr. Manucci. I will return the money in one week, as promised." What cool! I wish I had a lot of customers like that.

All right, if I need Riller for camouflage, it's just for a while. Meantime I wanted it understood I was running this show, so I played head man over the dinner, motioning the captain, things like that. Riller was keeping his end up, telling some story about a theater critic who realized he was in the wrong theater when the curtain went up. It was funny, but Mary was laughing too fucking loud.

Riller, his wife, and Mary were all looking at me. I realized the captain was hovering on my left like a penguin, waiting for the joke to be over. Then he handed me this envelope and said it was left with the doorman just a few minutes ago. MR. NICK MANUCCI, CONFIDENTIAL. I know Bert Rivers's handwriting. "Excuse me," I said, and tore it open.

Dear Nick,

Sudden circumstances have made it necessary for me to suggest that one of the lawyers on the enclosed list would have experience with theatrical deals and might be able to represent you on your investment in The Best Revenge *and perhaps in your other affairs as well.*

I'm sorry to do this on such short notice but I have no alternative. I'm sure you will understand.

Sincerely,
Bert Rivers

I wanted to throw the table over with all those fancy plates, the food, everything.

I looked at the list of lawyers. I never heard any of those names. I wanted a gun, not a list.

Bert was fucking involved in everything I did, he can't quit just like that.

Somebody got to him.

"Excuse me," I said. "I have to make a phone call."

You can imagine what shot through my head as I sidestepped people through that long lobby, and took the fancy staircase down to where the phones were. At least I didn't have to do this from a wall phone, there was an empty booth with an accordion door. I sat down, closed the door, glanced at my watch, remembered that Bert's private line rang in his home as well as his office. I plunked my coin in, and dialed.

Would you know a recording machine answers?

"This is Bert Rivers. There is no one in at the moment, but if you'll leave your name and number . . ."

"Bert," I yelled into the phone, "don't fuck around, I know you can hear me, pick up the goddamn phone."

"Hello, Nick," he said. Just like that.

"Don't give me hello Nick, I just got your note, you can't quit like that, you never said anything, I got you on retainer. Everything seemed jake when you brought Mary down. What happened?"

"Nick," Rivers said, "it's extremely important that you remain calm. We'll settle all our financial matters when this blows over. I just can't represent you now."

"They got to you, Bert, didn't they. How much?"

"It isn't money, Nick, I swear it. You shouldn't be in a phone booth. It's a bad place to get trapped in."

"This is the Four Seasons, Bert."

"Nick, this is my last favor to you. It'll cost me if they find out I said anything. They've got someone there right now from out of town."

"Here?"

Suddenly the phone booth was no place to be in.

Rivers said, "Don't phone me again, Nick. Don't come to my office. Try to stay away from me as if your life depended on it."

watched Nick's anger fan across his face when he
got the note. I thought he was going to throw the table over as he
pushed it away from him before the captain could help.

The minute he was out of earshot Mary said, "It's probably one of
his girlfriends." She was half smiling. Half a joke.

Jane got up before the captain could restore the table to its rightful
position. "Back in a minute."

When she went off to the ladies' room, I felt Mary Manucci's knee
touch mine under the table.

"Excuse me," I said, thinking I had bumped her knee by accident.
She smiled. What I felt on my thigh was unmistakably her hand. A
touch. Just for a second.

Louie once said, *The daughters of the women who made passes at me,
Ben, will make passes at you. Don't refuse them in a hurtful way.*

I smiled at Mary Manucci. Her hand, having delivered its message,
had gone back to where it belonged.

"Do you come here often?" she asked.

"I come when I can."

She reacted before I did, laughing greedily and, I thought, suddenly
radiant.

"There's Nick," I said, relieved.

As soon as he sat back down, his gaze panned around the room.

The waiter asked if any of us wanted a refill. I waved him away.

Nick's gaze had stopped. I had to turn a bit to see who he was looking at.

A man who looked as if he'd been in the sun a lot was sitting at a banquette alone.

"He's the only one in the restaurant who's not with somebody," Nick said.

"Do you know him?" I asked.

Nick shook his head. "They wouldn't use someone I knew. They'd get someone from out of town."

I'd hired Nissof to put pressure on Nick, but not this.

Jane returned.

I'd opened Pandora's box.

Mary Manucci's voice overrode my thought. "The four of us ought to go away on vacation together, in the Caribbean. Under made-up names so nobody'll know. We could have a good time until this blows over."

Nick kept his eyes on his assassin.

Jane, the slightest trickle of irony in her voice, said, "Nobody'd look for us in a Club Med."

I looked at her as if she were crazy. She went on, "We'd meet all kinds of people we'd never met before. It'd be a lark."

Don't blow it, Jane, I thought. His money isn't in the production yet.

"I'm pleased the two of you are partners," Jane said. "With Manucci money and Riller command of the theater, you two could conquer New York like Romulus and Remus."

"That was Rome," I said.

"Getting to be the same thing, isn't it, dear?" Jane said.

I heard Louie's breath at my ear. *Zipporah talked the same way.*

You're nuts, Pop.

If you think it's a coincidence you don't know how God works. Pay attention, He doesn't have time to give you private lessons.

The four of us, I thought, are sitting here in four separate worlds.

The five of us, I added.

The only one paying attention to reality was, of course, Nick.

Mary's left hand fidgeted with her pearls. "Nick?"

"Yeah?"

"Do you see something? Somebody?"

I could see the pulse in Nick's neck.

The waiter set the main courses down in front of us.

Jane said, "If the food tastes as good as it looks, why don't we plunge in?" She looked at me. I was looking at that lone diner. "Ben," she said, "that man you're staring at probably's never been in the Four Seasons before. I bet it feels dreadful eating alone in a place like this."

Nick laughed.

"I, for one, am going to eat," Jane said.

"I for two," Nick said.

My fork was going down to the plate, it hadn't yet touched the food, when Mary Manucci said, "Nick, tell Bert Rivers to give Barone what he wants."

Nick looked at her as if she'd farted.

"We can't live this way, Nick," she said.

Nick smiled at me and then at Jane as if Mary didn't exist. "I think Rivers gets Mary nervous," he said. "He didn't want us going back to my sister's. He was going to put us up at the Carlyle for tonight. Jack Kennedy used to stay at the Carlyle." He laughed. "It's got to be safe."

Jane put her knife and fork down on the side of her plate. "Why don't you both stay at our house for the night?" she said. "We have a very nice guest room on the second floor, with its own bath."

"It'll be an imposition," Mary said, glancing at me.

"Not at all," Jane said. "When businesspeople stay over, it helps at tax time. Mr. Rivers will tell you that."

Nick looked at his wife, whose fork was picking at the food in her plate. "They have terrific desserts here, Mary. You loved their Chocolate Velvet." To Jane he said, "I appreciate the invitation."

I said, "I suppose Bert and Ezra will be getting together first thing tomorrow morning to get the papers worked out."

Jane seemed relieved at the shift of subject.

"I guess you'll all know sooner or later," Nick said. "Bert isn't representing me anymore. That note was from him. Somebody got to him. I'll have to find someone else to work with Hochman in the morning."

The heavyset man with the dark suntan who'd been eating alone put his utensils down. He was staring at the entranceway to the main dining room. I saw what he saw, a reporter I knew from the *New York*

Post. The man with him carried his camera down at his side, but his mission was unmistakable.

"I think we'd all better look like we're having a good time with each other," I said.

The maître d' was hurrying along behind the reporter and the photographer, trying to stop them without touching them. Better a camera, I thought, than a gun, just as the photographer exploded his bulb. Ringed by restaurant personnel, the reporter and the photographer, having gotten what they wanted, surrendered. They allowed themselves to be escorted out of the restaurant.

"It'll be good publicity for the play," Nick said. "Won't it, Ben?"

He wasn't looking at me.

"I have an idea about that fellow with the suntan," I said, motioning for the check.

"On me," Nick said.

"I wouldn't think of it. I've been chewing over the idea of introducing myself to him," I said.

"You feel bulletproof?" Mary said.

"Now listen, you know where the limo's waiting. I'm going over and have a word with him. As soon as I sit down at his table, you all head for the limo. I'll be down in three minutes."

"Ben, be careful," Jane said.

"I know what I'm doing."

I looked straight at the suntanned man as I walked toward him so he'd be certain I was coming to him, and when I stood in front of his table I said, "Excuse me, I noticed you were looking at us. Do I know you?"

I could see Nick, Mary, and Jane heading out. So could the fellow I was talking to. I slid into the banquette, boxing him in. I extended my hand. "Ben Riller," I said. "You're not from Texas, are you? Someone who looks just like you invested in one of my plays." I signaled the waiter. "Please bring this gentleman an amaretto and charge it to my account."

"I don't know you," the man said, straining to see Nick and the others, who'd left the room. "I got to go."

I signaled the waitress. "Would you have the waiter cancel the amaretto, please. My friend here needs his check. And could you hurry it, please." To him I added, "I wouldn't try leaving before you have your check. They're very efficient here. They'd stop you before you got out the front door."

There was no way he could get up without my getting up first. When the check arrived, he just glanced at the bottom number and started to peel bills off a roll.

On my way past the maître d', I said quietly, "Those may be phony bills, Maurice. I'm certain you know how to distract him while the bills are checked, but do ask your person to be careful. I wouldn't be surprised if he was armed."

"Thank you," Maurice said, as if this were an everyday event.

I took the stairs two at a time. Outside, I quickly spied the limo with three occupants and slid into the jump seat. "Let's go," I said to the driver.

I told the others what had transpired upstairs. Nick loved it. "How does a guy like you," he said, "learn to think like that?"

"Oh," I said, taking Jane's hand in mine, "I saw a lot of gangster movies when I was a kid."

· · · · · 27

Gordon Walzer

The best revenge, of course, is living well, but something always comes up.

After all these months of run-throughs, rehearsals, midnight meetings to discuss changes, and all-night sweat sessions at the typewriter, there was suddenly a black hole in life: nothing to do! On the morning of opening night, I sat at the counter in a Chock Full o' Nuts half a block from the theater, drinking my fourth cup of coffee, hearing the clink of plates, the thunk of the cash register, people giving orders to the waitresses in near whispers so as not to wake themselves too much.

On this day I expected to hear drum rolls, crowds shouting as we long-distance runners neared the tape. Hey, everybody, it took five hundred fifty thousand dollars and *pain* to get the words I wrote into the mouths of the actors in that theater next door, and you're not even looking at me.

Wrong. The black counterwoman is looking at me to see if this nut is going to have a fifth cup of coffee. Don't look at me, look at all those other people sitting at your counter, bags under the eyes, wet armpits, burbling stomachs, do you think each and every one of them is loved? Some of them not even their mothers loved, why am I so angry at these strangers for not being aware that as of tonight I'm a produced playwright! The playwrights whose work made Broadway in my lifetime wouldn't fill one car of a subway train!

The last two weeks out of town all I heard from Mitch was "Walzer, stop improving. Don't change any more lines, don't rattle the actors." Night after night, seeing the play in front of audiences, I heard the coughing, saw the fidgeting, detected gaffes, gaps, the pimples in the way of perfection. Walzer, I told myself, shut up, the play is out of your hands. I had no way of knowing whether *The Best Revenge* would last a week. How would you feel, mother, if the hospital told you we don't know if the baby will live long enough for you to take it home.

Never mind, there'll be a revival some day. I'll improve it for the revival.

"Yes, please," I said, "another cup." Coffee makes cancer in the pancreas. Is that too slow?

In Baltimore, the audiences were lukewarm. "Don't worry about it," Mitch had said. "In Baltimore they don't know how to feel until somebody tells them. It's not a place to try out a play, it's a place to bring a road show after it's a hit in New York."

In Washington, I hugged Mitch, I was ready to dance. "Hey, look at this, two out of two good notices!" Mitch said, "Those aren't selling notices, Gordon. They are fucking reverent about your play. They treat it like a classic. Nobody'll come."

"The house seemed pretty full to me."

"Don't be stupid, kid," Mitch said. "From the ninth row back those are students from Georgetown. We're papering the place. Those aren't real people. They didn't pay."

I asked Ben Riller, "Is it true the house is being papered?"

"I'll talk to you about it later."

"Is the play a flop?"

"I said I'll talk to you about it later."

I could have killed Riller with my bare hands. I didn't exist. The only one he ever talks to is Manucci. It may be Riller's shirt, but it's my play. I called Pinky.

"Sweetheart, fly down on the shuttle. There isn't a single human being here."

Would you believe those pricks made me buy her a seat for the play? They're giving all those freebies to students and Alex the Pencil has the nerve to tell me, "There's nothing in the Dramatists Guild contract that says you get free tickets."

Pinky had to sit alone. I'd forgotten how to sit except when there was a typewriter in front of me. I watched from the back, standing.

After the show, I took Pinky to an all-night diner.

"Well, what do you think?" I said, as if I were under Niagara Falls waiting for the water to be turned on.

Pinky kissed my right cheek with Danish still in her mouth.

"What's that mean?" I said. "Condolences?"

She swallowed the rest of the Danish and said, "Gordon, you're crazy. The play is terrific. It's better with the actors than it was reading it."

"Then why are the audiences not breaking down the doors? What am I supposed to do, hawk to street-corner crowds?"

"You said Riller told you it was building."

"Yeah, but what the hell does that mean? Three more customers!"

"Everyone is looking at you," Pinky said. "Tone it down. Bertha Goodman said to me a quality play takes word of mouth."

"How do you get enough mouths going to keep the theater full before Riller closes the play down?"

"You're getting yourself all worked up, Gordon. They're running ads, aren't they?"

"Those ads wouldn't make me want to see that play."

"You don't have perspective."

"Right. I'm one-dimensional. I want the play to be a hit."

"It'll be a hit in New York."

"If you're going to have fantasies, Pinky, let's go back to the hotel. I like fantasies better in bed."

Pinky left Washington. She didn't even suggest coming to the next stop in the tryout tour, Philadelphia. "I make you nervous," she said.

"Masturbation makes me nervous," I answered.

Mitch made me admit that in Philadelphia the cast was developing a certain confidence. He called it polish. I told him he was mispronouncing Polish. He told me you didn't get three curtain calls for a flop. I said they're applauding the actors, not the play. He said what the hell do you care what they're applauding, as long as they like it. I wanted to kill him and I hadn't even gotten around to killing Riller, so I went to the hotel and made myself watch television. I woke in a cold sweat. The clock said three a.m. Jesus, the TV was still on and it was showing a commercial for the other play in town! Writers have the hearts of murderers!

Back in New York, I didn't know what to do with myself. That fifth cup of coffee tasted terrible. My tongue was rotting. My teeth were decayed. My alimentary canal wanted to burp and fart at the same time. Hasn't anyone got a body bag I could crawl into?

I felt the hand of authority on my shoulder. A cop? I'll go quietly. Then the familiar voice. "Hello, Gordon." I looked up and saw him in the Chock Full o' Nuts mirror before I turned. Ben Riller slid onto the stool on my right. "How goes it?"

"If you're running out of ideas, I'll be happy to write early morning dialogue for you," I said.

He laughed. "You're a bag of nerves," he said.

"I don't know how we're doing."

"Even if the play's a smash, there'll be a lot of work to keep it going."

"I'll settle for a minor hit right now," I said. "Where's your Italian friend?"

"I'm meeting him at the theater in ten minutes."

"I haven't seen you without him since our little money crisis five weeks ago. I thought you guys were married."

Riller had the nerve to laugh again. How can a guy laugh on the day of opening night? Is it possible you shower, shave, and shit today as on any other day?

"I have a suggestion," Riller said. "See that counter lady? Every time she takes a warm hot-dog roll out of the bottom of the machine, she puts in another one at the top to get warmed up. Why don't you go home and start a new play on page one?"

"Today?"

"What better day?" Riller said. "Start a new one just before the old one opens."

"You can't be that cool."

"No," he said. "There's Manucci heading for the theater. Got to catch him. See you tonight, Gordon. Remember, it's black tie."

Black tie? Why didn't anybody tell me? Who owns a tux? Could I rent one the right size on short notice? I could see myself in a monkey suit four sizes too big. "That's the playwright," they'd all point.

In the taxi I sat on the edge of the seat all the way home, as if by keeping my body weight off the seat the cab would go faster.

"Pinky," I shouted, "start on the Yellow Pages. I need to rent a forty-long tux for tonight. I hope you've got a gown to match."

Pinky said she was busy with the kid, why didn't I do the phoning. How could I, I said, I had something *urgent* to do.

A half hour later she came into the tiny room I use as a place to work in and found me at the typewriter.

"You're not making changes for tonight?" she said.

"Get out of here!" I shouted without looking up. "I'm trying to write a new one!"

Nick

I told Mary, "After twenty years in this business, I don't see too many new situations anymore, except for Riller and this show. This has been like five weeks of foreplay and the thing still to come. What are you looking at me for?"

She doesn't say a thing.

"You biting your lip? I'll give you something to bite. Don't you turn your back on me. I can't make the house grow back where it was. We were lucky to get this rental where the kids could go to the same school, which is what you wanted, wasn't it?"

I am not going to lose one night's shut-eye about the house burning.

"I don't care about the house," she says.

"You better care I collect the insurance. They're talking 'suspicious origins,' maybe I need to feed them a few clues to Barone. This isn't the South Bronx where you can torch a house and forget it."

"Your father says you deserved it. He's only sorry that it's my home, too."

"Listen, why don't you marry the old man you like him so much. You think he never made mistakes?"

"Oh sure," Mary says. "He made one helluva mistake the night you were conceived. He should have worn a condom."

Out she goes before I can grab her. I used to like her smartass mouth better when it wasn't shooting off at me.

I don't care. I'm having a helluva time with this whole Riller deal. I try to be useful. For instance, when Ben filled me in on his old pal Sam Glenn wanting to waltz backward, I said, "One phone call is all I need. Give me his info card."

Ben says, "Can I listen in?"

Why not? I let Ben pick up the extension, but I warn him, "Don't breathe." I dial the number, and I tell whoever, "Mr. Sam Glenn, please."

So she says, "Who's calling?" and I say, "Ben Riller," winking over at Ben. I hear some intercom back and forthing and then he comes on. "You fuck," he begins.

I motion Ben it's okay, relax.

"Mr. Glenn, Ben is kind of busy right now. This is Ben's partner. I'm in the money business, like you. I do lending and collecting. I assume you know people in the money business in New York, like Mister Forty-four?"

Dead air. "Are you there, Mr. Glenn?"

"Yeah," he says finally.

"Good, good. You might want to call Forty-four and ask him about Nick Manucci, that's my name. I can give you other references."

He cuts in. "I know who you are."

"How nice. I understand that now that the play is fully financed, you want your piece out, is that correct?"

"That play's a dud."

Ben is motioning me, but I wave him off. This is no time for interruptions.

"I'm sure your opinion is right for you, Mr. Glenn. I don't want to disagree with you. Just I think *The Best Revenge* is going to make a lot of money. Your sour grapes would just bother the hell out of me if you complained afterward, so I'd just as soon . . ."

"Just as soon what?"

"Take you out."

I drum my fingers on the mouthpiece. Then I says, "I could send somebody to see you about that. I have a friend in Chicago."

"I know about your friend in Chicago. I don't want him on these premises."

"Easy, easy. I was going to suggest he meet you at . . ." I look at the card in front of me. ". . . thirty-five Ann Street."

"I don't see anybody at my home."

"Oh, that's sad, Mr. Glenn. I understand you threatened Mr. Riller a while back. That's not true, is it?"

Dead air again.

"It's okay to lie if that's what you want to do. All I care about is your investment. I'm perfectly happy to buy out your piece."

"For cash?"

"I'll leave that up to my friend in Chicago. Maybe cash, maybe a note, maybe just his word, he's a man of his word."

I hold my hand over the mouthpiece. It seems like minutes before he says, "Mr. Manucci, I'd rather discuss things with you than with one of your delegates. Do you want me in or out?"

I wink at Ben.

"But Mr. Glenn, you are in. Maybe you should stay in. Otherwise people could misinterpret your withdrawal. Mr. Glenn, I just noticed the time, I'm late for a funeral. Tell me quick, in or out."

I can feel his sweat on the phone line.

"In," he says.

"Glad to hear it," I say. "Gotta run."

I hang up. Ben looks like he's going to do a jig.

"Forget it," I say. "Any time."

I'm beginning to think that when Ben fell into my lap, I was ready for something different. I used to get excited one and a half times per transaction. Should-I-or-shouldn't-I is like a vibrator on the brain. Do I or don't I lend money to this guy sitting across from me? What would it take to cash in on the collateral if the loan went bad? Is this a one-shot or the beginning of a steady? When I say okay to the loan, the vibrator stops.

The half-high comes at the end of the line, the due date. Sometimes, not a ripple. But usually there's a phone call and the vibrator dings. Could I give him another week? Could he repay the loan and have his brother-in-law take out the same amount, only could his brother-in-law take it out a few seconds first so he'd have the money to repay the original loan, shit like that. You can't believe the things people will try.

Sometimes it's smart to go along if you're getting your vigorish and you're pretty sure you'll get the principal eventually. Money's no good to you unless it's out there working.

The only time your brain has to work in high is when the customer first starts dancing. He's looking for a delay. A delay is okay if a guy knows what he's delaying for and it's just a matter of time. The amount of time doesn't matter. But if it's an act of God the guy's waiting for, you've got to show your knuckles. Showing knuckles to Sam Glenn was nothing.

A week before the opening, Mary and I were at the Riller's town house for dinner and for Ben and me to shoot a little pool before Mary and I headed back to our rental. When Ben and I were down in the playroom, I asked him, "You ever get bored putting on a show?"

Ben concentrated on his bridge shot. Then the cue went straight forward just an inch, hitting the cue ball which hit the five perfectly, and only when the ball dropped into the pocket did Ben look up at me and say, "Are you kidding? It's the longest horse race in the world and there's no place or show."

I waited my turn. Using the bridge for a difficult top shot, I said, "Loaning money is boring compared to your kind of horse racing."

I chalked the stick too much.

"Stick around," is all Ben said.

"Ben, I been meaning to kind of apologize about hassling you on your deal at the beginning. I almost missed the fun."

"Suppose the play flops?" Ben said, his eyes at me dead cold.

"I've thought about it."

"What have you thought about it?"

"I'll write it off my income tax. Maybe the next one will make it double. I can afford fun."

I concentrated so hard on giving the cue ball a little backspin it nearly missed the ten ball. Instead of plunking into the pocket, the ten ball moved just enough to position it for Ben.

"Like that," I said. "I missed, but I'm still ahead. I'd like to have a serious talk with you sometime, Ben."

We heard the doorbell ring upstairs. Ben took his turn, aiming carefully.

I said, "Last night I was thinking, if I was to get married all over again, you know what kind of woman I'd go after?"

"Shhhhh," Ben said.

When he pocketed the ten ball, still bent over the table he looked up. "What kind of woman?" he said.

"Like Mary. She's got eyes for you."

Ben straightened up. "What are you talking about, Nick?"

"I'm not fucking blind, Ben. I been neglecting her for a long time. She'd pick up on a guy like you."

"Don't get jealous, Nick, it takes two."

"Not always, Ben."

Ben's wife was on the last stair coming down to the poolroom. I hoped she didn't hear anything.

"The UPS man wants your signature for the package, Nick," she said.

Instantly Ben said, "Stay here, Nick." Like a shot he was up the stairs. I followed him. His hand on Jane's arm got her away from the door. He opened it.

The UPS man said, "You Mr. Manucci?"

"Mr. Manucci isn't here. Where's Lenny?"

"Who's Lenny?"

"Our regular UPS man."

"He's off today."

"Where's your truck?"

"Down the block. You going to sign for this package?"

"Get the hell out of here or I'll call the cops."

Ben shut the door in the guy's face. I started to say something and Ben said, "Hold it." Then he opened the door a crack.

"Just wanted to make sure he didn't leave the package. It's all right, the guy's gone and so's the package."

"What's this all about?" Jane asked.

Mary said, "Nick's head." She was asking Ben, "Isn't it?"

Ben looked like all the blood been drained out of his face. He said, "UPS never delivers this time of night. Why would UPS deliver a package to Nick here? Who would know he's here?"

"Hey," I said to him, "You didn't send the package, did you, Ben?"

Ben just stood there.

I felt the stubble on my cheek. You shave it off every morning and by evening it's pushing its way faster than weeds.

I'm thinking I'm happy, and that package shows up at the door. I got the damn computers back to Barone's guy, didn't I? My new lawyer said Barone accepted the parcel in Jackson Heights, didn't he? We're supposed to be even.

They were all watching me so I looked straight at them and said, half-laughing so they'd know I wasn't taking it too seriously, "Hey, maybe that was a real UPS package. You guys order anything from Bloomingdale's?"

Jane shook her head, "He asked for you."

"Maybe it's a present. Maybe Barone forgot his little game is over. I better remind him."

"How?" Ben asked.

I never got the chance to answer because Mary said, "This is no way to live."

B e n

O n opening night, when the usherette showed us to our seats in the back row with a "Good evening, Mr. Riller," as if I were the only identifiable person in the party of four, Nick said, "What's the matter, Ben, don't you know anyone who could get you better seats?"

"I've already seen the play," I said. "From here I can watch the audience."

Nick shuffled us in so that it was Jane, me, Mary, and Nick last, which left Mary where, concealed by the wrap in her lap, she could move her left thigh as close to mine as she wanted to. The more I had warmed to Nick these past six weeks, the queasier I felt about Mary's heavy need to get her battery charged. At the same time I had to admit I felt a surge from attracting the wife of the man who'd had me in a half nelson when we first met. Why was Jane getting up? Had she seen anything?

"I'm going to use the facilities before the lines form," she said, moving past us to the aisle.

Nick, who'd been riffling through the program like an excited school kid, was trying to attract my attention. "I like that," he said, hitting the title page with the back of his hand. BENJAMIN RILLER, IN ASSOCIATION WITH NICHOLAS MANUCCI, PRESENTS *THE BEST REVENGE*, A PLAY IN THREE ACTS BY GORDON WALZER. Then in a voice of old friendship he had started to use with me, a breathy, confidential near-whisper, he said, "I didn't think my old man in the wheelchair'd be such a good idea for tonight. I want to bring him down later in the week, what do you think?"

I knew the feeling. I'd craved for Louie to see my first production. At every opening, I felt him all over the place, watching the play, watching the audience, watching me.

If you want to understand a people, Louie had once said, *listen to their special words.* That's when he told me about the four-thousand-year-old secret of the Jews. *In Yiddish, Ben,* naches *means the pride a parent gets from the achievements of a child. Who else has an untranslatable word that means that? Nobody. And who else gives their kids such a need to provide* naches *to their parents?*

Suddenly I remembered Louie saying *You run faster than Ezra. Make sure you're running in the right direction.* I'd forgotten to send Ezra tickets to the opening! Distraught, I glanced around, saw him sitting eight or nine rows down, next to the critic from the *Times.* Thank God Charlotte had remembered.

Tell the *Times* what a louse I am, Ezra. At openings, he and Sarah had always sat in the seats that Nick and Mary were now occupying.

Ezra had understood Louie better than I had. He had the distance. He was someone else's son.

We both chased Louie's *aperçus* to the mouth of the grave.

Louie had outrun us. We were too young, stopped at the door, not let in. Louie was too young and he was let in! After thirty-five years I still missed him. God in Heaven, I thought, now that You've got Louie, keep half an eye on him or he'll work himself to death up there, too.

A woman way up front in the fourth row turned in my direction. My heart jumped. Zipporah! Was she staring in my direction because I had thought of Louie and not of her? In a second I refocused; the woman looked very little like Zipporah. My brain needed brakes.

"How long till the curtain?" Nick asked.

"Couple of minutes."

"Never been so nervous," he said, forcing his voice to chuckle.

"You were right, Nick. We should have bribed the critics."

"Yeah, but how do you bribe the audience?"

Nick had a first-class osmosis factor. He picked up fast.

Why was that woman turning around again and looking in my direction?

In 1954 I was up in New Hampshire to catch a local production of a new play that two or three people had said might be worth considering for Broadway with a better cast. The play was as good as the publicity. Backstage I introduced myself to the local producer and we arranged to talk deal over breakfast at nine the next morning.

When the phone in my motel room jangled me awake the next morning, it was only seven a.m. I'd left a call in for eight.

"I have a person-to-person call for Mr. Benjamin Riller," the operator said.

Ezra was on the line. "I've got bad news, Ben."

"Who's suing me this early in the morning?"

Ezra's silence got to me. "Say something."

I could hear him swallowing. "Zipporah is dead."

I'd talked to her yesterday morning. Zipporah was in perfect health.

"I'm sorry," Ezra said.

How could she die in New York when I was in New Hampshire? "Just a minute." I put the phone down. I found Kleenex in the bathroom and blew my nose.

"What happened?" I said into the phone.

"She was uncomfortable yesterday afternoon. When she couldn't get you, she called me and I called the doctor and told him to get his ass over there. He told her to take Bromo-Seltzer. It was a heart attack, Ben. It's very hot in New York now, and the funeral people want to pick the body up as soon as possible."

"Before it starts to smell," I said.

"Stop it, Ben. There's a flight out of Keene an hour and a half from now. You can make it. I'll meet you at LaGuardia."

I left my apologies for the producer to find when he woke up. It cost sixty dollars for the local taxi because I wouldn't wait for another passenger heading in the same direction. Ezra took my bag when I got off the plane, and shook my hand the way Jews do to seal a death.

When we got to the apartment, the front door was open. I headed straight for the bedroom. Two men—they looked like furniture movers—were heaving Zipporah into a body bag, her left breast flopping out of the nightgown.

Jane, just getting back to her seat, said, "The curtain's going up."

Jane

Gordon Walzer was prickly the one time I met him after reading the play.

"It's very clever," I said.

"You mean insightful."

"Okay, insightful."

"And you're wondering how a hippie-looking slouch who doesn't look like the people you associate with can have a brain that produces interesting work."

I told him, "Mr. Walzer, you are not reading my mind successfully."

"Oh yes, I am, Mrs. Riller. If you knew that Henry James picked his nose, you might not have read *The Princess Casamassima*. Anyway, how come your Broadway-smart husband picked a verse play to risk his ass on?"

"Because he wrote one once."

"Riller?"

"Riller."

* * *

During the first act on opening night I felt that I was seeing the play for the first time. Perhaps because I could feel the audience. A shared cigarette is not half a smoke, but a different experience.

Gordon Walzer was now working a whole theaterful of people.

On stage, Ruth Welch seemed to billow to twice Christopher Beebe's size, as she said:

> *George, you're wrong. Harvey*
> *discovered the circulation of the blood*
> *and thought there were humors in it.*
> *A politician has to study history.*
> *A doctor has to study his precursors,*
> *who were mostly wrong. You need*
> *to study yourself, George.*

I measured the beat as the audience waited. Then Beebe said:

> *What's that supposed to mean?*

And Ruth replied:

> *I love you, George.*

George said:

> *You love yourself.*

Ruth waited a second, then said:

> *I'm beginning to. When will you begin?*

Beebe stood frozen as if in mid-breath. It was a fabulous silence, manufactured by Mitch.

Ruth, playing chicken with the audience, waited a beat, another beat, and then simply repeated, *When?*

The applause was shattering. The auditorium seemed to vibrate. I could see people at each other's ears. The curtain was down on the first act.

I found myself searching the audience to see if I could spot Walzer. "What is it?" Ben whispered.

I shook my head. "Nothing." Ben was right to risk this play.

Nick, having a good time in an alien world, seemed to want to do something with his hands in addition to applauding. Was he echoing the audience's reaction, or had the play's magic walloped him, too?

Ben said to him, "Relax, Nick. A great first act makes it harder for what's to come. The audience won't forgive us if we let them down now."

Comment by Mary Manucci
▮▮ ▮▮ ▮▮

At the end of the first act the four of us were touching each other. Ben wasn't pulling away. Jane touched me and meant it. When we stood up, she hugged Nick for a second, I couldn't believe it. Theater makes people crazy. Look at Ben, he's moving through the intermission crowd, eavesdropping.

Nick said, "I want to do this."

"Do what?" I asked.

"This, what we're doing."

"Don't get carried away," I said.

"Too late," he said. "I'm away, I'm away."

• • • • • 31

Ben

The second act held. In the last thirty seconds, no-body breathed till the bottom edge of the curtain touched the stage, then the applause came on like thunder. Some young people in the back shouted *Bravo* as if they'd never heard a verse play before. I felt like I was standing outside under a spring rain.

Louie's voice was so clear.

Stand up!

Was I the only one still sitting? I stood up.

It feels better standing, Louie said, *if you've climbed up on your hands and knees.*

I said to Jane, "It'll be harder for act three."

The audience was one large porous membrane now, exuding the smell of success. Laughing, we wrapped our nerves with sound.

"Hey, hey," Nick said, "looks good, looks good. Mary, look at old sourpuss Ben, he must be used to hits."

"Nick," I said, "there are fourteen men sitting on the aisles who are making notes instead of gossiping in the lounge. Six of them count. One counts more than the rest of them put together. I don't know what they had for breakfast or lunch. What the state of their lives is. Who they're mad at, including themselves. I don't know what's going on inside their heads. Each of them is like Jane's father in his chambers just before he comes out with a decision. Jane's father is not more objective than the rest of us. Why should critics be what judges aren't?"

"Hey, hey," said Nick. "Enjoy."

Mary said, "Considering the number of good plays you've produced, the critics must look forward to reviewing one of yours."

I remained silent for a moment because one of the critics was coming up the aisle close to where we were. He saw me and, stone-faced, nodded. I nodded back. Normal people who'd known each other for fifteen years would have exchanged a smile.

"Where's he going?" asked Nick. "Isn't he waiting for the third act?"

"I would guess he's going to the men's room. Better he pisses in the loo than on the play."

Mitch, who'd just sidled up, heard me. "That's what I like about you, Ben, an optimist who won't count his chickens because all the foxes are out tonight."

"Where's Walzer?" I asked.

Mitch said, "His woman took him out to the alley so he could have his heart attack in private."

"You guys are in some business," Nick said.

"We guys," I said.

During the first week of out-of-town tryouts, Nick had suggested an early dinner with me alone for a briefing on the economics, how the money comes in to the box office from brokers and charge-outfits, how much the theater gets to keep as rent. I told him the theater charges a percentage of the box-office gross. Nick wanted to go over the budget line by line, asking questions.

When I put the paperwork away, Nick said, "Tough racket this is. It's like lending someone a lot of dough to play Vegas. If he wins, he can win real big and you get your loan back and half the profits. If he loses, you go on to the next player. The only *business* in Vegas is owning the tables. Maybe you should have owned theaters, Ben, instead of putting on the shows."

"I'm not a landlord type," I said.

"I was only kidding. I appreciate the fill-in. You know . . ."

I had a feeling he was thinking about whether he wanted to trust me with something other than money. Then he said, "Where I grew up, in the Bronx, the kids traveled in dog packs. The ambitious kids wanted to be chief dog. Sometimes it took fists, knives. My old man was king of the hill, and I could have been chief dog in any of the gangs. I didn't want to be chief dog and I didn't want to be a hydrant for the other dogs to piss on. The power I wanted was to be let alone."

"I can understand that," I said.

"My old man," he said, "was a loner, but when it looked like I was shaping up as one he thought I was a freak. He used to say look at the Jewish kids. The father is a nobody, they want to be doctors. The father is a doctor, they want to be a bigger doctor."

"I never wanted to be a doctor for five seconds," I said. "The flops would kill me."

Nick laughed. "I tell you," he said. "I wanted to build buildings, but the old man said did I want to spend my life bribing building inspectors? Once I had an idea. I saw all these Italian people going downtown to buy their boat tickets for a summer trip back home, buying tickets for family to come over here, all that money going to midtown agencies, I thought I'd start a travel agency right in the middle of Little Italy, in the Bronx, and a branch down near Mulberry Street in Manhattan, and maybe later on in Brooklyn, in the Spaghetti Zone. Well, my father was right there with his cracks, saying, you think I brought you up to work for commissions like a salesman? He put the kibosh on every damn idea I had, and this one time I couldn't stop my mouth. I said right at him, 'Pimps *give* commissions to the women instead of taking them.' He punched me in the belly like a maniac. If there was a baseball bat around, he could have killed me. I was down on the ground and he was going to stomp on my head when my mother came in and started screaming. He ordered me to my room. How dare I criticize! According to his code, when I was little I had eaten the food that came from his business and I should be grateful, whatever that business was. He was right, but who knows that when you're a kid?

"What got to me about the travel business was hearing that travel agents get to go all over the world for next to nothing. I liked that. My old man went straight from Naples to the Bronx. After he made it, he moved his ass out of the Bronx only to his farm in Italy and back. He never went anywhere except to that farm. What kind of living is that? I wanted to find out what the world outside the Bronx was like, Yellowstone, California, Mexico, Europe, even Japan. Crazy?"

"Not as crazy as investing money in plays," I said.

"You know what, Ben? I would never have seen you if the old man hadn't ordered me to."

"You sorry?"

"Ben, I'm having one of the best times of my whole life. Besides, this play's going to be a hit if I have to get everybody that owes me out there dragging people to the theater."

"You ever been to Europe, Nick?"

I knew the answer before he said no.

"South America? Mexico?"

"No."

"San Francisco?"

"I've never been west of Minnesota, and that was just to visit Mary's folks. Maybe with my end of the profit from the show," Nick said, "you know, maybe I should start a travel agency."

"Nick," I said, "you don't need an agency to go anywhere. Just open the door."

Mitch had told me he had a little surprise coming for me in the third act. I don't like surprises, but we were less than a minute from the third-act curtain, and I hadn't seen anything that wasn't in the last performance I had caught out of town. I thought I must have missed it.

On stage, Christopher's arms were being held by his friends. Ruth was coming over to deliver an obligatory slap to his face. Instead she kissed him on the mouth, then raised her hand to deliver the delayed slap, and instead kissed him again, and as his friends let go, his arms went around her. It was a stunning idea. Not a word of the play had been changed. That move, I later learned, had come to Mitch only two days earlier, and he and the actors had risked it.

The cast took three curtain calls before a standing audience. Ruth and Christopher came out together, holding hands, then Christopher alone, then Ruth alone, and that's when the audience went wild. She was probably the largest woman on a stage since Kate Smith, and they were applauding her with affection the way they applaud Hepburn.

I thought of the investors who had run for cover. I must buy Harrison Stimson a ticket for this play.

The instinct to crow, I thought, is the instinct for vengeance. It was too early to crow. The critics got their turn next. And then God, with His weather. At least this early in the season it couldn't snow for ten days straight as it once did so that not even the treasurer could get to the box office.

I glanced over at Nick and Mary. Though the cast was gone and the asbestos curtain down, they were still clapping like tourists.

All sorts of first-nighters were stopping to shake my hand. I moved each one to Nick, introducing him as my co-producer. What the hell, Nick was on a roll, blushing from the gush of compliments, thanking people, introducing Mary, soaring.

Where was Gordon? Out in the alley, Pinky holding his head? He knows about the party, doesn't he?

I said to Nick, "The limo will take us to Elaine's." He looked as if I were interrupting his wedding night. There were still hands to shake.

"We ought to get there before the cast does, Nick."

"Sure, sure," he said, beaming at the last hand-shaker. I led him by the elbow.

In the lobby, the mob was thinning. Nick said, "How come the box office isn't open to sell tickets?"

"Union hours," I said.

"On opening night?"

"Any night. Don't worry, there'll be a line-up a block long before the box office opens tomorrow."

Nick grinned. "Eager beavers."

I shook my head. "Scalpers buying up the best seats."

"Businessmen," Nick said.

Outside, I spotted our limo among the four still in front of the theater. I let Nick and Mary have the back seat and parked Jane and me in the jump seats facing them.

As the driver plowed his way through the dense theater-district traffic, Nick said, "Come on, come on."

"Relax, Nick," I said, "the party doesn't start officially until we get there."

Nick

Jesus I was happy as a kid maneuvering Mary
through the crowd in the lobby. All that buzz was how terrific the
play was. And now my first opening-night party.

When we got to Elaine's there was this small crowd of gawkers on
the sidewalk. How do they find out about things like this?

The driver helped Jane and Ben out, then folded up the jump seats
so Mary and I could get out. Those people staring at us, I just beamed
right back at them.

"Come on," said Ben.

"Okay, okay." I told the driver to come back for us in a couple of
hours, and turned to go in when I saw Bert Rivers partway down the
block coming toward me. He had a nerve. I didn't care if anybody
heard me. I said at the top of my voice, "What the fuck you doing
here?"

Would you believe Bert moved his way through the gawkers and
held his hand out to me, saying, "I'm sorry, Nick."

"Sorry my ass. You deserted me. This is a private party," I said.
"You can't come in."

Bert's ball-bearing eyes couldn't make up their mind to look at me
or the ground. I was looking at that asshole mouth of his, waiting for

his stupid excuse when I heard Mary yelling, "Nick! Nick!" and I just turned my head when something in his hand roared into me. The street was dirty, I tried to keep standing, but I felt myself falling backwards to the curb, thinking my tux will be ruined for the party.

Comment by Mary
■ ■ ■

While I was sitting in the theater watching the actors, listening to the words coming at me fast, I felt like I was back in college, wanting to stuff everything into my head whether I understood it or not, keeping it like in a camel's hump, stored for the future. I kept glancing at Nick, wondering how he was taking this highbrow stuff, I never expected he could get turned on by anything like this, but he was going like lights running around the rectangle of one of these Eighth Avenue marquees. It isn't the play, I thought, it's the excitement of winning.

In the limo, it was as if we were starting all over again when he took my hand.

I saw Bert Rivers going over to Nick before Nick saw him, but only by a second, and my reaction was so clear my head had an instant ache: Why is Bert here? Nick, I was thinking, is vulnerable when he's high, and then in all that noise I swear I heard the crack as if I'd been waiting for it all my life. Then Nick fell back toward me. Before my hands could reach him, he was in the gutter, blood on his clean white shirt. Jane was holding me in her arms, but I screamed and screamed and screamed because I had wasted my life.

Ben

My first instinct was: chase Rivers. Louie's voice stopped me. *Go to Nick.*

Nick was conscious. The red stain seeped through his white shirt, a large amoeba spreading. I looked around as if the presidential limousine should be there to speed us to the nearest hospital. This was the swank East Side of Manhattan, dozens and dozens of people around, and, of course, one of the worst places in the world to get help fast.

Nick seemed to be trying to form words. I knelt down. The bubbles from his breath were pink.

The gawkers crowded around, swilling the excitement. "Hey, move back!" I yelled. The one that didn't move was the doorman of Elaine's. "I called for an ambulance, Mr. Riller."

"Thank you." I motioned for him to lean down. "Don't tell the people in there. It'll spoil their party." The man didn't move so I reached into my pocket for a twenty and gave it to him. "I won't say a word," he said.

One minute it looked as if Nick's eyes were pleading for life. I balled up my white silk scarf and held it tight against the wound. I had no idea what I was doing. This happening to Nick was my fault. I heard a siren. It's my fault. Could it be an ambulance so fast? I looked up. It wasn't an ambulance. It was a police car trying to get closer.

A cop got out and said, "He get hit by a car?"

"He was shot!" someone in the crowd yelled eagerly.

"You with him?" the cop asked me.

"I'm with him," I said, words that would remain.

The other cop was out of the car now. "The ambulance takes forever," he said.

Would the two cops have put Nick, bleeding, into the police car if he hadn't been in a tuxedo in front of Elaine's?

A cab took Mary and me and Jane to the hospital. The stretcher was already being wheeled inside. We followed through the doors marked EMERGENCY and saw a doctor and nurses gathered around Nick.

Jane had her arms around Mary.

The cop with the pad wanted to know the victim's name.

"Nick Manucci," I said, spelling Manucci.

"Address?"

"The Seagram Building."

"I mean home address."

I turned to Mary. She recited the address of the house that had burned down.

"Did you see what happened?" the cop asked me.

"The three of us saw it," I said.

Jane nodded. Mary turned her head away.

"Can you give us a description of the perpetrator?"

"You mean the man who shot him," I asked, "or the man who gave the orders?"

"Just what you saw."

"He's about fifty. Short, maybe five three or four. Very bald. His name is Bert Rivers. He's a lawyer."

"You sure?"

"Sure I'm sure."

I thought the cop was about to read me a lecture but we were interrupted by the doctor, who wanted to know if either of the women was Mr. Manucci's wife.

Mary held a hand up as if in school.

I thought of all those people at Elaine's. There was always mad gaiety until the first review was called in.

The doctor said, "He'll be in surgery for some time, Mrs. Manucci."

"Can I wait here?"

"It's nerve-racking waiting here. Why don't you go somewhere with your friends and leave a phone number. We'll call you in about two or three hours."

"Somewhere," of course, was Elaine's. I took Mary by one arm and Jane by the other.

"I can't go," Mary said.

"Sure you can. It's what Nick would want."

In the cab on the way over Jane asked if I wanted to call the party off.

"It's too late," I said, glancing at my watch. "They're probably well under way."

I looked at Mary. "Would you rather we went somewhere else?"

"They're expecting us," she said.

From amid the chatter and smoke, Mitch emerged saying, "What'd you guys do, walk? What was all that noise out there? Where's Manucci?"

"He had to stop somewhere," I said. And because my voice sounded like I was lying, I said, "He'll be along."

Mitch was about to say something when Spelvin, the play's press rep, grabbed his arm and said, "It's time for the *Post*."

We followed Spelvin to the phone. "Yeah," he kept saying as he scribbled things down on the back of an envelope. Spelvin's handwriting was execrable, but the message was all over his face. When he hung up, he said, "A class act. Christopher Beebe terrific. Ruth Welch fantastic."

"What about the play?" I said.

"Ably directed," said Spelvin.

"Ably my ass," said Mitch.

"What about the play?" I repeated.

Spelvin glanced at his notes. " 'Don't mind the poetry,' it says, 'the audience loved it.' "

Jane laughed and gave Spelvin a buss on the cheek. I glanced at Mary. "Why don't we find a place to sit down," I said, by which time Mitch was already leading us over to the big table where Ruth Welch and Chris Beebe were thanking the people who had run ahead to be the first with the news. Pinky had her arm around Gordon Walzer, who looked long lost to the world.

"Congratulations!" I shouted, as they made room for us. The waiter poured champagne. I couldn't make out anything that was said by the professional back-clappers. I just nodded and smiled and saw that Jane had her hand clasped over Mary's.

Spelvin called the *Times* twice and was unable to get anything. "He writes slow," Mitch said. "He's looking in the thesaurus for adjectives."

I realized Mary was trying to say something. Was she wanting to go back to the hospital? When I bent over in her direction she said, "If the audience likes it, doesn't it mean the reviews will be good?"

Jane, who'd heard, had to stifle the knowledge of dozens of opening nights. "Of course," she said, hoping that Ben the Cynic would not contradict her.

All I said was, "The *Times* is pretty much a monopoly. Ever since the *Trib* died."

I could see people at other tables looking at me. Among them were some of the smart ones who were so damn sure the production would never get to opening night. I owed them nothing.

I tried not to think of Nick. All I could think of was Nick.

Then there was the massive, rolling hush when the volume of the TV set near the bar was turned way up and I could hear Fliegel saying, "The play that wasn't supposed to get to Broadway did this evening and *The Best Revenge* is the best possible revenge against all the naysayers who say quality is dead on Broadway. There was a standing ovation tonight at the ANTA Theater for the best verse drama in three decades, starring Ruth Welch and Christopher Beebe in a heart-stopping play superbly directed by Mitch Mitchell, another hit for Benjamin Riller and . . ." Fliegel actually glanced down for the name. "And a newcomer to Broadway production, Nick Manucci." Hardly were the words out of his mouth when the picture switched back to the anchorman saying, "A bulletin just in says that Nicholas Manucci, financier and co-producer of *The Best Revenge,* was shot by a person or persons unknown just outside the restaurant where the open-ing-night party was being held. A spokesperson for New York Hospi-tal, where he was taken by police car, said he is still in surgery."

More than a hundred faces swung their gazes from the TV set to our table. And all of us at the table looked at Mary.

It was said that Aldo Manucci, when he heard, had Clara wheel him three blocks to the rectory of the Church of the Sacred Heart, where he woke the priest to open up the church. There he prayed, demanding some of the strength of his youth. The next day, with Nick in intensive care, his condition critical, Aldo Manucci set about hiring every free-lance hit man in the East who was fool enough to try to get Barone. The old man didn't want a lone assassin, he wanted an army, each man competing for the prize that went with the head of the enemy. He wasn't even interested in Rivers.

Many weeks later it was Mary who called to say the old man had invited us, including the kids, to Christmas dinner in the Bronx. Jane, who was closer to me now than on the day we married, wondered if it was safe to visit the headquarters of a man at war.

"It's as safe," I said, "as anything else we do."

As we arrived at the front door, Clara greeted us. I apologized for being late, blaming trouble with the car rather than with the kids who'd wanted to go to a rock concert instead of a Christmas dinner among what they mistakenly thought of as a family of strangers.

"We waited for you," Clara said, leading us in to the long dining-room table, at the head of which Aldo Manucci sat in his wheelchair, his eyes blazing the happiness of a man bent on vengeance. He shook my hand with the strength of centuries, then gave me leave to turn to the other wheelchair at his right hand in which sat Nick.

It is among life's difficulties to embrace a man sitting in a wheelchair, but somehow, with Nick straining upward on his strong arms and me leaning over, we managed a hug of brothers that drew applause from the others of the Manucci clan, and smiles from Jane and Mary, who, as wise women, had come to acknowledge more of the mystery of life in the weeks since our play had begun.

Clara sat me across the table from Nick and down a bit so that Nick and I had to shout at each other. Yes, the doctor hoped he would be rid of the wheelchair soon. Yes, he had read the new play I'd sent over, but he pooh-poohed his opinion. "You for it, let's do it." He was glad my office lease was up for renewal. What did I think about sharing his space in the Seagram Building?

"It shouldn't go to waste," Nick shouted through the din. "There's plenty of room for both of us when I get back."

I couldn't bring myself to tell a man in a wheelchair that even now our bond was like an affair, a convenience that would slip away in time.

Then Caesar clinked his glass with his fork. Even the grandchildren and my Matthew and Alice gave way to silence.

Aldo Manucci cleared his throat. "I have news from Sicily," he declaimed. "Everyone know my son's enemy Barone is there on a long vacation."

Of course we laughed.

"Barone . . ." he tried to continue. Nick was laughing the loudest.

"Please to shut up," said the old man, smiling. "The news from Sicily is Barone has fall into a well. My friends, they say Barone instead bringing bucket of water up to his face, fool put his face down to bucket of water!"

Jane, I saw, was laughing too.

"He no drown," Aldo Manucci proclaimed, his face mocking sadness, "but it be long time before he swim Atlantic Ocean back here."

He raised his goblet, and waited for all of us to raise our glasses also, including the children.

"To God," he said.

"To God," we repeated.

"My friend Louie once say to me, if Jesus Jew then maybe God must be Italian."

How could I not laugh?

Aldo Manucci, his goblet still raised, said, "To all Manuccis and Rillers around this table I say *Salute!* Special to Nick, who couple months back look like he going to visit God personally, then change his mind, *Salute!* Now Nick know what his old man know, to sit in wheelchair is hard on ass and good for brain. To my enemies, plague, to my family and friends, *Salute!*"

As we all applauded, I swear I could hear Louie's voice saying *Thank you.*

ABOUT THE AUTHOR

SOL STEIN has been a prizewinning playwright, novelist, publisher, software inventor, State Department official, and father of seven talented children. His novels have been translated into French, German, Italian, Norwegian, Swedish, Finnish, Danish, Dutch, Greek, and Japanese, and his second in Russian will appear in an edition of 500,000 copies. With Tennessee Williams, William Inge, and Robert Anderson, he was a founding member of the Playwrights Group at the Actors Studio. Stein has lectured on creative writing at Columbia, Iowa, and the University of California at Irvine, and through his computer program, WritePro, has students in all fifty states and thirty-seven countries, perhaps more than any creative writing teacher in history. He divides his time between Scarborough, New York, and Southern California.